D

Denying Ecstasy

Titles by Setta Jay:

The Guardians of the Realms Series:

0.5) Hidden Ecstasy

1) Ecstasy Unbound

2) Ecstasy Claimed

3) Denying Ecstasy

4) Tempting Ecstasy

5) Piercing Ecstasy

6) Binding Ecstasy

7) Searing Ecstasy

8) Divine Ecstasy

9) Storm of Ecstasy

10) Eternal Ecstasy

Denying Ecstasy

Setta Jay

A Guardians of the Realms Novel

Copyright:

Second Edition

Disclaimer:

This book is a work of fiction. Any resemblance to any person living or dead is purely coincidental. The characters and places are products of the author's imagination and used fictitiously.

Warning – This book is intended for an adult audience. It contains explicit sex; ménage M/F/M; an instance of M/F/F ménage; voyeurism; dirty talking males with bad language

Contributors:

Editor: BookBlinders

Proofreader: Pauline Nolet

Dedication:

This is dedicated to all the fans of the Guardians of the Realms Series. You have been so incredible. I love you all and appreciate the amazing support. It's been wonderful chatting with you on social media and through my website.

Acknowledgements:

A big thank you to all of the incredible Book Bloggers who've shown so much love and support for the series. I mentioned you all by name in the last book, but I'm scared I'll miss someone new on this one. Your kindness and critique have been highly valued. It gets my books in the hands of those that will hopefully enjoy reading it. That you take the time to outline what you like and dislike in a book helps everyone. I can't tell you how much I appreciate each and every one of you.

Thank you to the greatest friend in the world, Lindy. Without our weekly book store trips, lunches and tea, I would be insane. Kevin thanks you too. LOL. Your friendship keeps me level and your critique makes the stories better.

To my advance readers who are always so awesome. Rebekah, Laura and Lori you are the best!

As always, a huge thank you to my readers, I couldn't do what I love without you.

Lastly, to my wonderful and sexy husband, Kevin, who supports me even at my craziest, I love you!

Prologue

Outside the City of Limni, Tetartos Realm – A Century Ago

Another blow landed against his opponent's rock-hard jaw, splattering blood to the dirt at their feet. Dorian grinned wide and rolled his neck. He loved the surge of adrenaline running through his veins. The roar of cheers erupting around the ring fueled it. The Hippeus wiped blood from his lip and narrowed his eyes, forest green glinted in the firelight that surrounded them. They'd been circling and dodging for long minutes now. He never liked to end a fight too soon. He hated disappointing the crowd, and he didn't have any intentions of making his friend look like a pussy. Only his brothers were a true match for him, but Cahal was a good fighter.

He grinned when he heard Brianne's bloodthirsty shouts of encouragement from the sideline.

He looked over and saw his sister Guardian behind the rest of the crowd with Conn, another of his brethren. Her long titian hair was in braids, and she was in her leather fighting gear, the top backless. No Geraki liked to have their back covered, it had to do with freedom to unleash their wings. Of all his sisters, he had a soft spot for her loud and wild behavior. Both had too much energy to fully control, so they understood each other.

"Will you tell your damn sister to shut up?" Cahal growled.

"Oh, you better pound that damn pony into the ground!" Brianne shouted back.

Dorian chuckled, and Cahal looked even more irritated. He was a Hippeus, half war horse, and his sister calling him a pony was a taunt she used often when he and Dorian were pitted against each other. Conn grinned wide, his amber wolf eyes glittering in the moonlight. Both Brianne and Conn were there for him, having his back when he fought.

"Why does she have to be such a bitch?" the male snarled.

Dorian shook his head before kicking Cahal's feet from underneath him. The male landed, and dirt filtered up around him.

Brianne's loud cheers amplified, and he shook his head.

Cahal jumped up, looking furious. Dorian cocked a brow at the male. "You know better than to say shit like that."

"That's right!" Brianne shouted down to them from the rise above the ring. They were surrounded by betting Immortals yelling just outside a circle of metal spikes, yet none were as loud as Brianne. The ring was set lower, allowing the masses a better view. Trees circled the rise above, and he saw Blaine's warriors keeping an eye on the crowds. He didn't see the cat himself anywhere. He might have already started his evening of fucking. The moon was bright, and the scent of arousal spiked all around them.

His was the last fight of the night. Immortals lined up for the opportunity to pit their skills against a Guardian, and he was always game for giving them a show. He loved the pull in his muscles from fighting with only his strength. He'd always struggled to relax unless he'd fought or fucked himself into oblivion first. That was what he loved.

He spun and jabbed at the big male's packed stomach. He and Cahal fought often, at least once every couple of weeks. The male was one of the Immortal warriors who guarded the city of Lofodes.

The big Hippeus' long black hair was pulled back at the nape of his neck. He wore a kilt in reds and black, leaving his chest as bare as Dorian's. The flexing of thick muscled shoulders signaled Cahal's next strike. One that Dorian easily maneuvered around. It was the one after that he didn't get away from, it landed right against his ribs, and the impact launched his body back almost to the iron stakes that comprised the barrier against the crowds.

"You're getting slow," Cahal taunted with a smirk, one that the females seemed to love.

Roars of excitement filled the air. They were always thrilled when one of their own landed a blow. He grinned to himself. They were a bloodthirsty crowd, and he loved them for it. He'd always enjoyed a bloody fistfight, something he could get from his brothers or sisters, but they tended to practice skills useful in their duties. Ones that helped when fighting hell beasts or containing demon-possessed humans. The Tria in Hell liked to fuck shit up. Those triplet bastards were the reason he and his brethren were so damned busy. The twisted fucks, birthed from an incestuous coupling between Ares and Artemis, were powerful enough to send creatures and demon souls out into the other Realms, but not strong enough to gain freedom from their prison.

He and his brethren honed the abilities suited to cutting down hell beasts and containing the demon-possessed humans. One worked best with blades; the other required more finesse. Humans were never to be harmed by a Guardian, even the possessed, or he and his brethren suffered the same injury tenfold.

"Lucky hit," he responded, with a grin.

He jumped to the side as Cahal charged. Dorian enjoyed the freedom and wildness in these bouts, and they kept his energy levels balanced. His side hurt from Cahal's last hit, but the cracked rib would repair soon enough. He healed faster than the average Immortal. He was like them, yet not. The Creators had enhanced the Guardians' abilities when they charged them with the protection of the Realms: Heaven, Hell, Earth and Tetartos.

He heard Cahal's breathing change and spun away before the male could take him down to the ground. It had been a good fight. Cahal was one of his favorite opponents. He just liked the male in general. They loved fighting and often enough ended up sharing females after their match.

Another dodge and he spun low, kicking the male's feet out from under him again. The ground rocked from the impact of the fallen warhorse. "Bloody bastard."

He grinned down at his friend's irritation, then saw Cahal's smirk before he grabbed one of Dorian's feet and flipped him back.

He felt the hard dirt at his back as he landed and quickly rolled away, just marginally missing a foot to the ribs. The male was strong and faster than most of his race. He'd gotten better and better each time they were matched. Fighting in the ring always challenged Immortals like Cahal, those that were used to battling in their beast forms. The Limni ring was for human form only. Opponents were allowed no use of magic or powers. Only strength and cunning were permitted; that was why Dorian fought there. It was a different set of skills he was able to hone, and he enjoyed the excitement of it.

Each of the races had their own grounds for training their clans in whatever way they chose. This was different. His brothers and Brianne sometimes fought there as well.

Brianne continued shouting in the back of the crowd. The other Immortals gave her plenty of space. He saw that she and Conn held big mugs of ale and were smiling and sloshing the shit everywhere.

He shook his head. They enjoyed the fights even if they came mostly to watch his back.

Drake, the leader of the Guardians, had long ago instructed him and the others to be cautious in their dealings with the Immortals of the Realm. The bastard was suspicious as shit, and in the early years it had been more than warranted. They'd dealt with several centuries of strife within the Realm. The Immortals and Guardians alike were nearly feral back then. Not all Immortals had been happy to be exiled and forced to live among the beasts of Tetartos Realm. Many had wanted to get back to Earth, and had been convinced that the Guardians could get them there no matter what the Creators had decreed before leaving the world.

Admittedly, some had been out for the blood of the sleeping Gods, and he didn't fucking blame them. He wanted to kill the majority of the bastards as well, but the Creators had forbidden any harm to come to their sons and daughters, no matter how fucked up the assholes had been. Damn, they'd nearly destroyed humanity and the Immortal races in their madness. He mentally shook his head, sending the bastards to take a nap was not a fitting punishment, nowhere near what they'd deserved for their crimes. The Creators assured them that the Gods would be needed one day. Dorian just didn't see how they could ever be needed for good.

The exile happened long centuries ago. In his opinion, Drake needed to ease up on some of the paranoia. The majority of the Immortals had settled into their lives, accepting the fact that Tetartos was their home. He mentally shook his head that Drake hadn't seen that. The Guardians kept the Immortals well supplied with different goods from Earth Realm, giving them trade options and entertainments.

A quick strike landed against his stomach while he was distracted with thoughts that didn't matter. His breath left in a rush;

he righted himself quickly and spun before another hit landed. Cahal flashed a grin in his direction, obviously pleased with himself. Dorian chuckled.

It was time to end it. He was ready to find some female entertainment for the night. He was sure his brother and sister had shit to do as well. He'd dragged the fight out long enough for Cahal.

He winked at Brianne, and she grinned brightly back.

His fist hit Cahal's jaw, sending the male just shy of the metal spikes. The sharp metal surrounding them added a bit of danger that got the observers off. He'd made sure to hit just hard enough to knock the male out, but not hard enough to send him flying into the spikes.

He only impaled the assholes that deserved to be skewered. There had been more than a few that met the spikes for pissing him off. Some behavior was not tolerated by him and his brethren, and the inhabitants of Tetartos were well educated on those rules. It was his duty as a Guardian to make sure the weaker were not mistreated; if he ever saw that happening, getting speared would be the nicest part of the punishment he'd mete out. If they dared harm one of the mortal Mageia that agreed to live in the Realm, they could only hope to face him rather than suffer the wrath of his sister Guardian Sirena. He repressed a smirk at that. He loved his sisters, but they were ruthless and had no problem kicking any ass they felt needed it.

With the match over, and Cahal slowly shaking off his short nap, Dorian listened to the mixture of cheers and angry roars filling the air. Those who'd lost bets weren't nearly as loud as the ones who'd obviously won. He looked around and saw hot looks from the females and pissed-off glares from some of the males. It had been a longer fight than most, but many were still unhappy that it was over. He was more interested in choosing who to fuck than what they thought.

He never engaged in the normal festivities. The night generally ended in fucking in the middle of the ring. A prize would be offered up. There were those that bet or offered up their females to the winner. It was a common practice that generally ended with wild orgies under moon and firelight. He could already scent the arousal and anticipation in the air. His was the last fight of the night, so there would be no stopping the revelry, but the crowd was aware he would not take part. He may be one of the more reckless of his brothers, but he wasn't stupid enough to put himself in a vulnerable situation in front of so many Immortals, even if he thought Drake was over the top with his edicts on that shit.

He was fine picking a female or two to enjoy his victory where he wouldn't be risking Drake's bad attitude. He smirked to himself.

He saw Brianne smile and finger wave as Conn shook his head. They were both gone, teleporting away in the blink of an eye. Always knowing him well enough to know what he'd be doing after his bout.

Dorian's cock was starting to twitch at the delectable scent of wet pussy and pheromones beginning to fill the night air. It was heady. An enticing combination of scents, with so many races in attendance. Immortals as a whole liked to fuck, and each scent differed in some edible way or another. To remain in prime condition, they usually required sex as much as they needed to feed from the world's energies. He bet many would be getting their fill that night, he planned to. He just needed to find a female or two out of the crowd.

He heard Cahal approaching. Turning, he saw the big male rubbing his jaw and scowling. He chuckled at his friend and clapped him on the back as they walked through the now open gate. The usually sociable male sported a sour look. "Bastard," Cahal grumbled.

The crowd parted for them to make their way through. He was just about to respond when he caught Calista's scent. He turned, and the seductive blonde was giving him a heated look that promised a good night ahead. She had the sultry silver eyes of an Aletheia, a race well known for their sexual excess and she was no exception. The bad part being she was a bitch, which accounted for the months between fucking. Spending too much time in her presence grated on his nerves. She would do for a night, but nothing more. She had two good things going for her. The first was her enjoyment of females and males alike. One female usually wasn't enough to fully satiate his needs. He also liked to share with Cahal or one of his brothers if the mood struck. Options were something he enjoyed. Calista's other redeeming quality was her eagerness to have her ass filled hard, that thought alone made his dick stand at attention.

"Dorian." She nearly purred as she slid her small hands over his bare chest. She was dressed to entice. He'd never seen her otherwise. Tonight she wore a tight dress of blue that hugged her sleek curves. The top was cut deep to show her shadowy cleavage. Two slits at the sides were so high they nearly reached her waist. She had a nice tight ass that he liked to hold on to while he fucked her hard from behind.

"Calista." He acknowledged with a nod. "Your place?" He made no attempt at small talk. That was not what she came to him for. Since he would never take her to any place of his, her home was their usual destination. He only trusted her enough to fuck her; allowing her in his space would never happen.

"Not yet, lover. I have something dirty planned." Her eyes flashed, and he saw a raven-haired, dark-skinned Kairos teleport in near her. Another Aletheia female with bright red hair and silver eyes reformed with the Kairos.

"I feel in the mood for a show and some variety," she whispered, and his cock pulsed. Calista was an enjoyable lover, and he hadn't set his sights on another.

He looked to his friend. "Are you heading out now, or did you want to join us?"

The redhead looked up at the big Hippeus, and her silver eyes swirled with interest. He smelled her heat, and he watched the male flash a wicked smile in the female's direction. "Home can wait."

"My place." Calista's eyes flashed for a split second.

He frowned at the odd response. She was always up for adding another dick to the mix. He honestly didn't give a shit if she had other plans, he did as he pleased, and she was easily replaced. He looked down at her and cocked a brow, challenging her to make her decision. She smiled brightly before placing her small hands on his bicep, expecting him to teleport her away. He assumed the dark Kairos would teleport the redhead. Kairos were the only race whose sole power was teleportation. They provided transportation to the others throughout the Realms for a fee. The Creators gifted all Guardians with the ability, so he grabbed onto Cahal's arm as Calista snuggled into his side. They were air one moment before reforming in front of her place in the city of Efcharistisi.

The home was built atop a cliff overlooking the sea. They entered through an ornamental iron gate that led to a pool. His senses didn't pick up anyone there other than them and the sweet scent of the flowers that bloomed near the path leading to the water he sought. The Kairos and redhead reformed a few feet away and walked in just ahead of him. Once they neared the pool, Dorian slipped off his confining pants and dove in. As a Nereid, he loved gliding through the liquid, letting it cover his skin. He felt more at home enveloped in its soft caress than anywhere else. His muscles instantly relaxed. He wouldn't shift in the small pool, but his skin tingled with the desire to let his beast free. No, he only needed a quick swim to get the dirt and blood of the rings off his skin. He felt the water move, Cahal likely entering to clean up as well. He heard a slight screech and grinned under the water. Knowing his friend, the redhead had likely been carried in to the water as well.

The temperature beneath the surface was cool. It felt perfect against his heated skin. His head and chest broke free of the water, and he pushed his short blond hair off his face. Judging from the heated look on Calista's face, his eyes were near glowing from being within his element. She loved fucking him in the water, got off watching that change. Several times she'd begged him to fuck her in his beast form, but that was something that didn't appeal to him in the slightest.

"Such a sexy male?" he heard Calista muse to the Kairos, who also stared as he stepped back out of the water. He cocked a brow. Was he some prized beast to be inspected?

He looked over and saw Cahal pushing the redhead's naked body up against the side of the pool. Their hair was wet, and Cahal wasn't paying attention to anything but the full tits he was sucking on. The female's head had fallen back over the stone, and her keening rose above the splashing from each thrust of the male's big body.

Cahal joined him whenever the mood struck, and the redhead in his arms had definitely caught his friend's attention.

Dorian rolled his shoulders before focusing on the other two females. Though the water relaxed him some, he was still wired and ready to bury his cock. Calista had already undressed and was helping the dark-haired Kairos do the same. Her pouty lips were trailing down the other female's neck as her hands moved to unfasten the black dress that clung to the Kairos' taut curves. There was a bed set up on the patio. Calista was always hoping someone would see her fucking. She loved an audience, but in reality her neighbors were a ways off, closer to the city center.

The dress fell in a pile on the ground as Calista seductively prowled around the other female. Her pale skin slid up against the Kairos' bronze body. She lifted her small palms and caressed the other female's heavy breasts. The Kairos was an attractive female. All of her kind seemed to have an aloof beauty. Calista pushed the heavy tits together, the brown nipples pulled tight, and he could smell both females' arousal. Tanned hips pushed back.

"Doesn't she have fuckable breasts, Dorian?" Calista said, peeking from around the other female.

"She does," he agreed while walking naked toward the two. Water clung to his skin, and the warm night air blew against him. It felt especially good against his hard dick, which had gotten stiffer with every step.

Silver and black eyes tracked his movements while Calista's pale hands roved down until one had inched its way between the Kairos' thighs. He heard the female's erratic breathing as her lids lowered. Her head fell, and her smooth bronze hips circled in enjoyment against Calista's fingers, her tits were swollen, her back arched. He moved in and slid his hands over her ribs to the soft flesh being offered up for his pleasure. Leaning in, he nipped at her full lower lip, taking a small sample of what he planned to have wrapping around his cock soon. She tasted of spiced wine, and the sweet flavor made him impatient to get on with it. His hand moved over her jaw and neck down to a plump breast. He broke the kiss as he caressed a thumb around one hardened bud. His other hand plumped her other breast while Calista continued to toy with her pussy.

He looked down at her. "Do you want her to lick your pussy?"

Her eyes flashed before she let out a faint moan. Those of her race didn't display much emotion. Just the small indication said exactly how much she wanted Calista to eat her pussy.

"Do I get to feel these soft lips sucking my cock while she buries her lips in your wet cunt?"

Her breath caught, and he scented the liquid flowing from both females. Indication that the Kairos was interested in the play ahead.

"On the bed," he instructed, briefly glancing over at the hard pounding Cahal was still giving inside the pool. One big hand was visible at the ledge, and water sloshed against the sides with each hard pump of his hips. Harsh grunts and whimpering noises issued from the two as they fucked with abandon. He felt more in the mood for that than the entertainment Calista had prepared. He just wanted to get his dick hot and wet.

When had fucking become a habit? An itch beneath the skin that was never fully eased. He wondered if finding his mate would change that. That thought was quickly shoved aside, mates were rare. It was the one thing all Immortals sought and he'd likely never find his. He frowned and shook off the random thought to focus on what was happening in front of him.

The Kairos lay on her back, her legs spread wide, and Calista wasted no time. She was on her hands and knees, ass in the air as her face moved down and her mouth greedily worked between the Kairos' thighs. He repositioned the darker female's body so that her neck fell off the bed. After a few hard strokes of his cock, he was ready to slide between her full lips. "Open your mouth and suck hard," he instructed.

She obeyed, even though she seemed uncertain about the position change. Calista seductively crawled back between the

Kairos' thighs. Her eyes latched onto him as she pleasured the other female. Silver swirling eyes flashed as her tongue darted out and teased the female's clit. She wiggled her ass in the air as she sucked on the Kairos' labia, taunting him. The suction around his cock grew broken and sporadic, so he settled his thumbs against the Kairos' jaw and controlled the movement for her. It was a necessary precaution, preventing her from clamping down. They stayed that way, him slipping his dick between her lips while Calista ate her cunt.

His focus kept moving to Calista's ass high in the air and just begging to be filled. One of her hands had disappeared between her own thighs as she teased the Kairos with her tongue. That pale ass was where he wanted to be next. He planned to fuck them both all night.

"Swallow around my dick," he instructed the female on his cock. She moaned around him before doing as he said. He nearly groaned at how good the vibration felt. He didn't fuck her mouth hard like he wanted, not sure the Kairos could take it. He kept his thrusts shallow; his hips pumped as she sucked until he felt the tingling in his balls. "Swallow it all," he instructed as he groaned and jetted come down her throat. Once he was sure she had it all, he withdrew. Her dark eyes closed, and her hips ground up into Calista's mouth. She was lost in her own pleasure as he slipped away.

He started hardening again as he watched the two females. Water splashed, and hard footsteps on the stone warned him that Cahal was moving the redhead to the bed.

Glancing down, he noted the tensing of the Kairos' body, and a single tight gasp tore from her lips. There were no overtly vocal acknowledgments that she'd come against Calista's lips.

He moved around the bed and grabbed Calista by the hips, sliding her body back to the edge of the bed. He'd always enjoyed the sight of a female's round hips and narrow waist bent over in front of him. Her soft skin was lit with the silvery sheen of moonlight, and in one quick thrust he was inside her hot, wet cunt. He wanted to get nice and slick before getting into her ass. He liked an easy glide even though it'd be a tight, hot fit. Calista always greedily took his dick no matter where he put it.

The Kairos shared a glance with Calista before moving off the bed. She clearly looked to the other female for direction in their play. He watched, unsure why her seeking direction from the blonde Aletheia bothered him. He shook it off and continued thrusting. When Calista tightened her pussy around his dick, he groaned.

He peered to the side, where Cahal was standing with the redhead impaled on his cock, her pale legs wrapped around his waist. His hands gripped her ass tight, slamming her onto his cock over and over as she pleaded for more. Instead of giving her what she begged for, he slipped her off his dick and dropped her to the bed with a cocky grin. She let out a throaty laugh as she bounced.

Dorian continued sliding inside Calista with swift and smooth motions, her cunt tightening around him as she pushed her hips back for more. "That's it, take it. Fuck my dick. Get it good and wet so I can take your greedy ass." He smacked her round flesh as she pushed back. Soon it was the hard fast fucking he wanted, his thumb pushing into her small back entrance. "Yeah, suck my thumb. I know that's where you want me."

He barely paid attention to what Cahal was doing with the other females. He saw the bed shaking as the warhorse shafted the redhead, but from his angle, all he saw was the Kairos' bronzed thighs straddling the other female's face. From Dorian's vantage point, he could see her supple back and curved hips as they circled over the redhead's lips. Wet, red hair fanned out and moved with the force of the warhorses strokes. His friend's loud grunts echoed in the courtyard, right along with the sound of wet smacking flesh and moans of feminine pleasure.

Dorian pulled out of Calista's cunt, and she groaned in protest. His fingers moved down to gather her juices before slicking them over the small opening he'd been toying with. She pushed against him and made greedy noises when two, and then three fingers pushed in and out of that tight hole.

He gripped his slick cock and positioned it at her ass. "Take my dick," he demanded, and she thrust her hips back, trying to take him deeper. He watched it disappear, stifling a groan when his flesh was against her ass. She rolled her hips, still greedy for more. He pulled out and slammed in until his balls pushed against her again.

"Brace your hands. I'm going to fuck you hard." The scent and sounds of sex surrounded him, and he fucking loved it.

He saw the Kairos slide her leg back over the other female's head and crawl to the side. He caught her glancing to Calista for direction, again. He ignored their interaction. Instead he lowered his eyes to watch his dick slip almost all the way out of her ass. He rolled his hips and thrust deep as she held onto the bedding. He slammed deep over and over as she mewled into the blankets. He heard the slick noise of wet skin as his fingers gripped her hips. She tried to match his strokes, but he controlled her movements. He snaked a hand under her hips and toyed with her clit as she begged him to let her come.

"Come on my hand." His balls were tight, and he couldn't wait to empty his dick, but he wanted her to come first.

Calista screamed her release as he pumped his seed deep.

He pulled out and watched as Cahal started his next bout. His eyes shone as he toyed with the other females, he seemed more intent on the redhead, though he was kissing the Kairos. It seemed his friend was content; he'd leave the Kairos there.

Calista flipped over and writhed seductively into the bedding. A contented cat waiting for more. He was more than happy to continue. She gave him a sultry look as she lifted her pretty tits in both hands. Her nipples were hard and begging for his attention. She loved having them played with, and he leaned down and accepted the invitation. She was sensitive enough to come while he sucked them. It was a reward for her having been tame. He wasn't sure why, but nobody had bled yet. He nipped one hard nipple, thinking for a second that it tasted odd. He frowned. Why would she put something on her skin, knowing he would likely suck her fucking tits?

"Please suck them hard. It feels so good."

He palmed one swollen breast and massaged the other before lifting it to his lips. He almost made her get in the pool first, but shook his head and wrapped his lips around one tight tip and sucked like she liked. He got more of the taste and swallowed in annoyance. As he moved to the other, he heard a noise come from Cahal and glanced up. His friend was standing, more like swaying, with a confused look aimed at the Kairos. Dorian's senses went on alert as he jumped up. Just as fast as he stood, it hit him. Dizziness and disorientation. It slammed into him hard. He instantly searched for a blade and his link to his brothers, but it was like everything had slowed down. He wasn't able to focus on the connection.

"You shouldn't have invited the Hippeus, lover. His death will be on your head," Calista said, making a ticking noise with her tongue. "Cyril promised too much for you, and the brute is a liability." She chuckled as he tried to find a way out. He couldn't do more than sway. "Funny that you always discount females as a threat. You think fighting in the rings is impressive; it's galling. I'm not the only one that sees it that way." She clucked at him. "I've been promised so many beautiful perks to do this, and I've tired of your dick anyway." She smirked at him, and he saw the menace.

"Now, Cahal gets to die."

He collapsed to his knees, still trying to find the mental link to his brothers. Confusion was making everything too slow, like time had stalled. Even her words seemed stretched in his mind. He watched Cahal fall face first on the bed. Somewhere in the haze of his mind he heard Calista snapping orders to the others, "Quickly, get me a blade." He could see Cahal's eyes; fury and helplessness filled them.

"Lover, don't you want to fight me? Don't you want to save his life? Aww, so pathetic. You can't save him or even yourself now, can you? Cyril is so much stronger than you and your brothers. You really were too easy to catch." Her taunting laughter trilled in his mind. "Too bad you hadn't invited Conn instead. Mmm, that would have been fun."

He tried fighting the effects, but it had hit him hard and in a way that rendered him fucking helpless. He was impotent with rage.

"What, lover, can't do anything? Do you want me to spare him?" she said again in his mind while tracing the blade over Cahal's throat, slicing in a way that would bleed him dry.

Dorian saw the blood from the wound leaking onto the bedding, soaking into the white fabric as Dorian searched for a way to contact his brothers. He'd never felt so much rage and hatred in his long life. He'd also never felt so weak. It sickened him.

The Kairos smirked evilly as she came forward and took some of Cahal's blood and painted Dorian's lips and face. Her sick laugh of pure menace seemed altogether too lyrical for her actions. He roared in outrage, but no sound came other than a pathetic grunt. The coppery scent of Cahal's blood burned his nose, and he wanted it gone along with the slick feel of it on his skin. Hate was too mild for what he felt for the females. The Kairos smeared more of Cahal's blood over his chest. He couldn't fight, couldn't even call for help. Helpless infuriated rage poured through him. Calista and the other females flashed big smiles from above him. The bitch added more of his friend's blood to his cheeks with a twisted grin.

"Too bad I don't have more time to play with you." In a split second Calista lifted the blade, and in one harsh slice his friend's head rolled to the ground right next to him. Blood sprayed everywhere, all over him and the ground. He could barely move his eyes up to look at the sick bitches. His vision blurred.

"Pity," was all the redhead said, no emotion at all as she looked coldly at the headless male she'd just fucked. The scent of blood filled his nose as it coated the bed and ground. Inside his mind he roared for his mental link to his brethren. Something so simple, yet he still couldn't find it.

"Cyril thought he'd be out within moments. I'm impressed. I'll have to ask him to give me some more just for fun. I'll take that with all the other treasures he's promised."

How did he not see just how sick she was?

He roared over and over inside his mind. Not sure if it was getting to his brothers. The last of his strength left in a rush, and his body toppled onto the ground to lie in the blood of his slain friend. A friend that died because of him. It could easily have been one of his brothers. What would Calista have done to Conn? His body was numb. He felt nothing, not the cold ground or the blood. Whatever she'd given him fucked with everything. How was that possible? The three females stood over him, in total control of his fate. Calista held the bloody blade loosely in one hand as triumph gleamed from all three sets of eyes. Words were impossible, everything was—everything but succumbing to the darkness. His last thoughts were about how painfully they would die for this. Females or not, they deserved whatever vengeance he dealt.

Chapter 1

Miami Beach, Earth Realm

Dorian's dick was starting to piss him the fuck off. He was strung too damn tight. He sat in a dark bar in Miami, waiting for his brothers. He'd been avoiding them for days. Avoiding everything but patrolling while he wrapped his head around what was fucking happening to him. It was time to come clean. He needed to tell Drake too, but their leader was busy checking on the sleeping Gods. Drake had always handled that task personally, not wanting to tempt the others into killing the bastards for all the destruction they'd caused before mommy and daddy sent them to bed and forbid any harm to come to them.

"Another, hun?" a dark-haired waitress asked.

He nodded. Another beer was just what he needed. His eyes tracked the female to the bar. She was built for pleasure. Her dark hair was pulled back in a ponytail. Her round ass swayed in the tight black shorts that barely covered her ass. Tanned skin peeked between her low shorts and the tight black tank that was her uniform. He knew she was putting extra hip action into her movements in order to entice him. It was wasted effort. He ran his fingers through his hair. Days ago he would have already arranged to fuck her, now he knew it wouldn't be happening. His mind and his body both rebelled at the thought.

He saw movement at the door and watched as Conn and Bastian

walked in. Out of the nine male Guardians, they were his closest brothers. Uri would be there soon as well, and he hoped to hell that Uri had the answers he needed.

The waitress was already there smiling at the males before they even sat down. “What can I get you two?”

His brothers ordered while Dorian tried to get his shit together.

He needed to get things under control, needed to find a way out of his current nightmare. He’d been jacking off constantly since Gregoire’s mating ceremony. Ever since he smelled that sweet intoxicating female and known just what she was to him. He’d hated her for it, once he’d gotten over the initial shock. It had only gotten worse when she’d been abducted and he’d actually touched her skin as he carried her from the enemy compound. He hated her hair, her pouty lips and those fuckable tits. He’d dreamt of nothing but those soft lips surrounding his cock while bright aqua eyes flashed with heat, her tits shaking as she sucked him hard.

He looked around for a blonde instead, finding a few on the dance floor. He scanned the area for one that looked like her. None of them were right. Too tall… too plastic… none with the ability to fool his beast into allowing him to fuck them, to relieve some of the biting need preventing him from figuring out a way around what was happening.

His brothers eyed him. They looked out of place in the beach bar. Bastian wore a black tee shirt and cargo pants, and Conn sported the usual flannel mostly covering a dark tee shirt beneath. Some of the wolf’s tattoos were visible from under the rolled-up sleeves. Conn’s eyebrow was pierced, and his amber eyes usually shone with dark mischief. Now they held curiosity, concern…

“You gonna finally tell us what the hell is up with you?” Conn finally asked. When you'd spent centuries fighting and sometimes fucking beside someone, you tended to notice when shit wasn't right.

"Yeah." He saw the light from the door opening and watched Uri walk in. The crowd parted as his brother moved forward, no one wanting to cross paths with the six-feet-eight-inch-tall, dark-haired male with pitch-black sunglasses. Uri's eyes were sensitive just like all the Aletheias, becoming a Guardian hadn't changed that.

The tension rolling off his brothers was thick as they waited for Uri to give their waitress his order. He finally lounged into the other chair and cocked a brow. Dorian had called them all there when he knew it'd be a while before he could talk to Drake. He couldn't keep avoiding the manor without them getting on his ass.

"I need a way out of a mating."

They sat there for a minute; three sets of brows lifted.

"What the hell are you talking about?" Uri asked.

"I'm mated." He clenched his jaw tight. "You know I won't claim her. I can't." These were a few of his brothers that knew just how fucked up he was. He was the last one that should ever have been given a mate.

"Who?" Conn's narrowed eyes indicated he already had the answer to the question.

"Rain." They knew who she was, the mortal Mageia that was friends with Gregoire's mate and currently living at the Guardian manor in Tetartos.

"Fuck, man, so you plan to try to get out of it?" Conn bit out, shaking his head. The harsh tone to his brother's voice said he wanted to say more.

He gave Conn a piercing look. He was in no mood to be fucked with on this. It was his life, and no one would force him to go through a mating. The little mortal was dodging a bullet without even knowing it.

They all sat there looking at him, and he dared them with his eyes to challenge his choice.

Conn asked the question that had been constantly on his mind. "How is it that we go centuries with hardly any Immortals finding their destined mates, and then within weeks, Uri, Gregoire, and now you? Not to mention Erik, all at the same time." Erik was Uri's brother-in-law and the reason Uri and Alex even knew they were mated. If she hadn't gone to Uri for help finding Erik's kidnapped mate, they may never have known they were fated. "I mean, shit, four matings in quick succession when we've gone decades, sometimes multiple, between even a single Immortal finding their mate? This is weird, man. Have you at least talked to Drake?"

"Not yet, he's checking on the Gods, and then he'll be here." He refused to be a pawn in whatever cosmic shit storm was rolling in. There were too many reasons he wasn't going through with it.

"What about Sirena?" the wolf asked. Their sister Guardian, as a healer, was the logical person to go to for help, but he knew she would fight him.

They silently waited as the waitress sidled back and dropped off the drinks.

Once the female was at the next table, he answered, "There's no way in hell I'm succumbing to it, and I'm not stupid enough to go to Sirena for help until it's my last option. She's obsessed with finding mates. She would likely chain my ass like a sacrifice and send Rain in to force me into it." His skin crawled. He couldn't fucking do it. He was never mating. His jaw nearly cracked with the force of clamping it down.

They all sat there. Conn shook his head. He knew it was killing his brother not to argue, but they all knew Dorian wasn't one to budge, especially when his mind was so fucking set.

"It's not going to happen." The force of his words brought a surge of power through him. Uri cocked a brow as he looked around. Dorian tried to rein it in. He was always in control of his abilities. Drink glasses shook, and he heard the rattling of the water pipes behind the walls. The humans seemed oblivious with the loud music surrounding them. He took a deep breath, trying to get his shit together.

After a moment, Dorian got it under control. "I'm not a damn idiot. I know it's only going to get worse. We all know Erik suffered when he couldn't claim Sam." Uri's brother-in-law had had it rough. His mate, Sam's abduction had been a nightmare for them. She was freed, but not until after she'd been raped and experimented on. Erik had suffered the mating frenzy alone after saving and touching her. The poor bastard went through crazed pain while trying to stay away from her. Supposedly, Sirena had been working on a way to subdue the frenzy's symptoms. Sam eventually went to him before Sirena could do anything. As Erik's brother-in-law, Uri had been close during the hell the two went through.

"What did Sirena come up with for them? Were there any viable options?" He needed answers, and Uri was the only brother he could think to call. It was him or battle it out with Sirena. An option that was less than appealing, but if Uri couldn't help, that's what he'd do. Fully mating the little Mageia wasn't going to happen. He didn't fucking trust females as a rule, but even he could see the innocence in her, and mating him would destroy a female like that. She would see his nightmares, see his failure, and be fitted with a monster-sized target on her back because she was a Guardian's mate.

Then there was Cahal. He'd failed so fucking hard; he couldn't take something his friend would never have. Not when Dorian was the reason his friend had been denied the life he deserved. His skin itched at all of it.

Uri's voice snapped him out of his thoughts. "No. Her idea was to drug him to make him mellow enough for Sam to do all the work. Knocking him out delayed the effects, but after putting him under twice, he was still in bad shape when he finally woke up."

Fuck. Fuck. Fuck. He shut his eyes and thumped his head back against the wall.

He took a couple more deep breaths, trying to keep his powers in check. That was a new complication adding to the fuckfest. "Do you have any ideas?" He turned his head and looked over at Uri. He hated asking for help, but it was better than his other option.

Uri shook his head and quietly tried to push the issue, "Shit, I'm sorry, man. Sirena ran every option she could think of at the time. Vane was pissed when Sirena planned to chain Erik for Sam to take care of it, but he didn't have any other ideas either. None of us did." Vane was Erik's twin, and he, Erik and Alex, Uri's mate, were close. They'd avoided exile together, living and working as mercenaries in the human Realm for centuries.

Uri eyed him. "I know you don't want this, but Rain is a worthy female. She's nothing like the others..."

Dorian's vision blurred red just thinking of Calista and her band of bitches. Her death had been denied him, and that still ate at his gut a century after the fact. He was told that too much happened too quickly when his brothers stormed in and rescued him. After they'd cleared the rubble and accounted for all the kills, he was left knowing the females were already dead, and not by his hand. He hadn't exacted vengeance for Cahal's death, and his friend deserved more. Hell, he could still smell the male's blood.

There had been only one other kill left to him after Drake's fury had ignited the place, but Cyril had escaped and Dorian had spent the last hundred years planning the bastard's death. He still couldn't comprehend that the last kill left to him, the one he needed beyond anything, had also been taken from him.

Cyril had died days ago by another. He couldn't deny that the female had more than earned the right to kill the bastard, but he still felt fucked. That death should have been at his hand. There was no way left to avenge his friend, nor would he ever forget that it could have been one of his brothers that those bitches killed in front of him. The scent and feel of his friend's blood on his skin was burned into his senses. He would never forget.

"Uri's right. She is a good female," added Bastian, who rarely spoke. He sat there listening, assessing. His long black hair was pulled back with a band. His tanned face held no emotion, just calm.

Dorian shook his head. It didn't matter that his brothers liked the Mageia; there were too many reasons he couldn't, wouldn't claim her.

He eyed his brothers. "If she's good and worthy, then I'm the last male she deserves. She doesn't even need to know how screwed she could have been."

He looked over to the dance floor. Not one female had shoulder-length blonde hair that was tipped with purple. No vibrant, dancing eyes. Not one came close to comparing to the female his beast wanted. The one he was desperate to find a way out of claiming, for both their goods.

He took a long drink of his beer. The whole train wreck was unbelievable. He'd managed to avoid the manor since scenting her at Gregoire's mating. Then a few days ago the unthinkable happened. He'd lost his fucking mind and touched her.

He still couldn't believe he'd done it. When she and his brother's mate had been taken by Cyril, his beast had nearly gone insane battering inside his body. Up until that point he'd only had the scent of her. That had already been fucking with him, but if it had just stayed away, he wouldn't be so screwed. He closed his eyes. The moment his beast had learned she was in danger, it wouldn't let go, wouldn't let him stay away. Shit, it had been intense, a compulsion. He couldn't help but go to her, touch her, hold her to his chest and feel her heartbeat. What the fuck was that? He'd never even spoken to her, but his beast didn't seem to give a shit. It also hadn't given a fuck that *any* of his brothers could have easily taken her out of there. He'd felt it snarling and itching to lash out at anyone that touched her.

After delivering her safely to Sirena, he'd barely been able to make his legs work to take him out of the healer's office. He'd fucked up big. Touching her had made things so much worse. When all he'd had was the faint scent of her, it was bad enough. Now he knew how her skin felt. He'd felt her slight weight against him and dreamt of sinking deep inside her body.

That touch had triggered a nightmare. His jaw was so tight his teeth ached from it, and he needed that bit of pain because he wasn't keeping her. He fucking couldn't.

"You need to talk to Sirena. She's the only one that can come up with something."

Dorian nodded, knowing Uri spoke the truth and hating it. It would be a fight with his sister. Going against a mating would be like sacrilege to her, she was ruthless in her goal to find Immortals mates. That's why he'd been hoping Uri had the answers to his questions.

He took a deep pull from his beer and leaned back against the chair. The tension rolling off his brothers was intense. They wanted to fight him, he could tell. He was so fucking beyond hearing any of their shit. He absently banged his head against the wall a couple more times. His dick was hard and ready under his worn jeans. Ready for something that wasn't going to happen. He'd spent hours swimming around his island and out to the furthest points in the sea. Steering clear of the humans' shipping routes as he'd pushed his body.

Light flashed as the door to the bar opened again. He caught sight of Drake walking in, his seven-foot frame barely clearing it. They were all tall, but Drake wasn't just tall, he was built like the dragon he was. His power fell off him in waves, and the humans instinctually cleared a path.

It was time to come clean.

His brothers all got up to leave at once, each dropping down cash. They were leaving him to deal with Drake on his own. Conn shook his head and raised a pierced eyebrow. "Good call having him meet you in public. I doubt he'll burn the place down when you tell him."

He watched his brothers leave. Drake waved the waitress away and leaned against the wall. He wore a dark green tee stretched tightly over his muscled chest and shoulders, and worn jeans over his tree-trunk thighs. Half of his shoulder-length hair was pulled into a tail high on his head. Every female in the room stopped and stared when the seven-foot male walked in, and Dorian saw that the staring hadn't stopped. He and his brothers drew a lot of attention, but Drake was an entirely different animal. The biggest and most powerful of the Guardians.

"Speak."

He cringed, knowing what was coming would be fucked. "Rain is my mate."

Drake cocked a brow and looked at him for a minute, silent. "And you're trying to find a way out of it," he said, watching, assessing.

"Yes." He shouldn't have been surprised that Drake would know what he planned. He expected Drake to do more than stare at him. He felt like a kid, trying not to squirm in his seat. He got the distinct feeling his leader was seeing into his damned soul.

It was fucking eerie sitting there while Drake just watched him. Finally the dragon nodded once. "You're pulled from patrol the second it's a problem. Go."

He felt his mouth drop open. What the fuck was that? He didn't order him to mate the Mageia. Drake wasn't even going to guilt him? Tell him he was letting his brothers down by not mating? All mated pairs gained power and strength. They needed the added power from another mated pair. Drake cocked a brow, and Dorian got up and left before his luck ran out. He got the distinct impression he was still screwed, he just didn't know how much. His leader was intelligent and cunning, that thought made Dorian's neck crawl.

Chapter 2

Guardian Manor, Tetartos Realm

Rain didn't remember sitting, but she was glad she was. Her heart felt like it would beat out of her chest at any second.

"What?" Her mind was still reeling from what Sirena had just told her. Her head buzzed with so many emotions, ranging from shock, excitement to dread. She'd known something was wrong with her. She'd felt aroused and needy for days, even throughout everything that had happened in the last week, which had been insanity.

"Your blood shows signs that you've entered the mating frenzy," the healer repeated, concern painting her delicately stunning features.

She shook her head. She'd never imagined she was going through a mating. She assumed that arousal was the way her body dealt with the worry over everything happening to Delia, the young female that had worked in her shop before being captured and tortured by Cyril. She'd assumed it was some weird physiological issue about life and death, her mortality and needing to feel alive; she didn't think for a second that it was a mating. Those were so damn rare, and her best friend, Alyssa, had just found her other half in the Guardian Gregoire. So few Immortals found their mate, and only a select few of those were among Mageia like her, the odds had been more than miniscule.

She stared at the thick brown rug, sitting in the seating area of her room, still trying to process how she missed the clues. So much had been going on even before Delia was taken by the Realm's biggest enemy. She'd been uprooted from her home and business, thrust into the Guardians' manor, for her own protection... She and Drake, the Guardian leader, had shared words about his high-handedness, but in the end, after he'd nearly scorched her eyebrows off in his dragonish annoyance, she'd made the decision to stay. She wasn't stupid, and even though his behavior had set her off, she wasn't one to make a decision out of anger.

A week or so after she was taken away from her life, she and Alyssa were abducted. It was only for a short time before they were rescued, and she'd been unconscious through almost all of it. A thought that thoroughly disgusted her. She hated feeling weak. The only thing she remembered was being grabbed and fighting whoever held her, a sharp sting on her neck, and then waking up on Alyssa and Gregoire's couch. She still felt a little twitchy.

Damn it. It didn't matter why she'd missed the signs. Sirena was right. Her flesh felt heated, and her nipples strained against her bra as she sat there. Her body was telling her what it wanted. Those thoughts did nothing but jack up her heart rate.

Sirena's melodic voice relaxed her some. "Take a deep breath. We'll figure it out."

She would have snorted if she had the extra breath to spare. She hadn't been able to say more than a few words since the healer had shown up at her door and informed her she was mated.

"Can you tell me what you're feeling?" Sirena asked.

She put a hand up. "Just give me another second." She tried to do what Sirena instructed. Taking deep breaths was proving difficult, but she was finally getting it together. The air stuttered as if catching in her lungs.

"Rain?" Sirena asked in a gentle voice while crouching in front of her in a stylish pencil skirt and heels. It felt like her new cozy home was closing in around them. The stone fireplace seemed to be moving toward her.

What if Sirena was wrong and this was all some kind of mistake? "How do you know for sure?"

"The blood tests I took a couple of days ago, when we got you and Alyssa back from the abduction, indicate you've come in contact with your mate."

Wait. Contact? She furrowed her brow. Instinctually she was sure her mate could only be one male, but if what the healer said was true, that wasn't possible. Her stomach clenched as she shook her head. She needed to shake off the dread and get some answers.

"You're sure? Because the only one I can imagine it being has never touched me." She couldn't envision her mate being any other than the Nereid Guardian that had been haunting her dreams every night since she'd first seen him at Alyssa and Gregoire's mating.

She remembered the night, less than a week ago. She'd gone in with a heavy heart. Her best friend in the world had found her mate, but the minute she'd walked into the golden temple, that thought was gone. She'd been hit with the same seductive scent she'd only detected hints of while walking in the Guardians' manor. It'd been taunting her for the past couple of weeks as she'd gotten to know her new home.

Thoughts of her friend's new life and her own fleeting mortality had fallen away, and her whole world had focused in on one male. Her heart had slammed against her chest as her skin flushed. He was the most gorgeous male she'd ever seen. She'd been struck dumb by how perfectly edible he was. His hair was sun-kissed and spiked up with blue tips. She'd fantasized about ripping the clothes from his broad chest. Tearing her eyes from the big blond Guardian to watch her friend's mating had been nearly impossible. Her eyes tracked back to him over and over through the event, but it was his hard glare that was tough to shake. It jarred her. She had no clue what caused it, she hadn't even met the male, and his animosity was palpable in the ten feet that had separated them.

"Rain?" Sirena was watching her carefully.

She pushed back her shoulder-length blonde hair, realizing that he had to have known. That realization churned her stomach in knots. Why reject her offhand, because she was mortal? Was it the way she'd looked? That wouldn't account for the hostility in his eyes.

"There has to be a mistake." She felt certain it could only be him, and he hadn't laid a hand on her, except in her dreams. In those he'd done all matter of dirty and sexy things to her. His sexy-as-sin mouth had been all over her body as his eyes filled with lust that was only for her.

She bit off a snort. That was definitely not how he looked at her in real life. No, his eyes had glowed, but what had sparked in them should have cooled her wild attraction. Shocked animosity had shone in their depths, enough that her breath had caught in her throat. Fortunately for her, he'd left the ceremony the minute Alyssa and Gregoire started kissing. It had been the most awkward, yet, somehow, sexually charged experience of her entire twenty-five years.

"The extent of your blood work indicates touch. That's my concern. You were unconscious with the enemy during the abduction," Sirena said slowly, at the same time assessing Rain with her intelligent violet eyes.

Rain's heart rate accelerated all over again at the healer's words and their implications. She tried to shake off the anxiety. The abduction was for such a brief time, most of which she was unconscious. The experience could have been so much worse. She was safe by the time the drugs wore off. Both she and Alyssa had been taken, but Gregoire and the rest of the Guardians came for them within minutes. At least that was what she'd been told. Could she have been mated to one of the enemy? Alyssa had been awake and would have had some indication if one of Cyril's males thought she was theirs. She took a deep breath, more sure than ever about who her mate was.

She cleared her throat. "It wasn't the enemy. The symptoms started before I was taken."

Sirena's delicate brows furrowed. "Then you know who it is?"

She thought about keeping it to herself. What if she was wrong, maybe some weird part of her hoping it was him? She felt certain she wasn't, but she had no idea where that left her. If the Nereid Guardian was her mate, then judging from his angry expression, he wanted nothing to do with her. His senses were a million times better than hers. He knew; he had to. That meant he didn't want her for some reason. It was like a physical blow. She was generally a confident female, but she wasn't made of steel. If she was right, Sirena, who'd become a friend in the last weeks, would know what to do.

"Dorian," Rain admitted. All the inhabitants of Tetartos knew the Guardians' names. He was the only Nereid Guardian, and she'd always found the pictures of him to be the hottest, but they didn't even come close to the sight of him in real life.

Sirena snapped off a curse Rain didn't quite catch. Her violet eyes flashed as she started pacing. Rain was still dealing with her own emotions and wasn't truly processing Sirena's reaction. Somehow saying his name out loud made it more real.

"Damn him. He should have told me. He carried you in after your abduction. He also came to me around the time you moved in, having problems with his senses around Alyssa. I took tests, but at the time nothing showed up. I told him to let me know if it happened again. No wonder he's been avoiding me for the last few days. It started right after he brought you in." The healer murmured some more choice words about Dorian, but Rain's brain stuck on the part about him carrying her unconscious body from the enemy compound. Why had he touched her? He'd obviously scented her during Alyssa and Gregoire's ceremony. If he hated the idea of mating her, then why chance touching her and pushing them into this situation?

She frowned hard, irritated that logical thinking was completely beyond her. All she could do was picture being held in his strong arms, against his chest... Her screwed-up mind loved the thought of him carrying her away like some damsel in distress. She chose to pretend that the idea of being rescued by him had no effect on her.

"I'm sorry he's being an ass, but he has issues that have nothing to do with you. I shouldn't apologize for him, but knowing how stubborn he is, this won't be simple." Sirena paced the sitting area, going essentially around and around the comfy chairs that sat in front of the fireplace. The healer looked as if she were in her own world as she moved. Rain wondered what kind of issues Sirena was talking about.

After taking a bracing breath, Rain decided to start with basic questions. She still needed more answers, because she fully intended to confront the ass with a detailed list of his crimes. "His touch set the frenzy into motion? It wouldn't have shown up by just being in the same room with him?" She knew the answer. If he hadn't wanted her, then the asshole should have kept his damn hands to himself. Anyone else could have carried her unconscious ass out of there.

"Touch. Your mortal body wouldn't have shown anything in your blood work based on scent."

"What can I expect now? Judging from the pissed looks he was pinning me with at Alyssa and Gregoire's mating ceremony, he wants nothing to do with me. He sped out of there the minute it was over and has avoided me ever since, other than apparently when I was knocked out." She hated having to admit all that, but she wasn't naïve enough to think this would all just turn out perfect in the end. She needed to know her options, leaving her pride to take one for the team. She was fully capable of taking care of herself; she didn't need him to get her off.

The ugly sting to her ego wasn't making the reality any less true.

Her heart felt like it was taking a beating too. Not for him. She didn't know the Guardian, so it wasn't like she was in love with him. It was the loss of her childhood dreams. The fantasy of what a mating was supposed to be, of spending an eternity with a male who worshipped the ground she walked on for saving him from an eternity of loneliness. Never aging like her best friend, maybe having a bigger destiny than that of a small-shop owner with no real life or love interest. Not that she wasn't proud of her business accomplishments. It was just that the damn fantasies had been ingrained in her and Alyssa as children.

A thought hit her. "Is there a way out of mating?" Would he be looking for a way out? She got the distinct impression he would. She didn't want a male that didn't want her, but that would be a final ending to the possibility of having more. It was too rare, the chance would never come again, but that didn't mean she would consider tying herself to a male that didn't want her.

"No. There is no way out of a mating. It's rare, *sacred*," Sirena said, and the way she ground out the word "sacred" sounded as if the thought of Dorian going against it personally offended her. Mating research was Sirena's whole life. She took it seriously and worked her ass off to get potentially compatible Mageia to relocate from Earth Realm to Tetartos. Mageia were mortal and as such could choose to stay on Earth if they wanted to. They'd discussed it a few times since Rain started living at the manor.

Sirena took a deep breath and sat down. "It's not you," Sirena said, irritation bleeding into every word.

"Thanks, but can you explain what the hell I don't know. The only time I was near him, he glared at me as if I'd massacred his family. I've never even spoken to him so I don't know what his issues are, and I have no clue what's going on in my body and how it's going to affect me." She felt tired all of a sudden. So much had been happening and this was just one more issue she needed to deal with. A huge one and she didn't know where to start. She wished she could head back to Paradeisos Island and hide out, enjoying an endless array of spa treatments, but that wasn't going to happen. Her instincts were telling her to go and find that damn Nereid and have him fix this. Confront the bastard for not at least telling her what he'd done. He'd left her to fend for herself with no idea what was happening inside her body.

"I would have let him tell you, but he's likely in flight mode, and your mating has a time constraint now. You deserve all the information so that you know what you're up against. He can try to yell at me later for this, I don't care. He should have been upfront from the start, especially with me so I could figure out how to help you." She blew out a harsh breath before resuming.

Rain's stomach clenched, wondering what could be so bad.

"He was betrayed a century ago. Up until that point he'd spent centuries being reckless and a little wild. He was turned over to Cyril by a lover and two other females. They killed one of his close friends in front of him before turning him over to the enemy. I think he still blames himself for Cahal's death. Drake always cautioned against mixing too closely with the other Immortals, so I think it's that guilt that still eats at him."

Sirena took a deep breath while Rain reeled. She couldn't imagine being handed over to the enemy by someone she'd been intimate with. Jealousy mixed in with the anger that she felt on his behalf, which was idiotic. He didn't give a shit about her, so she was wasting energy being offended for him.

"Why would a lover hand him over?"

"I don't know exactly what Cyril promised, but with Immortal life spans and so few finding mates, Immortals can become mercenary out of boredom alone. It's a very dangerous thing when you're dealing with those with power. That's why we employ warriors to look after the Mageia and spell the cities against attack." Sirena sighed. She suddenly looked as tired as Rain felt.

The healer cleared her throat and finished, "Needless to say, Dorian distrusts and avoids most interactions with Immortals, especially females. He spends his off time on Earth Realm, avoiding Tetartos altogether unless he's patrolling the Realm."

Tetartos was the Realm where the Creators had exiled all the Immortals to keep them away from the fragile humans. Earth Mageia could make the choice to move to Tetartos, but it was a one-way trip, and some families had been there for hundreds of years. Only the Guardians could leave. Shit, her stomach churned. She couldn't even get to him if she wanted to. Damn him.

Earth was the one place she dreamed of visiting. Rain was second-generation Tetartos on her mother's side and four generations on her father's. It was her grandmother that had shared all kinds of stories about Earth Realm. Her gammy had lived in a very poor area with abusive parents and had little opportunity when she'd come of age. She said she'd jumped at the opportunity to leave Earth, and loved the life she'd found in Tetartos.

Rain had always been a little obsessed with anything to do with Earth. It just figured that her destined mate chose to live in a place where she could never go.

"I'm not an Immortal," Rain's irritation slid into each syllable. His attitude obviously wasn't reserved purely for Immortals.

"You're a female, and you will be Immortal when you two complete the ceremonies."

Rain saw the hard glint in Sirena's eyes and knew all hell was about to rain down on Dorian in the form of his fae-looking sister Guardian. She didn't want that, though. She wanted to be the one to personally kick his ass.

"What should I expect to happen physically?"

"The symptoms will intensify. The good news is that he will suffer more than you do. There won't be any relief until the two of you have sex. It will get worse and worse until it's unbearable. Damn it, he'll have to be taken off rotation at some point. It's been three days..." Sirena's violet eyes lit with a kind of evil mastermind look that surprised and, yes, impressed the hell out of Rain.

"Is there something you can do to dampen the symptoms?"

"Not that I've found. I only started looking into something like that when Sam and Erik were suffering." Sam was a Mageia abducted and raped by Cyril's males as some sort of experiment to try to circumvent the mating curse. The spell created by an abused Immortal who had been used as a breeder by Apollo so many centuries ago. It made it so that Immortals could only procreate with their destined mate. Cyril was finally dead, but he'd done a lot of damage before being taken down.

She shook her head. She had her own issues to deal with. Her nipples had been constantly hard. She was hot and ready most of the time. If her arousal wasn't as bad as his... He was likely out there on Earth, hard for her... while fucking someone else. "Is it possible to get relief with another?"

Sirena grew thoughtful, assessing. "I've never tested it. I've never known anyone to try to get relief from another when in the mating frenzy. I've known some who like to share and would include others, but I've never heard of a mate seeking ease from another during the actual frenzy."

Wonderful... She didn't like the idea that she was the first one experiencing that particular phenomenon. She was resigned and irritated by the fact that she knew the bastard was likely making his way through the female population of Earth at that very moment.

A twisted part of her wondered what those females were experiencing. She remembered his harsh glare. She couldn't imagine him as a gentle or even playful lover. No, he'd be raw and intense. She shivered.

He'd touched her, held her in his arms when she was unconscious and vulnerable. What else had he done to her? Did he touch her anywhere else? Run his lips over hers? Touch her breasts? She stifled a groan. She was too damn needy. She didn't have any intention of finding someone to take the edge off. She'd do it herself.

"Do you know any more about his relationship with the female that betrayed him? Where is she now?" Rain wanted to know what happened to the treasonous bitch that would sell out a Guardian to one of the Realms biggest enemies. Was there a bigger crime against the Creators?

"She's dead, killed along with the others," Sirena said with a hard look that only stirred more questions.

"Don't worry, Rain. I'll talk to him, and if that doesn't help, I'll send Drake," Sirena said with a deadly serious look on her beautiful face. She wondered just what Drake would do. Drake was his leader, and scary, but she didn't think his talking to Dorian would really help anything.

"Can you wait for a bit before having Drake talk to him?" She didn't like the idea of his being commanded to mate her. The thought alone made her stomach pitch.

They both turned at a knock at the door.

She jumped up and opened it. Layla, one of Sirena's assistants stood in the hall. She smiled. "Sorry to interrupt, but Erik and Sam have been waiting for a while for their exam."

"Son of a bitch, I forgot they were coming in. Sorry, Rain. Do you want me to contact Alyssa to come see you?"

"No, thank you. She was going to stop by in a bit anyway."

"Come see me if you have questions or need to talk. I'll see what I can figure out." Sirena blew out a breath, and looked sad. "Don't give up on him. This may take some time, he's stubborn, but he will be worth the wait. I promise."

Rain wondered what would happen next. She hated feeling so out of control of her own fate.

Chapter 3

Outside Limni, Tetartos Realm

Dorian was irritated and frustrated. The week since he'd touched Rain had been pure hell. He sank his blade deep into the side of another hellhound, slowing its progression toward the city. Another cut took the beast's head. Why had so many been sent by the bastard Tria? They'd sent packs over from Hell Realm often in the last centuries, but in the last week it had been a constant barrage, and the numbers ensured all the Guardians were needed to help. When they weren't sending beasts, they were sending demons to possess evil humans on Earth. It was all going down in greater numbers than he'd ever seen. It wasn't good. He and his brothers knew it had to be some kind of distraction, but from what, they didn't know, yet.

Drake had already instructed the head warriors in each area to have their people guard the city perimeters in events like these, making sure the mortal Mageia inhabiting the cities were protected. They were the most vulnerable beings in the Realm, and the Guardians had a responsibility to ensure their safety.

He, Bastian, and Sirena helped the other warriors down the vast meadow toward the small lake tucked up against a tree line. The city was at their backs, settled atop a steep cliff leading to the sea. The nice thing about fighting there was that the vegetation was much further from Limni than it was from the other cities. It gave the guards plenty of warning when hell beasts approached.

To your right. He spun and cut the head off another hound. The fact that Bastian's warning was needed just pissed him off. He was slow to find his footing in the fight. His dick was slowly starting to soften into a semi, but fighting with a hard-on was a hell all its own and only seemed to get worse with each passing day. The fact that it still rubbed up against the leather fighting pants wasn't making it any better.

Bastian and Sirena both sent him looks, waiting for him to lose his shit. Wasn't going to happen. He knew they could smell how fucking horny he was, and all of his brethren knew the cause and had tried to get him to go to Rain. Drake was the scariest of them all. He'd been quiet.

Dorian was on edge. Everyone was pissed that he held out from claiming the Mageia. Fuck them. They all thought he wouldn't be able to focus on the battle, but he planned to prove them wrong. He would get his head in the fight if it killed him. He clenched his jaw and finally gave himself to instinct and centuries of battle experience. He ignored the feel of the leather fighting gear and instead focused his power again, pulling water to douse the flames in the spots where the hell beasts had tried to set the hill ablaze.

Sirena, warrior down in Thalassa, and the healers are asking for help, Drake said through the link. Thank fuck, at least he'd get a reprieve from her dirty looks until she was done. If the other healers were calling Sirena, it usually meant dismemberment; he felt for whoever was down.

Bastian was further to his right, amid the city's warriors. The air was filled with battle cries and the pungent stench of sulfur from the downed hell creatures. The Immortals fighting were mostly Ailouros, a whole fuck ton of cats out there in half human form, using blades and claws against their opponents. He looked to where Bastian was finishing off another ophiotaurus. Its horned bull head rolled away from the still-twitching bulk of its body. The beasts seemed to be thinning, and so far no hell creature had made it up to the city and into the second line of defense. It would take a lot to make it through to the city's shield. They were still secure.

Report. Drake's booming voice filtered through the Guardians' mental link. He waited, half listening as the others reported in. It seemed the battle was coming to an end everywhere. It hadn't been waging for long.

P, or Pothos if you wanted to piss the male off with his given name, Sander and their sister Sacha reported thinning in Efcharistisi. Uri reported for the city of Lofodes, Conn for Thalassa, and Dorian knew Drake was in Ouranos.

Limni's fine. The horde is thinning. He informed the others.

Dorian pulled power and doused more flames as the hell beasts caught the meadow on fire in yet another spot. At the same time he engaged an ophiotaurus of his own. The key was teleporting around and lopping the serpent tail without getting kicked, bitten, burned or gored in the process. He managed it fairly quickly, dodging the heavy hooves. He scanned the area, still dousing flames as he sliced halfway through the beast's thick neck while porting out of the way of the horns. He hated the stench of tainted hell-beast blood. It sprayed and stung his bare arms, but he didn't like wearing full-sleeved gear. His leather protection only covered his torso, the acid like blood wouldn't kill him, and he found it less irritating than fighting without range of motion in his arms. It was bad enough his dick felt strangled, he wanted to at least be able to move his fucking arms.

Dorian teleported around and took another swing, barely missing a horn to the gut.

He mulled over why so many hell beasts had attacked in the last week? It all seemed to start a couple of days after Cyril's death.

He listened to the alarms going off in the city, alerting the mortal Mageia to stay indoors while they battled. It was a faint hum down the hill where he fought. So far, there hadn't been any casualties or shield breaches, just hell beasts let loose toward the cities. Not that the Tria were all that bright, sadistic and pure evil, definitely, but not necessarily intelligent. Now that the Guardians knew Cyril's bitch, Elizabeth, could contact the Tria in Hell, it was likely that things were more planned out than they'd ever imagined. A way to distract the Guardians in order to abduct more Mageia to experiment on.

Bastian and he continued to cut down beasts alongside the warriors. Dorian made sure to keep the Immortals as much in his sights as the hell creatures. It was going smoothly enough until, out in the distance, he watched three fucking ofioeidis come slithering between the trees. They were moving along the lake's edge toward the fight and the city beyond. Shit. He looked over at Bastian; his brother caught the movement too.

Three ofioeidis in Limni, Dorian sent through the Guardian mental link.

Son of a bitch. We've got the same shit in Lofodes, he heard Uri say through the link. More of the same was coming from his brothers and sisters about the other cities.

I'll be there as soon as I can. The warrior's in bad shape, Sirena sent.

I'll send help when I take care of these, Drake's harsh voice came through. They'd pissed off the wrong dragon. Drake was the deadliest of them all. Only P, son of Hades, was close to their leader in power.

Dorian started barking orders to the other warriors, who were still fighting the other hell beasts. "Keep the beasts from making it up the rise. When you've thinned them enough that the warriors in the city can take them, make for the ofioeidis on the left. Stay away from its head. Bleed it, but stay the fuck back."

Grunts of assent came from the warriors. The Immortal warriors generally respected the Guardians and mostly listened. They tended to be cocky and sometimes liked to pull out their dicks to show just how capable they were.

He took out another hound and saw Bastian working on his second or third ophiotaurus, making sure not to get gored or scorched in the fight. His adrenaline pumped, his body revving up for the bigger fight to come as he watched three of the deadliest of all hell creatures get closer. They fanned out in the meadow. The serpents were fast, and the poisonous venom could get even an Immortal killed. It was their speed and regenerative ability that made it so damn hard to take them out. Bulk alone prevented a swift slice of the head, which was the only way to kill the sons of bitches. He cocked his head. Something seemed odd about these creatures. They looked bigger, thicker. The red eyes and tough grey scales looked the same, but the barbed tails were new. What the fuck was going on?

These look different. A new breed? Dorian said through the link.

The ones we've been taking out in Hell haven't had barbed tails and weren't as big, P confirmed through the link. He and Sander were the Guardians on Hell Realm rotation.

I've got the one in the middle, he said through the link to Bastian after he decapitated one more hound that lunged for his throat.

He and his brethren would be a bit thin with three ofioeidis per each of the five cities and twelve Guardians capable of singlehandedly combatting the damn things. Fortunately they had Uri's Demi-Goddess mate, Alex, and her twin brothers, which evened the numbers if Sirena came back.

He eyed the creature, not liking the idea of a new breed popping up. He thought they'd nearly eradicated them from Hell. That was what Hell patrol was all about, cutting these fuckers down before the Demon Tria could send them to Tetartos or Heaven, the only Realms the Tria seemed able to send hell beasts to.

"Watch the ofioeidis' tail too," he bellowed to the warriors closest to him. He may not fully trust the bastards at his back but counted on them to work together and stall the serpent until he or Bastian could get to it. The warriors at the city had crossbows, which might slow it or maybe just piss it off. Either way, it would buy them some time.

I don't like this shit, he said to Bastian.

I don't either, his brother replied.

"Make sure the guards at the city stay put," he yelled as he slid his second blade from the sheath at his back. The last thing they needed was for Mageia to get taken by the enemy, again.

Before the words were completely out, he ported to the top of an ofioeidis and slammed a blade deep into the thick neck; the beast bucked and started to coil. He used his weight and jumped down, pulling the blade through the skin. It barely moved a foot, but would start bleeding the bastard some. Its skin was too fucking thick to cut through even with the sharpest of blades. He kicked off to dislodge his blade and teleported out of reach. The huge beast's thick middle nearly reached to Dorian's six feet eight inches of height. He quickly began slicing as he ported around the beast, narrowly missing big sharp fangs filled with poison. He let fighting instinct take him over again, anticipating the beast's moves. Blood sprayed from the cuts he'd made in the thick skin. It took a lot to finish off one of the fuckers, normally, but this one was even more advanced. He landed blow after blow as the thing bucked and coiled, striking out in quick succession.

He was confident that Bastian was making headway with his. As a Guardian, his brother's Kairos powers were enhanced. He was able to partially teleport unlike the others of his race. It was a gift of the Creators and something only he and Sacha could do. It was like fighting air when they were in battle mode. Bastian would solidify only enough to strike a blow. It was an impressive thing to watch. Not that Dorian could spare a glance. He had enough to fucking deal with. It was taking all of his concentration to keep the damn place from burning down while he fought the beast.

He dodged another strike. The ofioeidis coiled its long body so that the barbed tail was rattling near the right side of its head, protecting one side of its neck, leaving only the left vulnerable for attack. Its massive head was more dragonlike than snakelike and didn't bend back enough to guard against Dorian's blades.

Seems like the skin is tougher, he said through the link in irritation.

Yes, Gregoire growled back, making it clear his brother was not happy with that particular fact.

One down in Ouranos. Drake's voice was deathly calm through the link. Fuck, if they were competing, they'd all lost hard against him. He couldn't even use his dragon fire. Hell beasts were immune. No, Drake was just fast at cutting any creature down.

One more double slice from his blades and Dorian narrowly missed another strike. The big body was starting to uncoil while

Dorian moved, which was exactly what he'd hoped for. The heat of the fire coming from its mouth nearly scorched his skin. The good news was that it seemed to be moving a fraction slower as it lost blood. The tainted blood burned his arms, and the bite of pain kept him focused on the battle instead of his dick. This was what he lived for. He got off on the surge of adrenaline that fueled him.

The minute the tail was free of the coil, Dorian struck. He teleported to the tip and skewered it through the point right between two sharp barbs. Sparing no time, he used his other blade to hack into the thick scales. After two clean swipes, he managed to teleport away just as the creature roared and shot flames in his direction. The bloody tail flailed, but he was already on the other side of the beast's head. He pulled more water from the lake as he scented smoke from other flames erupting around them.

Drake's voice came through. *Brianne, go help in Limni.*

Good, Brianne would work on the other beast. A second later he heard a loud battle cry and grinned. Brianne loved a fight just as much as he did. He could imagine what was happening to the creature she was fighting. He'd known it'd made it closer to the city, but that was as far as he'd tracked it, too busy dealing with the beast in front of him.

Dorian continued making cuts, but the progress was slower without his other blade. He looked over to where it lay on the ground. The rest of the tail had finally slid away from it. He ported back and picked up the sword that was still stuck between the sharp points of the tail. The minute the creature opened its mouth to fry his ass, he launched the blade and tail down its throat using a boost of telekinetic power. He teleported away while the creature's harsh noises filled the air. It tried to dislodge the blade, but Dorian had made sure it lodged deep, the barbs cutting into its throat and rendering it incapable of spewing anymore fire. Thank fuck for that.

He went in for the kill. His muscles burned from the added strength it took to get through the thick, hard flesh and bone. The head finally made it to a pile on the ground.

Two down in Ouranos. Sacha, go help Conn and Jax.

One down in Limni, he reported and looked to Bastian, who had maybe one or two blows before his creature was down. More reports of one and, soon, two down in the other cities. There were still a few warriors dealing with the remaining hell beasts on the rise.

He saw Brianne working with some of the warriors to take out the last beast and shook his head. One cat was too aggressive and not nearly fast enough to miss the whip of its barbed tail. It struck hard into the male's stomach. The easily eight-inch spikes impaled him and then slammed him into the ground. Shit. There would be some damage for the healers to repair. He and Bastian teleported over, working as one they detached the tail. Getting the cat free of the area was priority if they were going to save the male from any more damage. The beast whipped its bloodied stump and sent Dorian flying into a severed ophiotaurus head. He looked down, irritated. He'd landed right on a damned horn. He dislodged it from his bicep as Bastian teleported the cat to the healers and other warriors up near the city. It bled like a bitch, but would heal. He checked Brianne's progress. She'd be pissed if he got in the way of her kill, so he cut down another stray beast as he glanced over.

Bastian appeared next to him a second later.

"Is the cat good?" he asked Bastian.

"Yeah, the healers said they'd be able to care for the wounds."

Dorian nodded at his brother's words, and they cut down a few more beasts, but didn't see any others. He and Bastian turned in time to see Vane teleport in. The Demi-God brother of Uri's mate immediately started 'helping' Brianne. Dorian shared a half-hearted smirk with Bastian.

We may as well get a front-row seat, Bastian said.

Dorian grinned, but it was tight. As the fighting ended, his dick was starting to make itself a fucking menace again. He needed relief, but what he gained at his own hand was little to nothing. His arm was bleeding, but he didn't care. He focused on Vane and Brianne, glad for a distraction. They weren't done yet; cleanup would take time once it was all over.

"So much for that chat we've all wanted to have with Vane," Dorian said to Bastian.

"She's a grown female, and Conn was right; she doesn't tell us who we can fuck." That had been the argument that had stopped the conversations about beating Vane for touching their sister. Well, that and Conn's taunt for them to do it because he wanted to see what she would do to them for butting in on her life.

He looked around, making sure that no other beasts were coming. All that was left was the ofioeidis and cleanup. Other warriors were gathering to watch Vane and Brianne. The remaining cats were only getting in the way of the fight. Dorian pulled power and doused more hot spots in the meadow, making sure that no more flames would flare.

You guys are missing out, Dorian said to the others.

Brianne glared over at him, and he grinned back at his sister.

What's going on? Gregoire asked.

We have two warriors, Brianne, and Vane, all working on the same ofioeidis. All we need is popcorn, Dorian said.

Chuckles sounded through the link.

He'll learn, Sirena said matter-of-factly through the link. *The warrior is all taken care of. Anyone else injured?* she asked.

Dorian would be damned before telling her about his wound. It would heal on its own, the bleeding wasn't as bad. He was much better off avoiding his sister Guardian for the time being.

He heard Brianne yell at the two warriors to get back. He could almost feel the bastards' cocks shriveling up. She was fierce when pissed off, and she was right to be angry. They should have backed off when she arrived. They were only in the way, trying to prove themselves, but their abilities wouldn't help them against one of those beasts. He shook his head. That stupidity was what had gotten the other warrior impaled.

Brianne's red hair was back in a braid, and she'd retracted her wings to fight. She tossed one warrior out of the way just as the beast's head moved around and shot flames in her direction. Vane teleported to her and flipped her out of the way. The Demi-God thought he was saving her from being scorched. Dorian shook his head at the male's mistake.

Bastian grinned in Dorian's direction. All the males knew what it was like fighting alongside their sisters. The females were fierce and more than capable of taking care of themselves. She would have gotten out of the way.

Each and every male, except Drake, had gotten multiple beatings in their early years after becoming Guardians. The males were forced to fight their instinct to protect the females. Their sisters hadn't appreciated those impulses. It only pissed them off, and shit, they fought dirty, proving they were more than capable and their skills were to be respected.

He fucked up big. She's going to kick his ass good now, Dorian mused through the link, still fighting to keep his dick down. He appreciated the small distraction from his personal hell.

Would you assholes shut the fuck up! Brianne snapped through the link.

What'd he do? Uri asked.

Spun her away from ofioeidis fire, Bastian provided.

He's outing their relationship in a big way, Jax said, and Dorian could tell that he was loving just how fucked Vane was going to be once the fight was over. He probably wished he could be there to witness the Demi-God's beating.

Swear to Gods, between your yapping and these stupid cats, I wouldn't be so worried over the Demi-God. Keep in mind that I don't care if any of your dicks work... and, Dorian, don't tempt me to get all up in your business, I've been cool as fuck even though you're in the wrong on this one. Rain doesn't deserve this shit, Brianne shot back through the link, and he could see her fighting with a perfect titian brow cocked high in his direction.

Silence filled the link, and Bastian cocked a brow in Dorian's direction. She'd single-handedly knocked them all down. Him more than the others. Dorian frowned. Brianne was one of the few that hadn't busted his balls. It hadn't been like her to keep quiet on anything, but they'd been fighting in different locations with all of the activity.

Report, Drake said.

All hell beasts are down, fire's out, and the last serpent isn't far behind, Bastian replied.

The others reported that they were all starting to help the warriors with cleanup. The fun was gone. None of them wanted to deal with an angry Brianne. They all liked their dicks where they were.

The remaining cat got in the fray, and this time Vane teleported in and tossed the male out of the way. Vane looked around for a split second, probably searching out Brianne, and it was if everything else happened in slow motion. The beast reared and struck as Vane was spinning. It latched onto the male's shoulder. If he'd moved slower, it might have been his head. Fuck.

Brianne roared while everything else went quiet. Bastian and he teleported and helped Brianne slice through the neck. They got Vane free as quickly as possible. He was unconscious almost instantly, which was scary as fuck. The male was a Demi-God. It shouldn't have knocked him out like that. They laid Vane's body out on the ground, the serpent's teeth still lodged in his flesh.

"Damn you!" Brianne shouted at Vane as they pulled the jaw apart, removing the teeth from bone and flesh. They didn't want more venom getting into him. Before they could do anything else, Brianne was yelling completely incoherent things at the knocked-out male while ripping his leather shirt with her sharp talons. Before Dorian knew what she planned to do, she put her lips to the gored flesh and sucked. She spit blood and hopefully poison over and over while Bastian and Dorian forced the serpent's still flailing body back. She quickly flipped Vane's body over and did the same to the holes in the back of his shoulder.

Sirena, Vane's down, ofioeidis bite. Dorian hated having to say it.

His heart clenched painfully for his sister. He'd never seen her with a male, and watching her now made him wonder just how long she and Vane had been seeing each other. It was obvious she cared for the Demi-God more than any of them imagined. He cringed hard. It could only end in more pain. She and Vane weren't mated. The races didn't mix. If either found their true mate, it would be painful if they were as attached as it seemed. He clenched his jaw, not liking the idea of his sister feeling that kind of pain.

"Shh, Brianne, he'll be fine. You'll get to beat the shit out of him later," he said to her as he rubbed her back, trying to soothe her. He glanced up at Bastian. The emotion coming from her was too raw, and he didn't know what the fuck to do to fix it. She was always a ball of energy and fire.

Bastian shook his head, sadness in his eyes as they looked at their sister.

Brianne was shaking under Dorian's hand, and he felt like a piece of shit as she continued to yell at Vane for his stupidity.

The beast venom was obviously stronger in the new breed, or it wouldn't have landed the Demi-God on his ass so quickly. With the other variety, the venom wasn't deadly for an Immortal, it only incapacitated so the beast could decapitate its prey. What would this breed's do? He listened for Vane's pulse. "His heart is beating, and he still has his head. He'll be fine." He tried to reassure her. It was likely the unknown that was scaring the shit out of Brianne.

Bring him to me, Dorian, and, Bastian, get me the ofioeidis' fang too, just in case something's different in the venom, Sirena responded.

Brianne got up and glared down at Vane. She looked pale and wobbly. The poison was getting her too.

"I'm taking him to Sirena. Are you good to meet us there?" he asked her. She didn't look okay. Her eyes were glassy. Bastian was already tearing off his spelled shirt and with a swift strike hacked off the area of the beast's fang to wrap in the material. His brother gently put a hand on Brianne's arm and ported her away. She'd looked dazed which was completely out of character; the venom was hitting her.

Dorian teleported with Vane's unconscious body a split second after that.

Erik, Alex and Uri were there before them. Erik lifted his twin out of Dorian's arms and carried him through the doors toward Sirena. Brianne looked worse than before. Fuck. He lifted her up into his arms, she could rail at him if she wanted, but she didn't fucking look like she could walk. She looked as if she was trying to speak, but no words came out. Son of a bitch. Uri held the door open, and they all went inside. The others looked as tense as he felt. He had the added tension of being in such close proximity to the female he needed to avoid the shit out of. He laid Brianne in the bed next to Vane. He felt her lose consciousness as he cleared the door to the infirmary.

"She tried to suck out the poison," he said to Sirena. Her eyes flashed with pain and sympathy when looking at Brianne. He wondered what Sirena knew of the relationship. Brianne cared for Vane in a way that made Dorian angry as fuck. They'd been playing a dangerous game, and Brianne deserved so much fucking more than falling hard for a male that could never truly be hers. She deserved a mate. He might not, but *she* fucking did.

"Dorian, get showered in the back, and I'll heal your arm."

"It'll be fine."

Sirena shot him a look that had him walking to the back to shower. Gods, she could be a bitch. It wasn't like he was going anywhere until she reported on Brianne. Cleanup in Limni could wait.

He wouldn't leave before knowing his sister was okay, no matter how much he wanted out of the place.

By the time the blood was off and he was in the flimsy pants from the stack on the shelves, he saw Drake standing inside the doorway.

Sirena started talking. "Okay, it seems like the poison is acting the same as with the other breed. Both are unconscious, but internally everything looks fine at the moment. I need to get working on whatever venom I can extract from the fang Bastian brought in. I have no idea how long they'll be out. We haven't had a bite in nearly a century, and this one was potent." The look on Sirena's face didn't bode well. He could see she was hiding something as she looked at Drake.

Chapter 4

Guardian Manor, Tetartos Realm

"How are you?" Alyssa asked as she walked up to Rain's seat in the courtyard.

Rain spent most days avoiding the shit out of the staff and swimming in the pool or in the lake by Alyssa's home. Her friend had been rescuing her daily since learning she was mated to a male that wanted nothing to do with her. It had been a week since she found out, and the symptoms were irritating the shit out of her, but it wasn't like she had much choice but to deal with it.

"Frustrated. How about you?" She grinned at her friend and then noticed something wasn't right. Her friend was wearing her usual cargo shorts and tank top; for someone that enjoyed making clothes, she dressed simply. Rain looked closer and noticed tension around Alyssa's pale green eyes. "What's going on?"

"More fighting. This time they're all fending off hell beast attacks." Alyssa rolled her neck.

"Are you worried?" She eyed her friend. Gregoire was a Guardian, and a few hell beasts were no match against them, no matter how many there were. She couldn't understand why her friend would be concerned about him fighting them, but Alyssa had been acting off in the last week. Rain suddenly felt like crap, she'd been so preoccupied with her own issues she hadn't pried it out of Alyssa.

"No. Yes. I don't know. I'm not used to being a Guardian's mate. My instincts are telling me to be with him, fight next to him, but he just about lost his mind when I told him I wanted to go," Alyssa said as she sat in the chair next to hers. "When steam started coming out of my ears, he explained that it wasn't that he didn't think I'd be able to handle the beasts. He just said *he'd* be too distracted with me there. The irritating part is that the big oaf is right." Alyssa blew out a frustrated breath. "I hate to admit it, but it bugs me that Alex is fighting by Uri's side. I'm perfectly capable of having my male's back. Logically I get it, but emotionally I'm losing my shit. He gets even one small cut and I don't give a damn, I'm there, and whatever beast dared lay a paw on my male gets dismembered."

Rain chuckled. She couldn't help it. Her mellow, sweet friend looked positively bloodthirsty, and it surprised and amused her all at once.

Alyssa scowled at her.

"I know I shouldn't laugh, but, Lis, I've never seen you so fierce. You're definitely coming into your own now."

Alyssa shook her head in frustration and blew out a breath before attempting a weak smile. "I just have a bad feeling about all these attacks, and I can't seem to shake it." She really looked tense and ready to teleport any minute, not to mention her face was flushed and she looked a little wild eyed.

"Is something else wrong?" Rain couldn't help thinking that there was more.

Alyssa ran her hands through her hair, and Rain cringed at how out of sorts she looked.

"I'm fine. I'm sure it's that I'm still getting used to the crazed emotions that come with a mating. Don't worry about me." Alyssa shook her head. “I’m sorry, Rain. We need to figure out what to do about your damn flounder.”

Rain let out a strained chuckle. “Nothing has changed, and he’s not mine.”

Alyssa closed her eyes and tilted her face to the sun. “Do you care if we just sit here for a bit? I need a break from my workroom, and I want to monitor the fight. It makes me feel better hearing all the chatter on the Guardians’ mental link.”

“That’s fine. I’ve been thinking about getting away for a bit. I guess I could stay with my parents. Or maybe at the shop until it sells.” She cringed. She loved her parents dearly, but the thought of crashing at their place went against every independent bone in her body. Her parents were very focused on their own lives and their shared passion for the research work they did. But, they’d worry about what was wrong and try to help. No one was capable of fixing her problems at the moment. Sirena had nothing that worked to dull the arousal. She’d gotten groggy but had still been aroused.

Alyssa raised an eyebrow. “Drake might have a fit. Your safety is still a concern. Cyril might be dead, but his people are still out there somewhere, and you have an ability that makes you a target. If what I heard when they abducted us was correct, they’ll come after you.”

Alyssa was right, but her parent’s cottage outside the manor didn’t feel far enough away. Though, she had no desire to get abducted again. Alyssa had heard the males saying that Cyril was looking for Mageia with rare offshoot abilities that were different than the usual, air, earth, fire and water varieties. Thank the Creators Alyssa had been with her last time, or they’d have likely never found her. The thought of being an experiment made her twitchy. She also wouldn’t be used against her friend if the enemy came. She was stuck.

“You can always stay with us.”

“Thanks, but I’ll think of something. You two need your space. You just got mated.” No way was she staying with them. When she’d woken up on their couch after the abduction, she swore she heard them going at it in their loft bedroom.

She rolled her neck. She hated the arousal; it was embarrassing. Sirena kept running tests, but the healer didn’t have a lot of time to help her. The Guardians were in constant battle in one Realm or another.

“Should we consider kidnapping him?” Alyssa said, and Rain knew she was talking about Dorian.

“Hell no. I’d love to chew his ass, but I won’t tie him up and make things worse. My pride couldn’t take that. If he doesn’t want me, fine. He doesn’t get me. According to Sirena, eventually he won’t be able to control himself, but I will... I just want to know why he touched me and started this. Any one of the others could have carried me out of there. I also want to rip into him for not saying a damn word to me about what he’d done. Even a letter would have worked. I was going through symptoms with no clue, and he knew.” She was so angry. The whole thing sucked. All of the Guardians knew what was going on, and she felt like unwanted trash.

“Everyone’s been nice, but I can see the pity, and it’s mortifying. Sirena told me some of his issues, but not one word from him.” She was so damned frustrated.

Alyssa just nodded.

“He’s really pissing me off.” They just sat there for a long moment, soaking in the sunshine. She needed to go for another swim. Being in her element soothed her, and she was riled up.

"How is the fight going? The cities are still safe, right?" She was sure they were or Alyssa would have told her.

Alyssa stiffened before speaking. "The cities are still secure. The beasts were thinning until ofioeidis came. I don't like it." Alyssa's jaw clenched, and her muscles were tense.

"Gregoire just assured me that they have it covered," Alyssa said, and her features softened when talking about her big mate.

"I'm sure they do." Though it seemed some of Alyssa's anxiety was bleeding into her. She never would have doubted the Guardians, but her friend's worry was making her question her own assumptions about their ability. Ofioeidis were the worst of all the hell creatures. They rarely made it to Tetartos Realm, and they could do some serious damage. They were scary as crap.

Alyssa looked off again, paying attention to the Guardian link even though Gregoire's assurance seemed to soothe her.

They sat there silently for a while. Rain needed to come up with some sort of plan. What if Dorian never came for her? Never tried to court her or even attempt to make up for his asshole behavior, what would she do then? Her body wanted him. There was no help for that. Her pride wasn't accepting anything less than an apology and some show that he wanted to be with her. Groveling would be good. A lot of groveling. It wasn't like she had any choice in the matter either. She would theoretically be tied to him for eternity, without knowing a damn thing about him. When she was a child, it had all sounded exciting and romantic. Her mate would sweep her off her feet, and they would live happily ever after. She nearly snorted at that now.

They sat there looking toward the pool house, each lost in their own thoughts

"Anything else," Rain asked, hoping there was a good update.

"It sounds like the beasts are mostly taken care of... They should be done soon." Alyssa looked relieved, and Rain smiled at her. "Sorry I've been so distracted."

"It's fine. We've talked the Dorian thing to death. Nothing has changed. It's all dependent on him now. I hate it, but I'm hoping Sirena will find something to help with the symptoms."

A few minutes later Alyssa's brows furrowed and she tensed up again. "Vane's hurt. Sirena's having Dorian bring him here. Sirena sent me a private message for you to come down to the infirmary in a few minutes."

"Is Vane okay?" Rain's stomach flipped. Not only with concern for Vane but thinking about finally having it out with that damned Nereid.

Alyssa looked off again before letting her know what was happening. "He was bitten by one of the ofioeidis. Gregoire says he'll be unconscious for a while, but he'll be fine."

"Poor thing." She couldn't imagine the teeth on those creatures leaving a small hole.

Alyssa nodded her agreement.

Rain stood up and looked in the direction of the infirmary. She suddenly wasn't sure if confronting him was the best idea. "I want to talk to him, but will getting near him take us further into the frenzy?" she asked Alyssa.

Her friend smiled sadly at her. She knew Alyssa wanted everything to work. She appreciated that her friend was pulling for her and the Nereid to get it together. Yes, Dorian was a Guardian.

That meant the Creators themselves saw something worthy in him as a protector. That didn't mean he wasn't an asshole, it just meant that somewhere deep down—way deep down—he had some goodness in there.

"Rain, you're strong and stubborn. You can fight the arousal if that's what you want to do."

She wanted answers, needed to know what he was thinking. She looked down at her clothes. She had on her tiny purple bikini under the linen knit cover-up that Alyssa had made for her. The fitted tunic style hugged her body and dipped low, showing off a ton of cleavage. It was her favorite. Good. If she was going to see the ass, she was glad she at least looked sexy.

"I'm going to wait here for a bit in case you need me. Gregoire said cleanup was going to take a little longer. If you don't come back, I'll know you've got him by the balls."

Rain smiled at Alyssa's confidence in her ability to take no prisoners. She squared her shoulders and hoped to Hell something good would come out of seeing him. She wasn't sure that would be the case, but she needed to try.

She took the long way to the infirmary and finally came to the hallway she needed, more determined than ever to talk to him. He owed her an explanation. She almost tripped when she *felt* him. She braced a hand on the wall and took a deep breath. He was just behind the door to the infirmary. Emotion filtered inside her mind, anger, and it was building. It had to be coming from him. She stood glaring at the door that separated them. She wouldn't go in and interrupt what was going on with Vane, but he had to come out sometime.

She smelled that same delicious scent and knew it came from

him. After a second, she swore it was getting stronger. It was the sweet smell that filled the air right before a storm mixed with something else, something edible. Her nipples hardened inside the soft triangles of her bikini top, and she nearly groaned.

She heard talking through the thick door, but with her mortal hearing, she couldn't make out the words. She chewed her lip, hoping Vane was okay. He was sweet and funny. He might be miserable now, but he was Immortal and would heal fast. He'd likely have Brianne playing nurse for him. It was amusing that they thought everyone was fooled, but in reality, everyone knew about the relationship.

It felt like eternity had gone by while many of the others left the infirmary and greeted her before getting the hell out of there as fast as they could. First was Uri, Alex and her brother, Erik, then Bastian before Drake left. It made for a highly uncomfortable and awkward wait.

Finally, the door flung open with a harsh bang. It hammered against the wall before it slammed back shut. A wet, half-naked Dorian came stalking out. His brows were drawn tight over bright aqua eyes as he glared at her. There was no surprise, just anger. He'd known she was there, just as she'd known he was in the room.

He inhaled deeply as she looked at him. Her heart rate accelerated as she saw his bare chest for the first time. Both of his shoulders and biceps had swirling blue tattoos that tipped in points above his elbows. They were beautiful, and she had a visual of tracing them with her tongue. His chest was tanned and had drops of water glistening all over everything, including his small brown nipples. Her breathing turned erratic, and she felt hot, as if her skin were burning up. She forced her eyes away from his muscled body. The pull to go to him was intense.

She made a mental note to berate Sirena later. A warning that he was going to be half naked would have been greatly appreciated.

Her nipples felt like they would cut through her bikini top at any moment and her pussy ached. She blamed it on the amazing smell rolling off his skin. Her eyes roved to the vee of muscle that led under his loose pants and the hard erection pulling at the fabric. She lifted her eyes and caught a red and angry cut gouged into the ink on one bicep. She blinked and shot her gaze to his.

His eyes had been tracking her body too, and she felt it all over her skin, only his gaze seemed to get more angry as it moved. She'd truly underestimated the draw of the mating frenzy. Sirena had said it wouldn't be as hard for her. Shit, if this was easy, how was he dealing with it and why was it making her insecure that he could so easily resist her? The thought was barely out when he started stalking toward her. Her heartbeat kicked up. She straightened her shoulders and cocked a brow at him. She was thankful as shit that she was already against the wall; she needed the stability.

He narrowed his eyes on her and growled, "Did you think that coming here in that slip of fabric would make me claim you? Tempting me with your hot little body won't get you what you want."

She glared up at him, wishing she had heels on. He was well over a foot taller than she, and she hated that she had to look up. Was that the point he was trying to make? That he was superior to her?

"I came here so that you could explain what the fuck you were thinking? If you didn't want a mate, then why the hell did you *touch* me?" she ground out, fighting the need to lean in and touch his hot skin.

His eyes flashed. He obviously didn't like to be called out, and she didn't care. She lifted to her tiptoes to get closer to his face, but it only brought her up so that her mouth was level with his tight brown nipples. If she leaned a little closer... What the hell was wrong with her? She bit the inside of her cheek to get through it.

She could almost hear his teeth grinding. "You're really going to act as if you're not thrilled at landing a Guardian for a mate." His voice was harsh as he mocked her, completely avoiding the question and moving straight to defensive tactics. Other emotion was rolling off him, but it was hard to decipher with all the anger. Pain? Likely from his rock hard cock. She shook it off.

"You know what? You are an arrogant piece of shit," she snapped. "I'm not so desperate for Immortality and a mate that I would want an asshole. Guardian or not." She poked him in the chest as her anger boiled. The touch of his skin ignited her. It must have done the same to him because he hissed out a breath and pushed her up against the wall, trapping her between his skin and the hard plaster.

She wasn't done railing at him, and she hated that her emotions and his were confusing her so damn much. She didn't care that her pussy wept for him, and she closed her eyes against the feel of his hot shaft pushed against her stomach. He leaned over until his lips were near her ear. "Are you saying you don't want me, nymph? Because your pussy is calling you a liar."

He leaned back until his face was in front of hers, his eyes flashing with challenge.

"Oh, my body wants you," she purred back before taking a nip at his lower lip. "It's my mind that wants nothing to do with you, my little guppy." She would have smirked if she were capable.

His eyes flashed at the pet name before they narrowed

dangerously. “Bullshit. You’re saying you want nothing to do with Immortality and the power of being my mate? You’re not lining up to be a willing hole like all the rest?” He snarled. She felt the pang of pain and bitterness rolling from him. A hint of desperation flirted at the edge and it confused her.

His arrogance was pissing her off, making her a little sick. Almost but not quite killing her desire, that’s just how fucked up the mating frenzy was. She inched close to him. “I’m saying that you don’t know the first thing about me. You touched me, took away the option to ride this out slowly, and then swam off into the sunset. I had to find out I was mated from Sirena, who was concerned that I’d mated one of the enemy,” she bit out. Her cheeks were heated, and she had no idea if it was from excitement or anger—they were running neck and neck inside her. She saw something in his eyes, something that looked shockingly like regret, but it was gone too quickly for her to be sure.

She took a deep breath, trying to control the lust, feeding the anger instead. Big hands lifted her ass and pinned her to the wall before her next thought could form. Her breath exhaled in a rush as she fought the desire to wrap her legs around him. If he thought to bully and intimidate her and then just expect her to fall all over him, he was sorely mistaken.

“I will not be your mate,” he said so strongly it felt as if the walls shook.

“Then you might want to get your hands off me. Again,” Rain snapped back at him. It felt good to unleash her anger, but she knew her body was trying to take her over. She wanted to spread her thighs and feel his big hard erection where she needed it. It was cradled hot and thick between them. Wanting him just pissed her off. The desire to lash out was intense, almost as strong as the heat between them. His hands were holding her, his pinkie fingers dipping into the crease of her thigh and ass, massaging as he pressed his weight and hot cock into her.

“Put. Me. Down,” she demanded and then nipped at his lip again. That thick lip called to her, and she hated that it tempted her so damn much. She wanted to know what it felt like against her skin, over her lips, on her nipples. She glared at it as if the flesh itself were to blame for her torment.

Before she could do anything more, his lips were on hers. His mouth taking, demanding her surrender. She fought it, could have fought his rough tactics forever, but when he softened the kiss, she got lost.

Caught off guard by the gentleness, her lips parted, and his tongue slipped inside, soft and seductive. Everything fell away as it delved in and mingled with hers. He gentled, tempting and tasting her until she was wild for more of him. Her hands went to his wet hair and over his rough jaw. He tasted of something addicting. She was getting drunk on it as his lips grew aggressive and demanding again.

“Spread your legs.” He demanded harshly, his hands moving to her thighs. Her vision was getting hazy. She felt drugged and needed so much more of it. She groaned, unable to stop from parting her legs to make room for him against her pussy. His lips took hers again, his tongue sliding in, exploring, seducing. She moaned as he rode his cock against her clit and massaged her ass with his palms. She needed… her mind and thoughts were gone as they moved together. He was intoxicating her on purpose, rolling his hips into her until she was whimpering into his questing mouth and soaking the fabric separating them. She was almost consumed with lust, never had she been kissed like he was kissing her.

She raked her nails over his shoulders and back. He was so hot, burning up. His muscles twitched under her hands as he half groaned, half growled, and the vibration sent tingles over her skin, pulling her further into the haze.

His lips moved to her jaw. "Tilt your neck back." He growled. She gasped as one of his big hands tunneled into her hair. A slight tug angled her neck and the sensation made her pussy throb. His lips trailed over the sensitive skin. She was panting, barely able to breathe as his teeth tugged on her sensitive lobe and his warm breath at her ear left her whimpering for more. His thumb gently caressed the pulse point at her neck and traced down her shoulder, leaving gooseflesh in its wake as it moved further down to the side of her aching, swollen breast. She couldn't breathe, lost in what he was doing to her. She felt his muscles quaking under her hands as his tongue and teeth tormented her. His hot palm plumped her breast and one thumb slid over her tight nipple, wringing a strangled cry from her lips.

"You taste so fucking good." He growled.

Suddenly, his desperation crowded inside her mind, along with a sense of panic and anger. It was strong enough to pull her from the seductive fog she'd gotten lost in. She yanked at the back of his hair to look at him. Between panting breaths she watched the war going on in his overly bright eyes. What the hell was wrong with her? She needed to stop this. She was no one's doormat, and she could see how he was trying to fight through the lust. She also saw something else. More than the pain and regret she'd felt before. Longing. The frenzy was fucking with them both. If she did nothing, he would fuck her right up against the wall. Her pussy tightened, dying for him to do just that. She closed her eyes, desperately trying to find the anger. It was the only weapon she had to fight through the haze.

"You don't get to be a dick and then think I'll let you fuck me." The words didn't come out nearly as strong as she'd hoped, more a panting whisper.

He dipped a finger under her bikini bottoms, and she bit her cheek to stop the moan that welled up. He brought his finger to her lips. "Don't lie to me. The fact that your legs are wrapped around me and your pussy is soaking through my pants tells me you'd love it if I fucked you right here, right now. You want to ride my dick as I pin you against this wall."

She flicked her tongue out and tasted her own desire. It was a compulsion she regretted succumbing to when his eyes flashed with heat and she felt his arms shaking with tension. "Yes, but you still haven't earned that... or me. I'm not lining up to be another hole for you."

She heard his heart beating against her chest, it matched hers. He frowned. His cock pulsed between them, and she bit her cheek again, nearly drawing blood that time. She wouldn't have him claiming her, and then leaving to look for a way out of the mating after she'd put herself out there.

"Put. Me. Down. Now." She infused steel into her words. "You don't get it both ways. You don't get to treat me like some mercenary bitch without knowing a thing about me, and you definitely don't get to hate-fuck me."

He set her down, but she saw his tendons tightening as if he were fighting himself. He probably was. She slid from between him and the wall, feeling slightly sick to her stomach. Her instincts were urging her to claim him, but at the moment she needed to get the hell away. Running was not in her nature, but this time it was her only option. They were both too far gone to talk. If she stayed another second he'd slam that big, hot cock inside her and she would beg for more. If she let that happen, she'd hate herself as much as he obviously did.

He needed to figure out his own issues. She slid out of the first door she could find and walked on wobbly legs around the back garden toward the wing that held her room. She still felt his lips on her neck, his warm breath against her ear and her pussy ached with need.

She inhaled deeply, hoping to replace his scent with the fresh mountain air. It was futile, she'd never get the scent and taste of him from her lungs and lips. At least she'd gotten confirmation that he planned to fight the mating, she thought grimly. She really didn't know how she felt about any of it. She was angry, and the rejection stung even harder than before. She hated that her mind conjured up bits of tenderness from the experience. He was an asshole and had been toying with her. If she didn't know what had happened to him, she might hate him now for making her feel so damn weak and cheap for rubbing all over him.

She shook her head. Sirena said fighting it wasn't possible, so where did that leave her? She hated that he turned everything around when they spoke.

It ate at her that he hadn't explained why he'd touched her. Some instinct? Something to indicate that he wanted a mate, even subconsciously. One of the others could easily have taken her out of the enemy compound. Why him?

She closed her eyes. Too many emotions had washed between them and she was confused by the whole damn experience. She was left feeling sick and achy all at once. All she knew for certain was that she needed to get to her room and gain some relief for her tormented body. Talking to Alyssa while soaking wet was not happening; she purposely avoided that side of the manor. She hoped her friend would go home when she never came back through the courtyard.

She walked as fast as she could, finally slipping inside the door to the sitting room near her suite. She let out a deep breath and thanked the Creators that no one was in there to scent her. It was awkward as hell living in a place with so many Immortal staff members. She made it to her room and immediately went to the shower. She needed to get his scent off of her skin. It was only making matters worse. She turned on the water and slipped out of her cover-up and bikini and sat on the edge of the tub; it was cold against her skin. She quickly turned the nozzles and listened to the water. The room itself was cool, and it started to take some of the heat from her body. An orgasm or three might take the edge off.

No doubt Dorian was getting his own relief from some human female. She frowned at how much that pissed her off. It had to be the whole mate thing. He'd started them on a road of torture, and she couldn't do a damn thing about it. She wanted to knock him over the head, just to see if sand came out.

She touched her lips, tasting him there along with her own heated arousal. Her traitorous pussy ached for his touch. She just needed to go through her options. She had friends she knew would help her. She had a few more questions for Sirena, and she needed to get the hell out of the manor for a while.

Chapter 5

Dorian's Island, Earth Realm

What the fuck was wrong with him? He'd been pissed and frustrated that she'd tracked him down. No doubt Sirena fucking helped her. Dorian couldn't believe how close he'd been to claiming her against that wall. She'd looked fucking sexy as shit in that tiny bikini. It had infuriated him when he'd seen her standing there with barely any clothes on.

Her sea-colored eyes flashed with anger while her body wept for him. She smelled like nothing he'd ever known. His dick hurt like a bitch, so much worse than before. He refused to fall further into her thrall, but if she hadn't stopped him, he would have. It would have been so easy to slide the tiny bikini aside and slip inside her hot wet cunt. He groaned in pain.

He shook his head at how fucked up the situation was. What had he been thinking? He needed her to hate him, to never search him out again. She had to realize that she was better off without him, but then he'd fucking kissed her. Just one fucking taste, yet when she hadn't yielded to his angry kiss, he'd been caught off guard. Instead of breaking it off, he'd seduced her, coaxing more liquid from her pussy. Tempering his strength, he'd sampled her sweet lips. His beast had whimpered like a damn pussy as he'd allowed himself a taste of her. A taste of what he could never fucking keep. Ambrosia. His muscles ached from holding back his strength when he's pinned her to the wall.

The desire to seduce was completely foreign to him and it had totally backfired. He'd tormented himself right along with her. The feel of her small, soft hands and sharp nails on his arms and back had nearly made him lose all control. It wasn't like she'd stroked his damn cock.

He knew the frenzy would make him out of control, but had every confidence that he could overcome it. He'd been wrong as hell.

He barely held back the compulsion to find her and rip the small slip of clothe from her smooth skin and suck on those beautiful tits as he buried his fingers in her slick pussy. She'd be tight. He could tell she wasn't that experienced and his beast fucking loved it, but that knowledge had nearly killed him when he was touching her. He'd never been forced to hold back so much in his entire fucking life.

He knew taking her would only cement them deeper into the mating, and if she hadn't walked away, he would have claimed her there. He fucking wanted that more that he wanted to breathe. The raw need to make her his was what stopped him from following her.

He ran his fingers through his hair, hoping that Uri would come through with some answers.

Sirena was angry, but she was still trying to find something to dampen the symptoms. More for Rain than him, she'd made that very clear. His sister was not happy that he continued to resist claiming his mate. Sirena had come to him a couple of days ago. She'd tried to guilt him into claiming Rain. He knew his sister, though, and was aware of just how ruthless she could be; no tactic was off limits when it came to getting mates for the Immortals.

After seeing Rain, he knew Sirena had lied to him. The female was more than fine without him. She wasn't suffering. She smelled fucking incredible and was aroused, but she'd had no trouble walking away from him. It actually made him feel better and worse all at once. He wanted her like a fucking fiend. He'd wanted to hear her keen as she came all over his tongue, his dick. He'd make her beg for it.

His body jolted as if he'd been shocked. Mother fuck. What the hell was going on with his beast? That kept fucking happening. Electricity wasn't one of his abilities, and he didn't know what the fuck it meant, other than his beast was turning against him.

He dove into the crystal-clear waves, his body changing as he slid into the soothing liquid. He felt the transformation in his bones and enjoyed the rush that relieved some of the biting pain. His teeth grew sharp, his body got longer, muscle thickening. His tail wasn't like the others of his race, not shiny and iridescent. His was a sleek steel grey lined with spikes up the back. He shot through the water, all other sea life giving him a wide berth. They knew he was a predator that could rip them apart if they dared venture into his territory. He cut through the water, moving first around the island and then down, diving deep to the dark tunnels below. He needed to refuel his energies, and this was his private space. He tunneled through until it opened into a big cavern that glowed with rock in blues and green. A shallow ledge spanned twenty feet, where he could lay with his back in the water and look up to the ceiling above. He retracted the fin spikes and lay there in partial shift, soaking in the world's energies, fuel all Immortals needed as much as humans needed food.

He imagined her body. His female. He shook his head. No, not his. Never his. He could never trust a female even if he allowed himself the thought of happiness. He knew he would find a way out of it, but regret was starting to bite at him. He was beyond thinking clearly.

He closed his eyes and stroked a hand over his hard cock through the silky-smooth second skin. It wasn't enough to pull it free, he needed to spread his legs and tug at it hard, so he changed back to human form. It had become more and more difficult to come as of late. Like his body was storing it up for his mate. He frowned. Immortals needed a mutual damned release to keep at optimum levels. Jacking off wasn't helping.

Visions of her filled his mind. Her eyes glazed in pleasure as he held her small body tight to his, and then slowly the images changed. It was as if he was seeing through her eyes. She was in a tub, looking down through the heavy swells of her tits. His lids shot open. Fuck, he *was* seeing through her eyes. What they'd done, his tasting her lips, had obviously tied them closer. His chest rose and fell and his heart pounded at the implications. If he'd taken her, it would have been stronger yet.

He closed his eyes again, seeing so easily through hers; why wasn't he hearing her thoughts? His brothers had heard their mate's thoughts. He didn't like that somehow it was different for him. Had the little mortal shielded from him? Not if he was seeing through her eyes. He'd made sure to protect his own mind from her in the hallway. He shook his head and closed his eyes again. She was lying in a white tub, her smooth legs bent, and he watched as water caressed her heavy breasts. The way the spray moved wasn't natural. He cursed. Water was her element. All mortal Mageia had an element, and hers fit him perfectly; it wasn't always the case in Mageia-Immortal pairings. The water moved in a hard stream now, beating against her flushed breasts. Her small hands lifted and caressed the heavy mounds as the spray focused on both nipples at once before moving and sliding over her skin like a lover's hand. Her body moved and slid inside the space, causing his dick to pulse in his hand.

He could show her just what that water was capable of doing to her. Fuck, this was a sick invasion, but he couldn't stop himself. He couldn't have her in real life, so he would steal this small pleasure.

He saw goose bumps blanketing her tanned skin, and they were covered with sweet drops of liquid he wanted to lick off. He saw faint lines from where she'd obviously tanned in a very tiny bikini, and he wanted to rub his face all over that small triangle between her thighs. Her smooth flesh was shaved or waxed so that he could see every inch of her mound but not further from her perspective. He pumped his dick, feeling like he might blow the roof from the cavern when he finally came.

She firmed the water to a pulsing spray that pounded over her mound and lower, the water moving, tracking as her hips shimmied. Her slick body writhed in pleasure. His breathing was ragged, and sweat was beading on his chest. He could almost feel her heat through the bond. It was faint, but enough that his beast sent sparks of pleasure to his cock. Thank fuck for that. She tilted her hips up, and he caught sight of a small sparkle. He groaned so loud it echoed through the cavern.

His breathing was erratic when she moved the spray. It looked like she was pushing back and forth from her clit to her opening. Was she imagining him as she masturbated? Did she wish the water was his mouth gliding over her wet flesh? He shook off those thoughts. It didn't matter. His balls were pulling tight, and the fact that he was watching her get off made him the biggest of assholes, yet it didn't stop him. Nothing could. He was too mesmerized by what he was seeing.

She slowly moved the water over her thighs and stomach, teasing herself. He knew her sweet little pussy had to be aching like his dick, yet she still hadn't taken her orgasm. He pumped harder and swirled his thumb over the pre-come that was seeping from the tip of his cock. She tilted her hips, giving him another view of that sweet little piercing that made his dick pulse. He couldn't take his eyes from that tiny sparkle at the top of her clit, and he knew there would be another one lower. Damn, he wanted to see it, lick it. Son of a bitch, the thought of putting his mouth and teeth over that piercing made him ache. He knew how she smelled now, ached to have that scent all over him and down his throat. At the manor it had taken everything in him not to lick her liquid from his finger after painting it over her lips. Fuck.

The taste of her lips and mouth had him salivating. Her sweet come would set him on fire.

Damn it! She was addicting. He wanted to order her to give him more, show him more. He wanted her to find a mirror and position it between her spread thighs. He'd tell her to use her fingers or a fake cock, watching it slip in and out coated in her slick honey. Why wasn't she using her fingers? Fuck, she was tormenting him, teasing them both, though she didn't know it.

She teased the water over her breasts again, then back down. If he were there, he'd fill her pussy with the water she liked to play with. He could get it so much deeper, rushing inside her channel and sliding it back out to cascade over her ass. His muscles shook as he watched. He needed to stop the madness, but couldn't, not until he saw her come.

She'd said he hadn't earned the right to her, and she was right. He hadn't earned it, and he had no intention of trying. She was sexy as hell and had spirit. He knew there was more just under the surface, but he wouldn't ever know what that was. He didn't deserve to know.

He pushed those thoughts away as he watched her back arch and her body tremble as she finally came. His dick jerked at the sight of the water riding her pussy and gliding over her torso, bringing her down. Fuck. He pinched the bridge of his nose and shook his head.

Everything had gone dark. She'd probably closed her eyes.

He opened his and pulled on his dick, thoroughly disgusted with himself. His dick throbbed, but he knew it would stay that way. Painful blue balls were to be his constant companion until he found a way out of this fucked-up situation. His dick hurt, and all he could do was lay there and try to think of anything else. He couldn't stop himself from looking again. He gritted his teeth as he searched, only to see plain tan tile walls.

He was fucked. He didn't want to think about what would happen if he couldn't find a way out of the mating.

Chapter 6

Kane's Compound, Tetartos Realm

He hated the redheaded bitch with a passion. Kane truly wished she would fuck up and refuse to use her gift. Her ability was the only thing keeping her alive. He didn't want anything to do with her, but it was the only choice he had unless she decided not to work for him.

"Elizabeth." He infused the name with the disdain he felt for her. "You either use your power to contact Cynthia as I've instructed, or I finally kill you." She was testing him, and it was irritating. "Either way I'll get what I want. If you're unable to get me more females from Earth Realm for Ian and the others to work on, I will take my chances with finding some here on Tetartos." He would rather not risk getting test subjects in Tetartos again after the last massive failure.

The blame for that had fallen completely on Cyril's arrogance in taking the young Hippeus that interested the Guardian Gregoire. He'd had a bad feeling about taking her, and it ended up with the Guardians descending on Cyril's old compound. With the bastard dead, it fell to him to make decisions on how the place was run. He hadn't worked his way through the ranks and done vile things only to allow the research to fail now. Cyril had been a sadistic bastard, and he didn't mourn him in the slightest. He only wished the son of a bitch hadn't taken his knowledge with him to the grave.

Elizabeth's silver eyes swirled with a mixture of madness and calculation. She made his skin itch. He had been made her keeper by Cyril before he'd died, but it wasn't a pleasant task. She was a twisted and demented female.

She grinned evilly before purring, "Yes, you could get other females here, but you'd never be able to contact the Tria without me."

"I don't give a fuck about the Tria. That was Cyril's shit. They mean nothing to mating research, which is the only thing I care about. You really are expendable to me," he spat out. He'd never liked dealing with the sadistic fucks in Hell. It had always unsettled him, and he'd be damned if he shipped any other females to them. Their bodies couldn't go, those were trapped on Tetartos like all the other inhabitants, but Cyril had no qualms about sending their souls to the demented beings. That was one thing he wouldn't do now that he was in command. Elizabeth's grin fell, and he saw the moment she realized just how fleeting her existence could be under his reign.

He grinned wide at how pale her skin had grown.

He hated her with a passion that ran deep, but he would rather use her power than attempt to get more Mageia in the cities of Tetartos. Her ability was the one thing that kept her alive when Cyril was the leader, and it would be the only thing that kept her alive now. As long as the bitch used it. If she screwed with him, he'd kill her and be happier after having finally rid the Realm of her existence.

"Fine, Cynthia will be in desperate need of a fix by now, and she'll be in an entertaining amount of pain." Elizabeth's eyes shone with pleasure at the thought of the Earthbound Mageia suffering.

He clenched his jaw at having to work with such a disgusting creature. She'd treated him and his men sadistically for the centuries he'd worked for Cyril. That changed when Kane had been charged as her keeper; it was the only good thing Cyril had done in his reign. Kane had allowed his males to dole out some pain of their own, and she seemed only more twisted for it. She'd more than earned every bit of suffering she'd experienced, though, and those males had deserved the retribution he'd given them. She'd tormented them while under Cyril's protection, and before, when she was Apollo and Hermes' pet. None had dared to raise a hand against her, fearing that Cyril would punish them. He'd been a scary bastard.

He gritted his teeth, needing to focus on the task at hand. Ian and the others were going through the samples he'd taken before they'd left the lab. The male was attempting to understand why Cyril had ordered Kane to find more Mageia with rare offshoot powers. Not the normal air, earth, water and fire, but some mutation of the ability. Anticipation filled him. He knew Cyril had been close; he may have even found the answer before he was killed by the female he'd taken and secreted away. In the back of Kane's mind he knew that the only way she could have killed him was if she'd gained Cyril's power as a mate. He didn't believe even an ounce of the story the Guardians had fed to the cities. They were hiding the truth of that death. He wanted to know why. If Cyril really had mated the female, it would explain the Guardians' lies to the others in the Realm. They wouldn't want the others to know that Cyril succeeded in finding a way around the mating curse.

He glared at Elizabeth. After all the decades he'd suffered with Cyril's maniacal behavior, all the time he'd spent working his way through the ranks, the answers he needed were almost his.

"I've already made arrangements to transport payment. Do not screw this up." The fingers of one hand wrapped around her throat, and he lifted her off the ground to make his point. So easily he could snap her delicate neck. They were both Aletheia, but he'd been honed and battle ready for longer than he could remember, whereas she was merely a sick whore that spread her legs for any that would keep her safe from the Guardians' wrath. There were more Immortals than he could count that wanted her dead for her part in Apollo and Hermes' labs before the Immortal exile. She was hated nearly as much as Cyril had been. Her death would eventually be his gift to the Realm.

She looked at him, defiance bright in her silver eyes. Her long curly red hair ran down his arm and over her bare chest. He'd not allowed her clothing as part of her punishment. His cock twitched, and the response disgusted him.

He'd gone too long without a female if the sight of Elizabeth's naked body had any effect on him. He would never allow his dick to touch her. He would finish here and have Angus, his second, take her back to the cell he'd made for her. She couldn't be trusted outside of it. After his duty was seen to, he would go in search of a female to slake his needs with. He knew better than to wait too long, but with Cyril gone, there had been much to do in cementing himself as the new leader. He'd given many assurances that they would find the answer to the mating curse and fought all the challenges that arose. Most had stayed with Cyril for the promise of a mate, or like Elizabeth, to avoid the wrath of Immortals and Guardians for whatever heinous part they'd played in the Gods' labs those centuries ago. The minute they went to Cyril's side, it assured they'd never be accepted again by the others, so in reality they had little choice but to follow Kane.

Much as he disdained his own choices, they were the only ones he'd had. They were finally close to the answers that would make it all worth him having become a monster. He blew out a harsh breath and dropped Elizabeth to the ground. There was work to do. He'd bargained with evil, and he would see it through. He had to.

Chapter 7

Guardian Manor, Tetartos Realm

Rain rolled her shoulders, trying to relieve some of the tension that irritated the crap out of her. She'd taken to avoiding the interior halls and even the courtyard, where so many liked to sit when the weather was so beautiful. That meant taking the back path around the big mansion to the door she'd used to escape from Dorian the day before. She hated what her existence had become. She'd never snuck around like that in her life, always facing life head-on. Lack of sleep and the thought of catching the sultry or cocky grins from the Immortal staff members changed that. She hated that they scented her constant arousal and assumed it was for them. They weren't privy to the fact that she was Dorian's mate. Claimed or not, Sirena suggested keeping that information quiet.

Her symptoms were officially getting worse. Before it would hit at awkward times; now it felt more intense. She needed to ask Sirena if there was anything she could do, if there was anywhere she could go. She needed to get the hell away, but she wasn't stupid, she needed to be safe. She just wanted to be alone while she suffered, instead of having to put on a happy face for the world when she was a damned mess.

She slipped through the door to the hallway to the infirmary. All doors were magically coded to allow access to only those that were supposed to be there. A few more feet put her in the same place she'd been pinned against the wall and nearly screwed. Shit, she couldn't even look at the wall without wanting to rub against it. She frowned, thoroughly annoyed at having zero control of her urges. She knocked at the entrance to the infirmary and waited impatiently for Sirena to come and open it. No one else was in the hall for the moment, but who knew how long that would last?

Sirena opened the door. The beautiful female never had a blonde hair out of place, always resembling a petite version of an Earth pin-up girl. Rain wondered if she could pull off that look. She was tired of her purple-tipped blonde hair and had been itching for a change. She was itching for a lot of things...

Sirena frowned at her. "What are you doing here?"

Rain frowned right back at the Guardian. She was in no mood to take crap from anyone. "I have questions."

Sirena shook her head as if to clear it. "I only meant that I thought you would be with Dorian." Her gaze morphed quickly to concern. "What happened? Alyssa asked me yesterday, and I told her I thought you were off working through the frenzy."

She blew out a frustrated breath. "It was a bad plan. I waited for him, wanting answers, but all we did was snap at each other and make out. If I'd have let anything more happen, he would have hated me. I would have hated me. I honestly don't know if I could mate that asshole if I was dying and screwing him was the only option for my survival," Rain said with an annoyed bite. She was exhausted. Her sleep had been tormented. She felt unsettled and, oddly... stalked.

She found the nearest stool and sat. "He fought it?" Sirena seemed shocked, and that reaction set off Rain's defensiveness.

"I fought it." She felt ridiculous and childish that she'd said it. "Shit, yes, he was fighting it too. He said a lot of shitty things about not wanting a mate, and basically insinuated I was a Guardian groupie wanting him for power and Immortality." She inhaled deeply, managing to get it all out there without getting hit with all of the feelings that came from remembering all that was said. It had hurt, every damned word somehow striking her nerves.

She'd never been an emotional female, but her life had been flipped upside down. She was selling her business, her home and had a mate that was unlike anything she'd ever dreamed. Not in a good way. He was an asshole. An asshole she wanted to jump at the first chance, pride be damned, and she hated herself for that weakness.

Sirena gritted her teeth. "He said that?"

She needed to let it all out. She hadn't known Sirena long, but felt like they were friends, plus she had insight into all the mating stuff as well as Dorian. "Pretty much, and as much as I wanted to deny every bit of it, a part of me thinks maybe he's right. I don't know him. He doesn't know me and has no desire to get to know me. And I *would* rather be an Immortal with enough power to protect myself and those I care about than a mortal that's weak and a liability." She fidgeted on the stiff seat. "I don't want to get old and die. I've made the most out of my life, but now I'm supposed to live in hiding because I'm not strong enough to protect myself. If I try to go back to my old life, I risk being taken and used as an experiment or they take me to use me against Alyssa." She shook her head. Sirena watched her carefully. "That doesn't mean I'm willing to forgo my pride and open myself up to a male that hates me. I want a male that can't wait to claim me, not one that is forced to."

"He doesn't hate you, Rain. I think there's a lot going on in his head, but you're right, he doesn't know you, so he couldn't hate you." Sirena sat down on another stool that was under the counter along the wall.

Rain hadn't seen or heard anyone else in there. A curtain

divided part of the room, and she wondered if Vane was still out cold and recovering there.

"He used to be a completely different male, fun, playful, with way too much energy. When he was betrayed and his friend was killed in front of him, he changed." Sirena's eyes filled with sorrow. "Drake thinks it's because he was denied vengeance for Cahal's death. The females were killed when we went for him. The bodies were accounted for in the wreckage." The healer looked away. "I think there's more to it that Drake hasn't said. He refuses to push Dorian now, but says he will when the time is right."

"What do I do? I'm not forcing it. I don't even think I could live with myself if I went to him again. I refuse to let him fuck me while hating me. The thought alone makes me want to hit something." Her jaw clamped down tight at the thought. "Have you come up with anything for the symptoms? I'm exhausted and horny as hell. It's awkward since I'm basically trapped here at the manor. Add that to the new effects I'm feeling today and I'm hating my existence." She fidgeted in her seat.

"What new symptoms?"

"I feel odd. Something's going on in my head, and I feel paranoid like I'm being watched."

"I'm guessing your links are clicking in place. You'll start to feel his power too. Do *not* try to use it."

Crap, what does that even mean?

"I'll keep looking for something to dull the effects." Sirena's eyes held sadness.

"Thanks. I'm trying to understand what he might be feeling, but he's such an asshole to me. I haven't seen one redeeming quality about him. I know its destiny, but she's being a total bitch."

"He's really not an asshole. He's pushing you away," Sirena said softly. "He's loyal and will be a total sweetheart when he finally gets through his issues."

"Do you really think I'll see that side before I kill him?" Rain said without humor. If she started getting his power, she would not take responsibility for using it against him if he pissed her off. It actually made her feel marginally better knowing that she would get power even without being fully mated.

"So the weirdness in my mind is the start of a mental link with him." *Damn, this is really happening.*

"Yes, you'll be able to talk to him that way."

She knew that Alyssa was mentally linked to Gregoire and, through that, all the Guardians. "I have to direct the question to him, right? He can't just get in and take a look around, right? Alyssa explained how to do a mental shield, but I'm not sure I've done it right." She wanted a little reassurance that it worked the way she thought. It all seemed okay, but that stalked feeling made her nervous.

"That's good. I can tell you that I don't see your mental link connected through him to the Guardians so it may not have fully developed yet. Each mating is a little unique in how the powers start to meld together. If you're worried about him hearing your thoughts, though, Alex or Uri can double check your mental shielding." Sirena offered before adding, "And, yes, you direct your questions to him, but as a Mageia, you might project without thinking about it. Immortals have family links and are conditioned young not to project, but you'll need watch for that."

"I need to check on Brianne and Vane again. Do you want to

wait so we can talk some more?"

"Brianne's here too?" Rain was surprised. Alyssa hadn't said anything about Brianne being injured.

"She tried to suck the poison from Vane's wounds, and it affected her too." Sirena blew out a breath.

Rain could see a hint of worry flash in her eyes before she leveled them out. What wasn't the healer saying? "Are they going to be okay?" She'd originally felt confident that Vane would be fine. He wasn't just any Immortal, he was a Demi-God. A little hell-beast bite should've been nothing to him... Now she wasn't so sure.

"They'll be fine," Sirena said, a little too fast.

"Let me know if there's anything I can do to help," she offered, not liking that she lacked any skills that might prove useful. She had no purpose in general. In a week her shop would go to a new owner and she'd have nothing.

"I've got them covered." Sirena smiled warmly as she declined Rain's help.

It didn't feel right staying when Sirena was obviously busy. Rain had a sick feeling in her gut from the healer's reactions regarding Brianne and Vane. What was that all about? She shook her head; they would be fine. She needed to talk to Conn. She went down the hallway and upstairs to the room she remembered was the war room and where he said he always worked if she needed him. That had been part of his tour when she moved in. The wolf was so damn sweet to her. She knocked when she finally came to the door.

Conn popped it open in a second, and then frowned. "Rain, are you okay?"

"Actually, I was hoping you could help me."

"Come in." He held the door open so she could enter the massive room with electronics everywhere. There were a couple of desks in the back. A huge solid wood table sat in the middle with chairs surrounding it. "What's wrong?"

She almost snorted. What wasn't wrong with her situation? It didn't help to dwell on it. "Is there anywhere else for me to stay? Somewhere that's still safe but will allow me some more privacy. A place to cook so I don't need to go to the main kitchen." She bit her lip.

He just stared at her for a second. She knew he scented her arousal, but was kind enough to ignore it. "I'm really sorry, Rain. Dorian will eventually come to his senses. Don't give up on him."

"I don't even know him. There's nothing to give up," she said, and she knew bitterness hung on her words and hated it. She pinched the bridge of her nose. "I just hate that everything's dependent on what he wants. His emotional baggage. I haven't had a say in any of it, and everything comes from everyone but him." Damn it, she didn't go to Conn to have a pity party. "Never mind. I don't even want to talk about him. Can you help me out?"

She was so damn tired and knew it was only going to get worse.

"There are a couple of cottages on the property, and they're equipped with small kitchens. I'll get one set up with food and help you move in there."

She blew out a relieved breath. Good. A cottage of her own sounded amazing. "Thank you."

Chapter 8

Guardian Manor, Tetartos Realm

It felt as if she were in a cloud. Her body was weightless. She was dreaming? Brianne looked over the grass and felt a heated connection to the male she saw crouched there. A beautiful white lion with bright sapphire eyes.

He was more dangerous to her than any male had been in her long life. Even now, she itched to know what his fur felt like all over her skin. She'd never experienced a connection like theirs. They'd been playing the same risky game for decades. Those wild bouts of sex to fuel their body's needs had turned to something else over a month ago.

He changed into his human form as she watched, his bright eyes scanning the beautiful meadow. It was her dream haven and was safe. His gaze landed on her and heated. That look alone made her breasts swell. The gorgeous nude male stalked toward her with the grace of his animal, and she was transfixed by all his muscled beauty. Her stomach clenched. She wanted to launch herself at him as she always did.

"What's happening?" he growled out. He was frowning instead of thrilled to see her. She narrowed her eyes. He was always happy to see her; she scoffed at his attitude.

"It's my dream. Stop fucking it up, kitty!" she demanded with her hands on her hips. She narrowed her eyes at her dream Vane.

He furrowed his brow before smirking. When the smirk turned to a sexy and seductive smile, she was slightly mollified. "Do you always dream about me, my little songbird?" The words were a soft purr that made gooseflesh rise over her skin. She angled her body. She was just as bare as he was. Her nipples tightened at the way he looked at her, tracking over her body. His eyes were intense now. Nowhere was the playfulness he showed to the world, and she fucking loved that his intensity seemed like it was only for her. His eyes traveled back up her body, and she loved how his fists clenched at his sides. He wanted her, and she reveled in it.

In reality she'd been wrestling with the need to end things, but here she was free to experience all he had to offer as much as she needed. He was what she desired more than anything in her long life. Her body was always ready for him. She frowned at just how needy she felt. It deepened when she realized she wanted more than the usual violent coupling. She watched his hands flex as if he wanted to grab her. Dream Vane was no less thrilling than the real male. He was strong, and her beast loved and needed that in a partner.

"Come here, and show me what we do in your dreams." His eyes flashed with wickedness as he taunted her. His beautiful pierced cock glinted in the light, and she shook her head. Since this was all in her dreams, she wanted more than she would ever truly allow. She wanted to fall into the experience and decided to take what she was denied in the only place she was safe to do so.

She closed the foot-wide gap, rose to her tiptoes, and pulled him down gently by his long sun-kissed hair. She felt his body tense. He had been expecting her usual attack, and the gentleness surprised him. She grinned for a second before his lips came down on hers. He was just as hungry as she was. She tasted and explored him like she'd never done. She wanted him in a way that was foreign to her, desperate, dangerous.

He could never be her mate, the species never blended, but in her dreams it was possible. She swallowed back the sad thoughts. That was not how she was. She was strong, brash and a bitch. Not soft and needy.

His tongue seduced hers, caressing and taunting her. She felt his big hands trail down her back until they were cupping her ass, lifting her to straddle his hips. His hard, pierced cock lodged between them in the best way. She groaned deep as her fluid slicked along his length.

"So wet for me, mmm. What else do you dream?"

"I dream of making love for the first time in my life." Her mind said the words her mouth would never admit.

He stilled and then growled into her mouth. "You want me to be gentle with you." His words were a statement. The feel of him in her mind felt like the softest caress imaginable. An added intimacy that made the experience hotter. Her skin tingled in anticipation. She'd never wanted anything more in her long life.

He moved his hand up to her lower back and lowered them to a soft bed her mind conjured for them. The setting hadn't changed. They were still in the beautiful sunny meadow. Birds chirped happily in the trees far away.

Vane's tanned muscles were glorious in the sunlight. Why had she never stripped him bare in the middle of the day? She shook off the stupidity of the thought. Nothing about this was a possibility in their real lives. There, she made sure to keep everything that didn't involve fucking out of her mind. That had unfortunately gotten harder since his relocation to Tetartos.

"There will be no going back from this," he said as he gazed down at her. There was seriousness, a jarring truth in his eyes that

stilled her for a moment. She ran her fingers through his hair and pulled him down. She wanted to experience this, just once. He purred against her lips, and she moaned deep. Her back arched off the soft bedding, bringing her breasts and hard nipples up against his hot chest. He stayed that way, kissing her slowly as if he had all the time in the world. She reached between them to stroke his big, beautiful cock.

He groaned deep before whispering in her mind, "Put your hands over your head, Brianne. If you want me to make love to you, I need your hands off my dick."

She smiled against his lips and complied without complaint. He stopped and looked down at her with furrowed brows. She smiled up at a confused, dream Vane. She had never been a compliant female; she fought him, always forced him into proving his dominance. Her beast loved that. In a split second he was kissing her again, his hands roving over her sides up to her head. He held her head softly, caressing her jaw and neck as he kissed her to a point that left her feeling dizzy.

His lips trailed to her neck and ear, leaving heated tingles all over her. The sensation stayed even as his lips moved to other territory. She writhed and moaned under the tender assault. Never would she have imagined the sensations that rocked her, the disorientation she allowed to roll over her, giving herself permission to surrender completely to him because it wasn't real.

His mouth sought out her nipples, licking and sucking until she actually begged for his cock. "I need you." She gasped, and he groaned as he sucked harder. As soon as he moved from them, she was finally able to take in a stuttered breath. Soft kisses trailed down her stomach and mound before his lips met her wet pussy.

"Fuck, Brianne. I've never tasted anything as sweet as your

pussy. I want every bit of that sweet scent all over me."

She groaned at how pained his voice was. Her hips rose and circled against his face, and her beast beat at her to mark him with her scent and bite. She wanted to be all over him. Wanted all the Realms to know he belonged to her. Wanted so much more than they could ever have. She frowned that her mind was fucking up her fantasy. She shoved all thought away and focused on the things he did to her body. Thick fingers pumped inside her as he licked and sucked. His eyes closed, and he made soft purring noises against her clit, setting off a harsh orgasm that had her screaming into the sky.

He watched her, his eyes more beast than man as he crawled up her body. "You're mine after this, Brianne. I won't ever settle for less."

The harsh demand in his voice sent flutters in her stomach. If only... She shook off the sadness that wanted to invade her perfect moment.

His thick cock slid over her entrance as his fingers twined with hers. He pushed her hands into the bedding by her head, and he entered her so slowly. Her mouth dried up at how intense the experience was. She wanted to look away. "Look into my eyes as I claim you, Brianne. I want to see every emotion as I do this. Do you understand?"

Something inside her wanted that too. "Yes."

His cock burrowed inside slowly, and he circled his hips. She felt the jewelry on his cock rub inside her, and she moaned. Gods but she loved that he'd done that. "This is mine; you are mine now," he said as he claimed every inch of her while his hands held hers tight to the bedding.

"Mmm," she agreed.

She wrapped her legs around his hips and met every slick thrust. Every time she felt like she would explode, he eased her back. Their breathing was ragged and tight as he took her deeper, hitting the spot that would push her over. He held her like he never wanted to let her go. Her heart ached before her body overtook her completely. They rocked back and forth, his hands never leaving hers, his eyes never looking away, except when he kissed her.

Soon she crested in an orgasm that seemed to pull her soul from her body. She cried out at the same time she listened to him shouting his own release. His heated jets of semen bathed her womb, and she had never felt so incredibly sated. He rolled to his side and tucked her into his body. Snuggling against him was another first for her, they'd never rested together. She felt sleep come for her as an odd feeling settled inside her body. Sleep within sleep?

Chapter 9

Dorian's Island, Earth Realm

Dorian was addicted to looking through her eyes. He wanted her, had wanted her from the start, but knew he couldn't have her. Why would fate give him a mate? It was fucking unfair. It was what every Immortal dreamed of, and he hadn't been immune to those desires. At least not a hundred years ago.

He stood on the beach, looking out to the orange horizon. He inhaled deeply of the salty air and massaged the back of his neck. It had been nearly two weeks of pure hell. He wasn't able to stay out of her mind. He craved a glimpse before each battle, then again when he finally made it home, exhausted.

He was stalking her. For weeks he'd been fighting a war within himself. The need to suffer was a harsh pull in his gut, but seeing through her eyes countless times a day was pulling him in the opposite direction. Witnessing the toll it was taking on her was screwing with him. If he were only denying himself, he could do it forever. He was built to take the pain, but she wasn't. He fucked up by touching her. Later, he'd convinced himself that Sirena was making shit up. That Rain wasn't hurting with him, that the little Mageia was better off without him.

He couldn't get the tension to leave his neck, no matter how much he massaged the tendons.

She'd moved into a cottage at the manor. He saw her arranging her things and unpacking. Tiny clothes and even smaller lingerie. He fucking wanted to rip the bits of silk from her body. Make her stay naked instead. His cock throbbed with that thought.

He closed his eyes and felt a breeze over his bare arms. He slipped into the link with ease. Her face peered back at him. She looked over her shoulder before looking back into the mirror. His breath caught at how fucking beautiful she was, even with how exhausted she looked. The small mirror gave him a glimpse of her gorgeous breasts, peaked and ready for his mouth and hands. She brushed her teeth. Was likely getting ready for bed. Would he see her spread her tan thighs to work her fingers in and out of her pussy again? He moaned at the memories of watching her play with her little pierced clit. Fuck.

She was looking increasingly tired. Every day it was getting worse, and that ate at him. He saw it more in the last couple of days, making it difficult to deny that she was feeling the same effects he was. She didn't deserve to suffer any more than she deserved having him as a mate. He was a damaged piece of shit, and claiming her would only put her in more danger. Though it also gave her some power to protect herself. Damn it, Cahal wasn't weak, he was an Immortal, and he hadn't been able to save himself.

He felt the minute Drake appeared next to him.

He opened his eyes and looked at his leader. He knew what was coming. Had been dreading it. Sirena hadn't come up with anything to ease Rain. How long could he justify putting an innocent through this shit with him? That was the question he'd asked himself every time he saw her eyes in the mirror. Each time he saw the pain and sadness there and told himself it was for the best. That she was better off.

"Are you done punishing yourself?" Drake asked.

"When would it be enough?" he asked with derision.

"She's suffering with you," Drake growled at him. "It's over."

Drake's words pierced his gut. From anyone else, he managed to convince himself they were lying or exaggerating, but he heard the truth in Drake's voice and saw the evidence when he looked through her eyes.

"Sirena might come up with something to dull the effects until we can figure it out." He knew the argument wouldn't hold. He pulled at the back of his hair and looked out to the water again.

"Don't test me, Dorian. I let it go because you needed to feel like you'd atoned for Cahal's death. I don't need to tell you what having another mated pair would mean for your brethren and our fight. I also don't need to tell you that suffering any longer dishonor's Cahal's memory. He was a good male, fought alongside the other warriors with honor, and he deserves fucking better." Drake looked out to the horizon. "He would not want this." His leader took a deep breath.

He fought the guilt flowing in his veins. Cahal was denied the gift Dorian was given. Something he didn't fucking deserve, but desired more than anything. It felt like a lifetime had passed since he touched her, tasted her lips. The frenzy was a bitch, amplifying everything between them to the millionth degree.

"Rain is a good female, and I can't, in good conscience, give you any more time."

She was in pain and he was the only one that could make it stop. He was the fucking reason she was miserable.

Dorian nodded and pulled at his hair again. He wouldn't let his mate suffer.... He'd known it was coming. He would claim her, but he could still find a way out of Rain seeing his memories in the blood bonding. That was one thing he couldn't stomach. His last holdout. He imagined the guilt would always plague him for claiming her, for not punishing himself harder, but she hadn't done anything to merit suffering with him.

His leader pinned him with a hard stare. "Get it done. You're off rotation tomorrow."

We have hell beasts in all five cities again, Uri growled through the link.

"I'm getting really tired of this shit." Smoke filtered through Drake's lips as he spoke.

Chapter 10

Lofodes, Tetartos Realm

Rain was finally getting used to being teleported. Thank the Creators for that. The rest of her life was going to shit, but hey, silver lining, she didn't want to throw up all over her shoes as she and Alyssa reformed outside of Lofodes.

"Are you okay?" Alyssa asked in concern as Rain took a second to get back to normal.

"Yeah, I'm good." She tried for a convincing grin, but the look on Alyssa's face indicated that her attempt failed miserably. She blew out a breath. It had been a week since her encounter with Dorian. The increasing arousal was driving her crazy with it's consistency, but at least Conn helped her move into a small cottage. She loved that it was by a lake and had an intercom to the manor. There was a small kitchen, so she didn't have to see anyone, and she was settling in for the most part. The tension from the constant arousal was wearing her down. It was always there. That unsettling feeling of being watched was getting to her too.

"Why don't I believe you?" Alyssa said, shaking her head.

"How about, fine as I can be when I'm constantly horny and everyone knows it?" Rain tried for a laugh.

"I'm sorry you have to go through this. I hope you make him grovel on hands and knees when he does come for you. Gregoire assures me he'll make you a good mate once he gets his head straight," her friend said with a scowl. Alyssa really wanted her mated, and she knew why. She wanted Rain to gain Immortality. No one wanted to watch their loved ones die, and if Rain finally finished the mating with Dorian, she wouldn't. At least not from old age. A severed head, yes. She cringed at that gruesome thought.

"I'm not so sure, but if he does come for me, it better be on his knees." Damn. Her attempt at bravado conjured an image of him on the ground with her leg over his shoulder. She nearly groaned out loud, and her face heated. She could see Alyssa turning her back.

Her friend cleared her throat. "Maybe I should have used better wording."

She groaned. They needed to change to another subject. "Have you heard any more about Brianne and Vane?"

"Sirena says the tests keep changing, but she wouldn't elaborate. She thinks they'll be out for at least another week. She keeps getting pulled to help with hell beast and demon-possessed problems. There aren't enough Guardians to go around. The attacks are just too constant. I hate it."

"They still think the attacks are diversions?" Rain was privy to information no one other than Guardians and their mates had. It felt good to be in the fold even if she wasn't mated and might never be.

She shook off those feelings and focused on what they were talking about. As far as they all knew, Elizabeth might be in charge of Cyril's people, and she was purported to be one scary and sadistic bitch. Through her powers, she had access to the Tria in Hell and a Mageia traitor on Earth. They weren't sure if she was in charge now and having the hell beasts attack or if it was something more. The unknown was what none of them liked.

"Yeah, but there haven't been any other abduction attempts against Mageia, and that's what they were worried about." Alyssa shook her head, obviously frustrated. "They have the warriors in all the cities on high alert." Alyssa blew out a frustrated breath. "Conn has Earth Mageia going out and watching their territories closely. He's also got the covens on alert about Cynthia, the Mageia that was working for Cyril on Earth."

"It sounds like they're doing everything they can." Rain felt tired as they walked up the rise to Lofodes.

She breathed in the smells of fresh-baked bread as they walked into the city. She'd stop to get some to take to her cottage, but she just didn't have the energy. She needed sleep, although it constantly eluded her.

"Let's go to the shop first. It's too early to be open, and I don't have the energy to deal with anyone. I just want to do one more run-through." All her personal things had been moved to the Guardian manor, but she wanted to say goodbye to the shop that had been her home and life for the last five years. The new owner would be there in hours to start moving her things in. Maggie was about thirty, didn't have a mate, and was excited to have her own business. It made her feel marginally better knowing her baby would be in the hands of someone who loved it. Everything was set. The shop would continue to run without her there to see it.

The jingle of the bell sounded as she and Alyssa entered. She took a deep breath, smelling the soaps and lotions she kept on the shelf by the door. As she looked around at the books and magazines she'd personally sorted and shelved, it all felt different. She expected to feel a little sad, but she wasn't. It was like her mind had already moved on. The place felt empty, odd, like it didn't belong to her, even for another hour.

"How are you doing?" Alyssa asked, and when she turned to her friend, she saw the concern in her pale green eyes. She felt uncomfortable.

"It's weird. I thought I'd be a little sad after spending so many years running it, but I'm more anxious to get the hell out of here. I guess it finally hit me that it's not really mine anymore." She knew the road ahead wasn't going to be pretty, but she would overcome and make the most of whatever happened. That damn Guardian better watch his back.

She felt a sharp pang and her hand went to her stomach. Sirena had warned her that might happen. It was wonderful new symptom had been happening with greater frequency in the last day. She walked to the back of the shop, not wanting Alyssa to see her pain. It settled after a second and she took a deep breath. Once she got it together she came back out and saw Alyssa's flushed face.

"What's the matter?" Rain was worried.

"It's nothing. Just bizarre surges in my body that catch me by surprise. It started happening after the mating so I think it's our powers melding, I feel so much stronger now." Alyssa smiled.

"What did Gregoire say?"

"He's been busy, and when we get time together, there isn't much talking." Alyssa laughed as she waggled her eyebrows. "Don't worry. It's not a big deal; it doesn't feel bad. I just feel a boost of energy."

Rain nodded as she continued to do her last check on the store.

She moved through the space as quickly as she could. She didn't feel right being there, and that threw her. After a minute she settled her key on the counter and locked the door from inside before closing it behind them. She blew out a breath. "I don't want to be here and I don't want to go home either... I feel so out of it."

Alyssa grinned at her. "Maybe we should go get some spa treatments at Paradeisos? Tynan has intense security there now, and it would be more fun to get pampered there than at the manor." Gregoire nearly lost his mind at the idea of them coming to Lofodes alone again after the abduction, but they'd been incredibly vigilant about their safety and watching their surroundings. Even so, Rain was fully aware her friend had been giving him constant updates on her whereabouts the entire time.

"That sounds amazing, but do you really think Gregoire won't lose his mind if you go there?" It was just what she needed, but Gregoire was beyond protective of Alyssa, and she figured that option would get shot down quickly.

"He won't be happy, but he can't argue that we won't be safer there than we were coming here," Alyssa said with a grin.

Rain let her mind go back to the sight of the gorgeous sea around Paradeisos. The water there was magnificent, and being at an island resort meant for pleasure, she wouldn't feel so uncomfortable walking around completely aroused. She bit her lip. Could she find a male to relieve some of the desire there? She hadn't considered it before, but Sirena had yet to come up with anything that helped the symptoms, and taking care of it herself wasn't really working anymore.

"I just told Gregoire. Let's go grab some swimsuits from the house, and I'll take us. He growled and postured, but my other option was taking you home and going to help him. That set him off even more. In the end he's having Uri tell Tynan to expect us. I'll be paying for taunting him later." Alyssa's skin flushed. Rain wondered just what the hell they did at home, but she quickly cut those thoughts off.

"Where's Gregoire now?"

"Dealing with demon-possessed on Earth, and he's got a few more hours patrolling after. He's going to let me know when he's done." Alyssa frowned.

"Why the frown?"

"I feel guilty, like I should be doing something to help. I have my business, and I have plenty of lingerie and clothing orders to keep me busy, but with everything that's happening, I feel like I should have some greater purpose. Fighting isn't an option in Gregoire's mind, and I don't have any abilities that would help Sirena. I don't like feeling that I'm falling short as a Guardian mate." Alyssa rubbed the bridge of her nose. "What would you do?"

"I don't know, Lis. I think it only needs to be what works for the two of you." She shook her head. "Gregoire has been fighting and patrolling for centuries. If you decide you want to fight, start practicing and see where it goes from there. Though, if anyone laid a hand on you in battle, he would likely be there taking them out before you had a chance to. Maybe with time he'll get control of some of that, but I don't know." She smiled sympathetically at her friend. "If it makes you feel any better, I feel the same way. They're all so busy, but I have no skills that would help any of them."

"I've already asked if I could spar when they train in order to hone the abilities that came with our mating. He said he'll take me and teach me the techniques. My father is possessive and protective of my mother, but Gregoire is on a whole other level. I always have to reel him in," Alyssa said, frowning again.

She loved that her friend had so much fight in her now she was able to rein in her big Hippeus mate. Rain grinned as they walked outside of the city's protection spell so that Alyssa could teleport them away.

Alyssa shot her a glare.

"I know, when he didn't want you even petting Havoc, I started understanding how much of a handful he was going to be, but you're holding your own, and I'm proud of you." Uri's pet hellhound was just a pup, and Rain still remembered seeing Gregoire stiffen when Alyssa petted the animal. He'd looked so out of sorts when Alyssa shot him a glare. It was actually about then that Rain finally started warming to Alyssa's mating with the Guardian. Her friend and Gregoire had started out rocky, but in that moment she'd seen how much he cared and struggled with his impulses. It was that tiny glimpse that gave her hope that he would be good for her friend.

She nearly sighed out loud. Dorian and she were starting out rough too, but that didn't mean they would end up anything like the other mated pairs. Her friend was happy, happier than she'd ever seen her, and they'd been as close as sisters since they were children. Rain had a feeling that kind of happiness was nowhere in her near future.

Alyssa's voice snapped her away from her angry thoughts. "Are you ready?"

Hell, yes, she needed a little pampering, and she firmed her resolve to take whatever else came with it.

They ported to Alyssa's home and were changing into bikinis within minutes. She grinned to herself as her friend flitted through her work room looking for cover-ups. It paid to know someone who made clothing and was roughly the same size, because she had no desire to make another stop to get her own things.

"We'll only have a few hours, but we can always go back again tomorrow," Alyssa said as they were leaving the house to teleport over to the island.

"I honestly just want to swim." She sighed at the thought of warm sea water soothing her arousal. She shot Alyssa a knowing look and winked. "Don't worry. I'll protect you."

"You better. Gregoire will lose his mind if I get even a scratch. Those damn serpents better back off."

Alyssa's frown made Rain laugh. Something about sea beasts always made her friend edgy.

Seconds later she was breathing in sweet sea air, and she felt lighter with the bright sun warming her skin. She let out a little noise of happiness and grinned at Alyssa. "Thank you, this is perfect." They'd landed on the big stone patio and were immediately greeted by a tall, dark-haired female.

She smiled genuinely at them. "My name is Cassia. I'm Tynan's personal assistant. He asked that I make sure you were given anything that you like. He will meet us momentarily. Did you have anything you'd like me to plan or would you like a drink first?"

"I would love a swim and a cocktail," Rain said and looked over at Alyssa. "Please have them make it a really big glass of something fruity with plenty of alcohol." What she planned required more courage than any small drink would provide.

Chapter 11

London, Earth Realm

Dorian, Bastian, Conn and Jax had gone from Tetartos, fighting hell beasts, to a big nest of demon-possessed reported on Earth.

They were in a dark alleyway not far from a nest of ten or more possessed. The other Guardians were divvied up in two other locations near Pakistan with the same number of possessed to deal with.

"What the fuck is going on? We've been all over the place for weeks," Jax complained. The dark-haired Guardian wore a scowl. His bright blue eyes flashed with the same annoyance and watchfulness Dorian and others sported.

Dorian hurt like a motherfucker. The mating was fucking his body up. His beast fought him, and his dick was constantly hard and painful. The two weeks since he'd first touched her felt like an eternity of agony. He pushed his fingers through his hair. It would all be ending soon and he felt worse for the thrill that shot through him at the thought of claiming his mate.

"Suck it up, Jax," Conn said, responding to their brother's bitching. With so much happening, Conn's usual office shit was on hold. Their accounts and investments would be fine. The Mageia in the cities were reporting possessed more and more, providing pictures of areas to teleport to and the directions to go from there.

The mortals were encouraged to stay away from the fight. Having elemental and some small magical ability wouldn't help them against the possessed's demon-enhanced strength and speed.

Dorian had spoken to Sirena in a private link before teleporting to London. She agreed to look for a way around Rain seeing his memories in the blood-bonding portion of the mating ceremonies. She said the blood bond had to be done, but she would look into something to dull or hide the memories. The thought of anyone seeing what happened a hundred years ago made him break out in a cold sweat. No way would he allow the innocent female he was destined to claim and protect see that nightmare. It would only mentally scar her.

He planned to go to Rain after the fight was over.

He rolled his neck. She would fight him when he came for her. She'd made it clear he hadn't earned the right to touch her. He wondered what she would do when she saw him.

He needed to get his head together. Demon-possessed were no match for a Guardian, but the fact that he couldn't harm them while fighting made it into a twisted game of dodgeball.

This would be his last time helping his brothers before changing his existence forever.

Conn looked over at him. His black eyebrow piercings moved as he cocked his brow. "Are you good, D?" the Lykos asked. Conn had already told him how good a female Rain was, making Dorian wonder if his brother wanted her. He narrowed his eyes at the wolf. Fuck. He was losing his shit. "Yeah, I've got this." He hoped it wasn't a lie.

He couldn't help taking one quick look to see what she was doing. He needed to see through her eyes before he went into the fight. He went straight to the connection and saw Alyssa's smiling face as she stood hip deep in bright crystalline seas. Where the fuck was she? He didn't like that she was in the water. She was mortal, and the sea beasts in Tetartos had deadly teeth; they wouldn't care that she was a water Mageia. Son of a bitch.

Gregoire, where are Alyssa and Rain? He clamped his jaw down tight as he waited for his brother's answer.

Paradeisos, Gregoire growled back. The male was possessive as shit of his mate and didn't sound happy about where she was. They all knew Tynan, and he'd heard that Alyssa and Rain had gone to the island before Gregoire claimed Alyssa. Fuck, even knowing that Tynan employed Nereids to patrol the water didn't settle him. *Tell them to get their asses out of the fucking water,* he demanded.

The silence lasted a moment. He assumed his brother was telling Alyssa to get out, and that settled him. His brother snarled through the link in obvious irritation. *Tynan is keeping an eye on them personally, and Alyssa has promised me that Rain would not allow a sea beast near them even if one got through the Nereids. Talk to your damn mate.*

What the fuck? He stood still for a second, processing what Gregoire just said.

Conn and the others stopped with him and eyed him. "What's up?" Conn said.

"Rain's affinity is with sea creatures?" He just stood there, surprised. That was rare, and in all of the little prompts from his brothers in the last weeks, not one had said shit about that. Not even Drake. Cyril's males were looking for Mageia with offshoot abilities. He'd thought she'd been abducted because she was with Alyssa, but maybe they already knew about her power. His skin tightened. They were protected for now, but his need to get to her just amplified, and his beast thrummed for him to go to her.

Conn raised an eyebrow. "Yes."

"Not one of you assholes thought to tell me that shit?" he said, pissed as hell. "All of you dickheads came to me. Not one mother fucker thought to inform me she had an ability that put a tag on her ass?"

"Everyone knew," Bastian said calmly.

"*I* didn't fucking know!"

"Gods damned, Dorian. We're really doing this now? Yes, Rain's a cool chick. She'll rule all your little sea horses, Flipper. She's also feisty as shit, and I don't envy you if you hold out much longer. That said, get your head out of your ass so we can deal with the damned possessed. I've got shit to do after we're finished," Jax said in irritated impatience. The big cat was likely just anxious to get back to his fucking harem.

Dorian narrowed his eyes at his brothers.

"Listen, we all get why you're fighting it, but it's affecting her. She's suffering and embarrassed, and that's on you, man. You better fix this shit before she truly hates you for it. You need to end this," Conn said, his eyes flashing. The wolf rarely got angry. He was the most mild tempered of them all, so his words struck harder.

"I fucking plan to," he snapped back.

The others assessed him before nodding. Not one of them liked that he'd been denying his claim. Shit. He might not be worthy of a mate, but fate had essentially given them the finger, and she was getting him whether she deserved it or not.

He rolled his neck. He needed to get his head in the game long enough to get this fight over with. They were less than a block away from the warehouse the Mageia told them about. He couldn't think of Rain now. He loosened his shoulders, thinking he'd rather be beating the fuck out of Jax for that Flipper shit than containing possessed.

The stench of rotting trash and evil filled the air.

Even after all the talking and anger, he was still fighting a semi. He deserved some kind of medal for his ability to fight with a hard-on. His dick refused to go soft. He hadn't bothered with fighting gear. He was in a bright orange Aquaman tee shirt with the sleeves ripped off and worn jeans. Not subtle, but he really didn't give a shit. Clothes fucking sucked ass. His dick hated him anytime he pulled on pants. For a split second he considered sweats, but didn't want his erection that free in the middle of a fight. He scowled hard at the dirty alley walls. His senses were on alert as they neared their destination.

The others looked much the same. Alert and ready. They hadn't bothered with gear either, other than cuffs. All but Bastian wore jeans; the Kairos preferred to wear black cargos. Conn wore a flannel over a dark tee shirt. His sleeves were rolled up, showing the tattoos all over his forearms. The wolf liked his ink, and his forearms were not the only things covered. Conn's eyes moved to Dorian, probably assessing whether he'd be covering Dorian's ass in the fight. That look snapped his thoughts back to the job. He would not be a fucking liability to his brothers.

"I'm good," he said a split second before they were swarmed by possessed.

Chapter 12

Kane's Hidden Facility, Tetartos Realm

"Has there been any change?" Kane asked, his stomach twisting at what he saw. He hated that he had no way of helping her. At least not yet.

"She still tries to harm herself when we allow her out. She's too strong for anyone to control."

Kane breathed deep as Jayr spoke. The healer had been sent to the secret breeding facility years ago. All the others thought him dead. The tall blond male had been the only healer in Cyril's employ, which meant he was under Kane's command now, and Kane planned to give him more to do.

He turned away from the cell, still trying to speak inside her mind, but it echoed back. She was blocking him. He wasn't even sure if she knew she shielded against him. Madness had plagued her for too long. So long that he knew Jayr worried that she wouldn't come out of it, even with a working formula. It was obvious in the way that the male avoided eye contact when discussing her. There had been many indications that it was too late for her, but Kane refused to believe she wouldn't come back.

He locked his jaw tight as they walked.

"What of the others?" He needed to know. It seemed to take a bit more of his soul, knowing that he no longer just condoned what was happening there; now he was in charge of whether it continued.

Jayr and his assistants had been hidden at the facility for over a decade now. To Kane's knowledge, Cyril had only shared this place with him. The bastard had been secretive until the end.

Kane felt in his gut that Cyril had finally found a working formula. Why else would he secret one of the abducted Mageia out of the compound? Kane had no idea where the bastard had taken her, and he was sure the hiding place and any clues there were lost to him. The Guardians had obviously found it and disposed of Cyril and then set up a memorial for the female. Kane didn't doubt that Cyril was dead. The mental link he once shared with the sadistic bastard was gone. He only wished he knew what the hell had happened. The truth, not the lies fed to the inhabitants of the cities.

He clenched his jaw in irritation. It was no help thinking about what he couldn't change. Being in the damn lab agitated him. Kane hated the hidden facility. It made his skin itch, and he couldn't wait to get the fuck out, but he needed the report first.

"They grow. I've altered each batch as Cyril had instructed, but we're still several years from seeing any real results. Do you want it to continue?" The other male looked haggard. He didn't seem any happier with what was happening.

"Is it viable?" Kane asked.

Jayr was lean and tall, his violet eyes assessing as he stood with his hands in his pockets. "I think if we are going to have a working serum, they will eventually be needed."

Kane nodded and said what he knew made him a monster. "Continue. I also want you to double-check the results Ian is getting with his experiments." Ian was smart enough, but he was a mortal and didn't have Jayr's abilities. He wanted every option for the serum checked and double-checked until they had the best possible formula before giving it to anyone. "We're close," he told the male, and he felt it in his gut. They would have the answers soon. They had to.

Chapter 13

Paradeisos Island, Tetartos Realm

Rain enjoyed the warm water while drinking her fill of the fruity cocktail in her hand. The push and pull of the current lulled her, soothed her soul. It was the best she'd felt in a while, but the arousal still nagged beneath the surface. The strain of holding it together was wearing on her body and mind, causing her to fully consider more drastic measures. She pulled her power and made sure that the sea creatures knew to stay back. She wanted to go to them, just beyond where the Nereids patrolled, but she wouldn't leave her friend, and no way would Alyssa swim out there with her. A small smile tilted her lips; no, Alyssa was not fond of being anywhere near the sea beasts. Rain had no such qualms. The creatures loved her, listened to her, and she enjoyed their company. In the seas near Lofodes the water was too cold, most of the year, for her to go to them.

"Do you want another?" Alyssa asked with a raised eyebrow and a smirk. Rain had taken down the first drink before they'd even gotten in the water. The second she'd sipped at, but it too was gone.

She took a deep breath of the sea air. The relaxed warmth, courtesy of her buzz, felt good, but she'd hit her limit. She only wanted a little courage, not to pass out. She was running a fine line. Any more alcohol and exhaustion would finally take over. "No, I'm good."

Alyssa took the glass from her hand and walked it up to the beach, giving it to one of the attendants up there. Such a good friend, closer to a sister. She didn't have any other siblings and neither did Alyssa; that was probably part of the reason they'd bonded so closely when they were young.

She caught sight of Tynan on his lounge tucked under a big blue canopy. The owner of the island smiled from his seat that was full of paperwork. He was gorgeous with dark mussed hair and broad shoulders. That smile of his was downright lethal, and the playboy knew it. She grinned back, shaking her head. This was not the first time he'd been on guard duty for her and Alyssa. Before Gregoire had come for Alyssa, Tynan had taken them out on his boat for the day. It seemed so long ago now. He was easy to be around.

Too bad she couldn't use him to relieve her needs. She'd thought about it when he greeted them earlier, but discarded it quickly. He was friends with Gregoire, and she wasn't sure how close he was to the other Guardians. She liked him too much to make things awkward for him. Not that she really thought Dorian would care who she screwed. She gritted her teeth at the thought. No, the Nereid probably wouldn't bat an eye if she fucked all the males on the island. He didn't care for her at all. That train of thought was quickly killing her relaxed buzz. Bastard.

Alyssa walked back into the water in her cream-colored bikini. "Feel better now?" She frowned a little, and Rain knew her expression had to be dark. She smoothed her features and tried for the calm she had moments before.

"Yes. Thanks for bringing me here. The water helps. It feels wonderful," she said, running her fingers through the crystal liquid. It was the perfect temperature as it caressed her hands and body like a lover. One that had never disappointed her.

"Do you want to do treatments tomorrow and just stay out here?" Alyssa asked without seeming to care, leaving it completely up to Rain to decide. She loved her friend so much.

"Thank you for rescuing me so much through all of this. I know you have work to do and a new mate."

"Whatever," Alyssa said, a soft smile tilting her lips. "It's not as if this"—her friend twirled in the water, hands up—"is a hardship to be around."

She smiled. "Still, thanks."

"Everything will be all right. Dorian will be groveling in no time."

She knew Alyssa was so hopeful for the match.

Alyssa kept smirking to herself and Rain got the feeling it had to do with some private conversation she was having with Gregoire. She shook her head at her friend. She kept assuring Rain that things would work out. Rain wished she had that kind of optimism, but she didn't. She didn't even want to think about him at all. "Let's go get the treatments."

They walked up to the beautiful golden beach. "Did you two enjoy the water?" Tynan asked, meeting them at the shore with a smile. The sand was warm and soft under her feet, and she dug her toes in, loving it.

"It was wonderful. Thanks for playing babysitter," Alyssa said with a grin, and Tynan let out a sexy laugh.

"It was my pleasure, I assure you. Watching the two of you frolic in those tiny bikinis is hardly an arduous task." He flashed a beautiful smile. Rain couldn't see his silver eyes through the dark sunglasses, but she imagined they were flashing with amusement.

"Are you ready for your appointments, then?" he asked.

"Yes. Thank you." Rain was glad Alyssa was holding the conversation, because Rain wasn't feeling capable of chatting. Her body was heating up again, had been since the minute they left the soothing water. She hated it. Tynan took a deep breath, and she flushed with irritation. No one knew that she was Dorian's mate, so he had to think her desire was all for him. He was beautiful, but it was the frenzy causing that particular reaction.

Alyssa went into one of the first rooms, and Tynan walked with Rain to a room further down the hall. "Rain?" He'd bent and whispered her name. She felt his warm breath at her ear, and she bit her cheek, her pussy wept with that small bit of stimulation. She swallowed and shook her head.

"It's not a good idea," she said as he took his dark glasses off and ran a knuckle down her cheek. The sensation made her skin tingle, but it really couldn't go anywhere.

"I'll be in the room at the end if you change your mind." He grinned at her playfully, and she was sure that damn male could melt a female's panties with his voice alone. She took a deep breath and tried to calm her hormones, sending him a small smile and nod before closing the door behind him. She wanted to get the waxing appointment over with. She turned on the shower that was set in the corner of the room. She needed to get the salt and sand off her skin, not to mention cool down her libido, fast.

She banged her head against the tile after she'd quickly stripped out of the wet bikini and washed. She rode through another sharp pain in her stomach while the water ran over her skin. She closed her eyes. Were they starting to come more often now?

She was barely settled under the blanket when a tall female

walked in. Luck and determination got her through the treatment without embarrassing herself. She thanked the Creators for making the female mostly mute and very efficient.

With the waxing done, she lay awaiting a massage, her final appointment. The escape for the day was at an end, and she was already second-guessing what she wanted to do. If it was a male, she fully planned to let whatever happened, happen. The arousal was hitting her hard. If a female came through the door, problem solved, she wasn't interested in a female's touch. She'd never tried it, but at that moment it was a hard male body that appealed to her.

Handling the desire herself wasn't helping anymore, she felt worse after trying, more needy and aching to be filled. She was desperate, but she was leaving everything to chance.

She blew out a breath, trying to calm her nerves, but lying naked, with tight nipples, under a whisper-thin sheet was not settling. She inhaled deeply, and that just slid the thin fabric against them again. She stifled a moan. Contemplating who the masseuse would be was only making her more anxious. The island was meant for pleasure, giving her no doubt that whoever walked through the door would be more than willing to help her out with the arousal, or get someone that would.

Shit, could she do it? Her screwed-up mind was running pictures of Dorian's bare chest when she'd seen him at the manor. Those images had been haunting her dreams and then filling her with self-disgust for still wanting such an asshole. She pinched the bridge of her nose and closed her eyes to control the riot of emotion. He'd caused this, and now she was forced to take care of it herself. She had to do something about the constant need; it was driving her insane. End of story.

She was sure Dorian was taking his pleasure with others; how could he not be? If she was this out of control and Sirena said he would be in worse shape, no way was he holding out. It wasn't as if he felt any attachment or loyalty to her. She chewed her lip, feeling defeated, angry, exhausted, and too damned aroused to make it through another day without relief. She'd been honoring the damn mating, and she didn't know why. It just felt wrong going to another. Plus, the arousal came with thoughts and visions of him and no one else. That was what messed with her sleep. She was miserable and, for some reason, paranoid. She knew their mental link was there, but she refused to talk to him. She was not going to chase after the asshole. She only hoped his dick would fall off for making her suffer.

A knock sounded before a big Kairos slipped inside. Male… That made her decision for her. She flushed when he inhaled deeply. She was really starting to hate Immortals' strengthened sense of smell.

His dark eyes glittered down at her. "My name is Cesaro."

The words weren't sexual on their own, but from his lips they were a soft, sexy purr. Gooseflesh rose on her arms, and she swallowed hard.

"Would you like me to start with the front or back?"

Liquid heat filled her at the thought of having her breasts and pussy massaged with oil. She closed her eyes to get a grip. She was nowhere near as experienced as Alyssa liked to paint her, but she wasn't a virgin either. She wanted this; she could do it. Something just kept niggling in her mind. Guilt, caused by ridiculously misplaced loyalty to a male that hadn't earned it. She clenched her teeth and firmed up her resolve at that reminder.

"Front," she said, and even to her ears it came out as an invitation to so much more. The sheet slowly slid away, and she felt cool air hit her naked skin.

Her eyes slit open when she felt his warm, oil-slicked hands smoothing over her stomach and ribs. She looked up and saw Cesaro grinning down at her. "You have a beautiful body. Your breasts were made for a male's hands."

She bit her lip at the sensation of his fingers and palms caressing her skin. His words only added to the arousal, making her feel sexy and desired. He hadn't even touched her aching swollen parts yet. He was going slowly, and she appreciated it. As much as she wanted to jump into pleasure and the blessed relief that she'd gain, she still felt that damn sense of wrongness in the pit of her stomach. It was throwing her off balance and making her angry, nervous... hurt.

He leaned down, his long dark hair brushing over her cheek as he whispered, "How would you like me to take care of you? I can smell your desire. Do you want more than a massage, little one?"

Her skin tingled as his hot breath touched her sensitive ear.

She swallowed back the trepidation and answered, "Yes." So far her desire wasn't being picky, his hands felt good. She was certain she'd be able to get relief from him, and she was going to see it through and hate Dorian for it later.

He gave her a wink. "I'll go slow."

She watched him take off his silk pants and vest to display a lean, muscular body and long cock. His chest was darkly bronzed and beautiful. She hated herself for comparing it to Dorian's, whose shoulders were so much wider, with tattoos that were mouthwatering as hell. She wanted to see what details were hidden in the blue ink.

A look at the Kairos' body showed no markings, just smooth, tanned flesh. She attempted a last mental pep talk, closing her eyes to the differences in the male's body from the one she craved.

She'd been with two males in her life. Not the huge numbers Alyssa teased her about. Both were Aletheia she'd met at the yearly Emfanisi, a Realm-wide event that anyone of age attended. It was the way Immortals found potential mates. It was also a big event full of all kinds of sexual invitations. The first year she attended, she had been naïve and excited about dressing up and actually finding a mate. When she and Alyssa arrived, she'd found no mate waiting to whisk her away to a beautiful eternity. That had been a very youthful, far-fetched fantasy. Instead of a mate, she was faced with plenty of hot, sexy males who were more than willing to help her forget what fate had denied her.

She hadn't been ready to give herself completely that first year, but the next she'd gone back and seen the same male. The disappointment was stronger after two failed attempts. She'd known it had always been a microscopic possibility, but that second trip changed things. She decided that she would enjoy and live her mortal life to the absolute fullest. Take whatever pleasures life offered her. She'd given Ryce her virginity that year. He'd been playful and seductive, but she'd felt like the experience lacked something. It had been pleasurable and enjoyable after getting used to it, but not what she'd dreamed. In the end her sexual encounters had been a once-a-year deal that left her not nearly as satisfied as she'd hoped. It had never been mind-blowing.

Would the fact that her body was on fire from the mating frenzy make sex incredible no matter who took her? She hoped so. She watched as Cesaro stroked his long cock. She sat up on her elbows in the narrow bed as he leaned in and caressed his thumb over her cheek. She felt the sensation of being watched again. It hit her at odd times. Most often it hit as she was getting herself off, but the last occurrence was while she was in the water with Alyssa. Only for a split second, but enough that it creeped her out.

It was an unsettling feeling as she watched Cesaro's hands slide from her neck down to her swollen breasts. She looked at his bronzed skin against her much paler flesh, hopeful that the paranoia would leave. His thumbs flicked over the tight nubs, and she groaned at the same time an animalistic roar filled her head. She shot up and covered her ears with her palms. She saw Cesaro's mouth moving, but couldn't hear a word the male was saying until the noise cut off. Her head buzzed from the sudden silence. What the fuck was that? Was madness settling in, or maybe it was her body's way of rebelling against the touch of a male that wasn't her mate?

Cesaro's hands came up to her shoulders. "What's wrong?" His dark eyes shone with concern.

"I don't know. I—" Her words were cut off by the sound of the door slamming open, the opening filled with a furious Dorian in jeans and a bright orange tee shirt. The sleeves were ripped off, showing his massive tattooed shoulders, and she heated for a split second, even more as the scent of him filtered in. He narrowed his eyes at Cesaro. He looked ready to rip the male to pieces. Cesaro's hands immediately left her and went up. Rain grabbed the sheet to cover her breasts as she stood with her back to the poor Kairos that seemed both shocked and horrified.

With both hands holding the flimsy material to her skin and a bright flush covering her body, she demanded, "What the hell are you doing here?" Then it all clicked in place, and she narrowed her eyes. That feeling of being watched... "You asshole! You've been spying on me?" Her voice was sharp, more likely shrill, in the small room.

Dorian looked between her and Cesaro as if deciding which prey to unleash his rage on. Without another word she was tossed over his shoulder and carted out of there with her bare ass in the air. The end of the sheet came up to cover her from view, and her breath left in a rush. She was slightly relieved not to have her ass and pussy out for the world to see, but she was still furious. She was boiling with so much anger and shock she didn't know where to start as she held the fabric over her breasts. She flushed when she looked up and saw Tynan, his dark brows raised high, but she shook her head. She was glad he hadn't tried to intervene. Dorian was too unstable to deal with anyone getting in his way; she swore she heard him growl. Felt it vibrate through his body. She wasn't sure why she thought she was capable of handling him. Maybe because she wasn't rational either, and she planned to take a chunk out of his ass the minute they didn't have an audience.

Alyssa came out of a door by the exit, and Rain caught her wide-eyed look. She started to come toward them, and Rain motioned her away too. She would have it out with the asshole once and for all, and she didn't want to stay over his damn shoulder any longer than she fucking had to. It was hard and jolting her with every step. She silently fumed, but didn't fight. She was saving her strength for the battle to come.

The minute he had her outside, they ported away.

They reformed a second later, and she was forced to squeeze her thighs together as she moaned in frustration. It was like no teleport she'd ever experienced. She gasped for breath, feeling wild with need.

He let out a single word. "Fuck!" His grip changed, and he moved so fast she felt dizzy. His hands massaged her thighs and ass as her stomach pushed into his shoulder.

She was mindless as she wiggled against him. Her arousal from before was nothing compared to what it felt like after their bodies had combined. At least that's what it felt like when they'd teleported to wherever the hell they were. For a split second they'd become one being, and she'd never imagined something so intense. She was desperate for release. She tried to fight it, knowing she was losing the battle as he removed the sheet from where his arm held it over her. His lips and tongue trailed over her hip and the side of her ass, leaving tingles all over her flesh down to her pussy, which was exposed to the sea air.

She was losing her mind; soon she'd beg for his mouth and cock. "Put me down!" she demanded, but knew the words hadn't come out the way she'd hoped. Her voice was too shaky, too damn needy. She might want him more than her next breath, but she had no intention of just letting him embarrass her and cart her around like luggage.

She heard the sound of falling water as he completely ignored her demand and carried her through a doorway. She couldn't see much from her vantage point. A few steps more and they were in a cavern room. It was dark, the walls made of stone. A light switched on as he tossed her onto a big soft bed. She looked around quickly as she bounced on the overly large, four-poster bed. The water she'd heard was flowing over an entire wall and washing away in a tiny stream. She saw two doorways and knew she needed to get to one immediately. Just as she wondered if she could make it, she saw his bright orange shirt flying across the room. Turning, she was faced with the sight of his naked torso and nearly swallowed her tongue.

She lost all thought as his jeans were pulled down over his narrow hips and she caught sight of his rigid cock. She wanted to lick the vee of muscle leading down to the long, nearly purple shaft. Shit. She felt paralyzed and completely unable to speak. His eyes looked brighter than before, and his breathing was erratic as he crawled over her body. Animal grace added to his seductive movements.

She nearly choked. "We are not doing this. Not without an apology and explanation." She'd hoped to hell she got one, because her body didn't give a crap how much he'd wronged her, she would give in. She'd let him do anything he wanted to her within seconds and then hate herself for being weak.

He narrowed his eyes. "You want me to apologize after catching you nearly fucking another male? If you want to be fucked, then you will be. By me." His voice was harsh, dark.

Her mouth dropped open. "You always turn it around, don't you? You made it clear that this"—she pointed back and forth between them—"was not going to happen. Don't even pretend you haven't been screwing other females," she challenged and instantly regretted it. She didn't want to hear about him with others. It actually hurt her heart and her pride equally.

The arousal was becoming painful as she crabbed back, trying to get out from underneath him. He stalked her. His biceps looked like they were shaking from holding back, and he looked furious. Good. She hoped he was fucking hurting. He was a total asshole.

"You would have let the Kairos have you, but me you deny?"

"Yes! He didn't call me a mercenary bitch or do any of the other shitty things you've done to me." Why had she felt guilty with the Kairos? She should have taken a male the moment her hand didn't give her any relief. Instead she had waited until she thought she couldn't take it much longer. Why did she have any loyalty to a male that clearly despised her?

His eyes flashed with what looked like surprised regret before his hand snaked around her back and pulled her gently beneath him. He groaned. "Damn it, Rain. I hated seeing another male's hands on you." The gravelly side to his voice hit her nerve endings. He looked confused and wild, and she wanted him like she needed water, but she pushed at his chest and glared instead.

“What now? I let you screw me, and then you leave again without a damn word? Is that your plan? To make me feel like a piece of unwanted trash? Again?” Were his eyes getting glassier? He looked feverish above her. It was obvious he was losing control. Damn it, couldn’t he leave her with one small ounce of pride. “Tell me this would be more than a quick fuck or don’t touch me, because I will hate you for it. Don’t make me just another hole. Not to you,” she said the words in a whisper. The truth made her stomach ache, and she was horrified that tears burned the back of her eyes. She was at the end of her rope. She refused to cry, so she bit her cheek and swallowed back the hurt. She wanted to rail against him, but desire and pain were suffocating all the anger. Her pride was going to get trampled, and she knew it. He was stronger, faster. She’d never make it to the other room, and she wasn’t sure her limbs would even do what her mind told them. They were both too far gone. The simple touch of his hot hand on her bare back ignited her to new heights of agony. It was getting harder to breathe.

“I haven’t fucked anyone else. I know you want and deserve groveling, but I don’t know how.” He looked uncertain and in pain, but there were so many other, softer emotions running across his face, and she didn’t dare trust them.

“I’ll settle for ‘I’m sorry,’ for now, but only if you plan on seeing this through and not using my body as if I’m nothing and have no feelings.” He was the one male in the world who she’d always thought would cherish her. She couldn’t stomach the idea of *him* using and discarding her.

“Fuck, Rain. I’m so sorry for hurting you. You’re not nothing...” He closed his eyes tight. “You’re the only one I want, the only one my beast craves, and you don’t deserve the life you’ll get with me.” Before she could fully process the sweetness behind the softly spoken words, his mouth came down over hers, softly, seductively...

When she gasped, his tongue slipped inside and took possession. She struggled, her hands going to his muscled back. He was drugging her senses, washing away all thought. She succumbed to the need and let him take her mouth in a way she could easily become addicted to. He tasted so damn good, better than her favorite sweet wine or the rainwater he smelled of. She wouldn't ever get enough.

His words ran through her mind. He wanted only her... His beast wanted her. She really hoped he hadn't been fucking Earth's female population as she suffered. It might make her gullible, but she swore she heard truth in his words. Saw it in the pained look on his gorgeous face. She probably saw what her heart wanted to believe, but it was too late. They were too far gone to fight any of it anymore. She was defeated. She might regret letting him touch her with so little fight, but she needed this, just once. At least she'd gotten an apology. It would have to be enough to ease her pride, for now. She ached and hurt too much not to get some ease. Her core actually throbbed. She'd take the lifeline and believe the words he'd given her, forget for the moment that he didn't really want her. This round was his.

He shifted her so that her head rested on soft pillows. His lips and tongue were on her neck, making her moan, before trailing to the sensitive spot behind her ear. His fingers tunneled in her hair as he gently angled her head. *Let me make it better. I'll take the pain away. Give you the pleasure you deserve, what I should have given from the beginning,* he murmured inside her mind, making her whimper at the intimate caress inside her head and the soft touches over her skin. *I need a taste of your sweet wet pussy more than I need to breathe. Will you give it to me, Rain?*

Creators, she'd give him anything. Her entire soul if he kept touching her skin and whispering sweet sexy things in her mind. He made it sound like he actually cared about her suffering more than his own. She moaned as his lips trailed along her collarbone. He licked and nipped at her sensitive skin, causing her chest to rise up. Her breasts were begging for his lips. "We'll talk after we feed this?" She was happy she managed to get the words out.

Yes. His lips continued to trail down, finally meeting her aching, swollen breasts. He rubbed his face all over them; the slight abrasion from his stubble only made it hotter. *So fucking beautiful,* he said as his tongue twirled around her hard nipples before he suckled at the tight tips. Jolts of heat raced from her breasts to her pussy as she pushed against his mouth, greedy for more. He gave her what she needed, his teeth nipping before he sucked harder. She almost came from that alone and groaned in protest when he moved to torture the other side. Her fingers dug into his hair and back, her thighs rubbed at his sides, and she couldn't get enough of touching and being touched by him. His skin was so hot against hers. She felt his muscles spasm everywhere she touched, and she wasn't sure either of them could take much more. Soft noises came from her lips, incoherent begging. All that mattered was his mouth on her skin. He used both hands, pushing her breasts up and together as he moved from one to the other. It wasn't enough. His chest was resting between her thighs, and her pussy clenched, needing his cock.

"Your nipples are so responsive. Fuck, I can feel your body jolt with each hard suck. What else is sensitive, Rain? Will your pussy pulse against my lips?"

His words alone were heating her as much as his tormenting lips. She had trouble breathing just listening to him. "Finish this. I can't take any more." Her hands ran over every bit of skin she could reach and then tunneled in the soft strands of his hair. It wasn't spiked with product like before, and she loved the feel of it over her fingers. The foreplay was killing her, and she was so wet that there was no need for it.

"I promise you can come all over my tongue, nymph." His breathing was just as harsh as hers. Why was he making her wait?

"No more torture. I need to be filled," she begged, sure that his mouth wouldn't be enough to feed the insanity.

"Spread your legs wider and tilt your hips. Imagine I've tied them to your arms. You're small, Rain. I want you more than ready before I take you."

Her eyes fell, she couldn't get that image out of her mind, nor could she come up with a hotter picture than being tied up and sexually satisfied by him. Her legs spread wider beneath him, her knees lifting up and back, leaving her completely exposed, vulnerable. The need was making her a different person, one that trusted him, at least with her pleasure.

His arms were shaking as he lifted his body away. Those eyes seemed overly bright, his skin flushed. He was holding back his own pleasure. Why? "Gods, this is the view I've craved. I'll gladly tie you up and feast on your wet pussy every damn day. You smell so good. I can't wait to tug on that piercing with my teeth and hear you moan as you come all over my tongue." Sweat dotted his forehead as he stared at her. So much intensity shone there, all focused on her as he sat on his knees between her spread thighs. She watched as his muscles twitched when he caressed her bent thighs and then dipped his fingers in her juices. A deep groan tore from his lips as he spread the liquid all over her pussy and ass. She wanted him so much her chest heaved as he pushed a single digit inside. Another harsh groan rang through the room as his head fell back. He looked like a God. Every inch of perfectly sculpted muscle had drawn taut, the tendons along his neck strained, just from touching her. Her eyes tracked the fine sheen of sweat along his hard chest. She wanted to lick every dip and rise, then use her tongue to trace the swirls of his tattooed shoulders.

The next sound from his lips was a harsh, pained noise that set her nerves on end. Her skin tingled at his touch, and she was so ready for more. So needy, but he was holding back. His eyes shone as they tracked over her body. He looked at her as if he'd never seem anything more beautiful. "I'm going to wreck you, Rain. You won't ever want another. You'll be mine completely after this. You may deserve more than you're getting, but I won't let go once I've had you..." His body bent, lips coming down on her wet pussy without warning, and she gasped before whimpering. It was so damn good, she was dizzy from it.

He added another finger as he licked her juices and growled against her pussy. "You're snug and so damn hot. You'll burn my dick when I get inside you, Rain." She loved the sound of her name on his lips.

He rubbed his face against her thighs in between lashes of his tongue that went from her slit down to her ass. His lips moved back up and sucked her clit and piercing, then growled against her flesh. The vibrations sent more fluid from her body, and her back came off the bed as she dug her fingers in his scalp. She was going to come. The second he tugged the jewelry with his teeth, she cried out as a harsh climax rocked her. He held her hips and gently laid a kiss against her waxed mound while her body pulsed. Her cries were incoherent and out of control. The release only seemed to whet her appetite. Her need hadn't abated, it'd grown harsher. Her chest heaved as she wiggled in his hold. She'd known. It wasn't enough.

"Dorian, I need... so bad."

"Look at me." His eyes were still bright, his muscles tense as he guided his cock to her pussy. His arms were quaking by the time the head was inside her.

"Fuuucckk, it's so damn tight. Mine." He groaned, and judging by the arch of his neck and the harsh look, she knew he was doing his best to hold back.

"Dorian, let go," she said, wanting him wild. So much emotion… she couldn't understand. She was so wet and needy that she put her feet on the bed, pushing her hips up for more.

He growled at her, and his eyes flashed. "I'm barely holding on. I shouldn't have tasted you. Fuck, I'm not sure I can do this without hurting you." His eyes were wild, panicked, and her heart clenched. His body came over hers, his arms twitching and straining at her sides. Each harsh breath he took rocked his chest into her.

She put her hands on his shoulders. "If it's too much, I'll tell you, but right now I need you to move. I can take it hard."

He looked down as she said the words. His eyes flashed with concern before morphing to something more feral. Beads of sweat dotted his forehead and chest. She could tell from his pained look he couldn't stop the thrust that took him all the way to her womb. Her back bowed off the bed in shocked rapture.

He made an agonized sound, but stayed there, eyes closed, neck straining as she adjusted. It was good, full, so very full, but so hot and intense. She moved her hips, and he groaned deep. "You have to stop moving." His voice was harsh, his eyes open and narrowed on her. He looked like he was in agony. "You have no idea what I'm holding back. You've got to stop before I hurt you." He stilled her movements with one hand at her hip. His strength almost too much. He eased his grip immediately, and she moved again, unable to stop it. She needed more of him.

"Rain, damn it, stop!" he roared, but she couldn't, she was too far gone. She wanted to come. A small part also wanted to be the mate he needed, one that fed this need for him. It didn't make sense;

it just was. Everything about it felt right, so right she couldn't help but move.

"You're so much more than—"

She didn't know what he meant to say, because his words cut off on a harsh groan. Her walls clenched down tight, and she held on, her fingers digging into his taut back.

He pulled out and pushed back, his jaw clenched, and another pained sound came from his lips. "Rain, stroke your clit. You're so damn tight. Come around my cock."

She groaned at his words and pushed a hand between them. She was close, circling her hips as his thrusts grew harder, faster, his balls smacking against her ass. A second later she came hard, tensing up as he hammered in and out of her channel. She met his thrusts. It was a rough, wild claiming, his breathing was erratic, and the wet sound of him taking her filled the room. She felt like she might come again even with the ache in her pelvis.

"Tell me you're okay? Tell me I haven't hurt you?" His eyes were filled with pained horror as he looked down at her. His hips continued to thrust deep, and she whimpered, needing to come again, not caring about the bruises she'd have later.

"More," she moaned as he continued to fill her. His chest came down over her, his hands cradling her head while his hips rocked, slipping his cock over nerves that were deep inside her. Some hidden place that made her pulse around him. He managed to hold her gently while his groans grew more animalistic. The sound mixed with the slick smacking of their bodies connecting. The noises coming from them drowned out the small waterfall and the screeching of the big four-poster bed rocking beneath them. It was so intense and all-consuming she bit his shoulder as she came hard, pulsing around him again.

"Fuck, the way you clamp down—"

She felt the moment he came. It was like an electric current pulsed inside her, igniting those hidden nerves all over again. She shot over the edge, crying out as she came over and over, her body bucking against his as she clawed his back. His cock throbbed as he continued to thrust, his body shuddering above her. They both came in another heated climax that would have shot her out of the bed if he wasn't on top of her, holding her down with his bulk. She cried out as that current electrified her again. The complete ecstasy of it caused spots to line her vision. She took deep breaths and fought to keep from passing out beneath him. Her ears rang, but she managed to fight back unconsciousness, barely.

She held onto him; she couldn't let go. She'd buried her face in his warm slick chest, and she thanked the Creators he couldn't see her emotionally bleeding out. She couldn't let go of him until she got it together. She realized that he had to be holding his full weight off of her or she'd be suffocating, and she closed her eyes. She felt his hands tunneling in her hair, massaging her scalp. Holding her head against him tenderly. The soft comfort only added to the crazed aftereffects of what they'd done. She'd never felt anything like it, and it left her more exposed and vulnerable than she'd ever been. Now that the frenzy was fed and her mind was free to feel the full impact of what she'd done, she felt splayed wide. Every bit of her, not just her body. It was like her soul was leaking out all over the bed. She couldn't look into his eyes, self-preservation had her avoiding the truth of their situation. She refused to be ripped apart by reality so soon after feeling something so magical. Her fingers were embedded in his back, and she didn't care. Knew he could take it.

She opened her eyes, hating her weakness. She was not this person. She was strong and defiant; she didn't hide. She took a deep breath and pried her stiff fingers from his skin. She hardened her heart and readied herself for whatever shitty thing he planned to say or do next. Now that her mind had some control back, she realized that he would have said anything to screw her. She was a naïve idiot if she thought any of the sweet words were real.

He kissed her hair, throwing her off her game. "Don't," was all he said before lifting his body from hers. Pulling from her body, it felt like a limb was being torn from her. He wrapped the blanket around her chest, and a towel flitted into his hand a few seconds later. His Guardian powers at work. His come was all over the inside of her thighs, and she closed her eyes for a split second. "Let me clean you up, Rain." The words were soft, he was still acting sweet, and she didn't know what to do with that. She had to get a grip. The blanket was moved, and her thighs spread automatically when the towel touched her mound. She was shocked her body obeyed him so easily. It had to be exhaustion making her weak and easy to manipulate.

She saw his jaw clamp down tight as he gently cleaned up the mess. She didn't have the energy to sit up, so she didn't. She just let him cover her back up, and she took another deep breath, bracing for it. She was too strung out to fling insults, but had no doubt they were coming. They'd gone from fighting and hating each other to mind-blowing sex that felt like so much more than it could be.

He blew out a breath and rubbed a hand over his face as he sat on the edge of the bed.

"I'm not going to fight you, Rain, and it was a lot more than mind-blowing." He inhaled again, and she braced for it. He looked at her, and she saw regret shining back, so strong it gutted her. "I know you're in pain. I know you hurt." He swallowed, and the look on his face was more agonized than before. "I'll have Sirena come check you."

Her mouth dropped open in shock. “No, you will not. Yes, I’m sore, but I’m not injured and in need of a healer.” How did he even know she was hurting? She hadn’t said anything. Had she flinched when he cleaned her up? No. He’d been answering her thoughts.

“Damn it, Dorian! Are you in my head?” Had he heard everything? She was mortified, couldn’t even breathe.

“Yes, you’re broadcasting. I couldn’t help but hear.” He at least sounded contrite.

Her heartbeat faltered, and she choked out, “The whole time?”

“Yes.” He sounded like he would have denied it if he could, and she wished he had. Her thoughts had been so vulnerable, raw. She looked away.

He leaned over her, looking worried and uncertain. His forehead touched hers. “You have every right to be angry with me.”

Hell yeah, she had every right! His lips tilted, obviously hearing her thoughts, and she frowned, gearing up to rip into him. She swore she’d shielded her thoughts the way Alyssa had instructed.

“Rain, I’m so much stronger than you. I’ll help you with a shield, but knowing what you were thinking was all that kept me sane while I claimed you. I couldn’t do it sooner, I was too out of control, and at the end I was too worried about your pain. I wanted to hear it all. I’m so sorry.”

He kissed her lips gently, but she was out of sorts, split open again. It was an invasion. How would he have felt if she was in his head?

“You’re right. I’m sorry, and I’ll find a way to make it up to you.”

Her heart clenched in her chest, and then his hands went to her head, and she felt him in there. It felt like a screen sliding up, and her thoughts echoed for a split second. Safe. Her thoughts were safe.

"When did it start?"

"The minute I picked you up in Paradeisos." Okay, so not every time he was in her head spying on her through the last two weeks. That meant she'd protected her mind, just not as much as she'd hoped.

"If you won't let me have Sirena look at you, I'll take you to the hot spring. You can yell at me and make me beg for forgiveness while it helps ease the pain." He still looked so damned concerned, and he cringed while giving her permission to rail at him. Not that she needed it.

Who was this male? Was it a trick? She blew out a breath, realizing just how paranoid she sounded.

He lifted her into his arms, blanket and all.

"I'm perfectly capable of walking." Maybe. She was sore.

"I'd rather carry you." Those words, mixed with the sound of his voice, shouldn't have made her soften, but they kind of did. She hardened her heart. He'd done and said some horrible things, too much to just let go. And even though she understood his reasons for listening to her thoughts, it was still a huge invasion that hit when she was at her most vulnerable. She firmed her jaw, but she was slowly losing the fight against exhaustion. Her eyes felt heavy; the hot springs sounded good. She'd rip into him once they were settled in the water.

"Fine." If he wanted to carry her, she just didn't care. The idea of walking seemed too daunting anyway.

He carried her through a hidden part of the rock wall into a dark tunnel. She couldn't see much but the iridescent rock lining the walls. She nearly snorted. She couldn't have walked down the tunnel if she wanted to. Not without feeling for each step with her toes and probably eating it hard. Would it have really killed him to put in a damn light? She got so irritated when her mortal limitations were thrown in her face lately. It never bothered her before, but now it did.

Chapter 14

Dorian's Island, Tetartos Realm

Dorian was grateful the manor staff cleaned his place occasionally. He'd built the place well over a century and a half ago and hadn't been there since Cahal's death. Instead, he'd constructed a home that was similar on Earth. He'd refused to live in a Realm he hated. Since taking Rain to his Earth home hadn't been an option, he'd brought her there. He'd had no desire to claim her in his suite at the manor, or even in her tiny cottage.

What did he do now? The hidden tunnel was dark as he walked her down to the cavern below. He hated himself, he'd hurt her, yet he was bastard enough to want her again. His dick bobbed against her back as he took each step.

"How far is it? You're not thinking of leaving me there, right?" Suspicion and irritation laced her tone.

He blew out a breath. He'd pushed her away, said shitty things so that she'd hate him. She might not actually hate him, but he managed to make his life a hell of a lot more difficult. Shaking his head, he followed the tunnel, offended that she thought he'd leave her in a cavern.

It looked as if he'd just begun groveling. He couldn't stop the growl infused in the words. "I'm not leaving you anywhere."

She was wrapped up in the soft blanket, yet he still felt her heat through the material. She smelled of his come; it mixed with her own sexy scent that had been rocking him from the beginning.

He wished to hell that he could hear her thoughts again. They'd been like a physical blow to the gut, but at least he knew what was going on in her head. He hadn't considered her pain or dreams when he'd run. He assumed she'd be better off without the danger that came with being close to a Guardian. He still smelled Cahal's blood on his skin. It haunted him, yet now he was taking what his friend would never have. Guilt churned his gut.

Being in her head showed him just how fucking perfect she was in every damn way. She was everything his brothers said, worthy, loyal, strong... His.

Every muscle in his body ached from holding back when he'd claimed her intoxicating little body. She was his to protect and care for, yet it was nearly impossible to temper his strength with her.

"Where are we?"

"My island on Tetartos."

"I thought you lived on Earth." She sounded... disappointed? He knew her business was selling Earth items; did she hope he'd taken her to the other Realm?

"I do. I used to live here. When I moved..." He cleared his throat. "I built a home almost like it on the sister island there."

The passage was steep. The wide steps were carved into the rock, and he was thankful he'd made the space wide enough to carry her down. He wouldn't want her walking after he'd abused her sweet little pussy. He hadn't been able to stop; he'd never been so rough with a mortal and was shocked he wasn't feeling the pain with her. Mageia were technically evolved humans, and a Guardian couldn't harm one without suffering. Maybe he was overreacting, but he'd feel better getting her into the soothing warm water of the springs. He would make it up to her. He would be fucking gentle with her if it killed him. He'd hold back the wild instincts of his beast.

"You've been in my head." It wasn't a question. He knew that the next hours, days, maybe even weeks would be filled with her itemizing all the shit he'd screwed up. She had every right to. She didn't know him or his reasons.

"Yes." Not something he was proud to admit.

"Why?"

"It just happened." He cleared his throat. He owed her after being in her head, but sharing wasn't natural for him. "After I nearly claimed you in the hallway, I knew we'd formed the mental link, but it was barely there." He paused. "I didn't realize I'd be able to see through your eyes."

"Just happened... What did you see?" she asked. Was her voice huskier, or was his dick just hopeful?

"Whatever you saw."

She let out a little yawn and then rested her head against his shoulder. Was she going to fall asleep in his arms after everything? She felt so small, vulnerable, and something inside him had changed since claiming her. He never wanted to put her down. He felt his life force so close to the skin, pushing to get out. It wanted to combine with hers. They were connected in a way he knew was only going to get stronger. He took a deep breath.

Hearing her thoughts while claiming her was what caused his change. It wasn't just the sex, though that had been more than the mind-blowing she'd called it. No, it was her. She was special. Guilt slammed him hard from all the pain he'd caused. He'd known how young and innocent she was, yet she had a core of strength that belied that youth. She'd been trying to honor the mating when she thought he hated her and was fucking any female that moved. She was everything a mate should be, loyal, strong, beautiful and so fucking sweet. Inside and out. The things he wanted to do to her, damn. He nearly groaned. Her pussy was a treat he planned to enjoy every day of their lives.

His heart had almost split open hearing just how low he'd made her feel. He would never let that happen again. He may not deserve a mate, and she may not deserve a male that failed those around him, but the choice wasn't theirs. He was responsible for her, and he would care for her and make up for the things he'd done.

If only he could just spend his days eating her sweet pussy until she forgave him. His lips tilted for a split second. He didn't think burying his face between her thighs would make her forgive that he'd been in her mind hearing her at her most vulnerable. It had been intense. Her body had trembled in shock, and her fingers had dug into his skin. She'd thought it was magical and forced herself to be strong and ready for him to hurt her again.

"Is something wrong? You just tensed." He heard the dread in her voice and cursed.

"I'll make it all up to you, nymph," he whispered and kissed her hair. Her small intake of breath was all he heard before the cavern opened up in front of them. It was full of rock formations, more brightly lit than the tunnel had been. The ceiling was high, and steam filtered up from the far pool. He walked around the side.

"The big pool below has tunnels that go out to the sea." He watched as she looked around. "I'll take you that way one day." He felt her move and saw her looking up at him. So beautiful. He wanted to taste her lips again. Suck on the pouty lower one.

"It's beautiful," she said, looking away, as he wound around to a small pool.

He set her down and quickly unwrapped the blanket. The fabric was tossed over the nearest rock, and she was back in his arms before she had a chance to argue. He needed to hold her. She felt so damn good, her naked body against his. He nearly groaned hearing the soft moan that came from her lips as he moved them into the warm water. It was a comfortable temperature from being fed by both hot springs and a fresh water stream above.

He hated that the water would wash away some of his scent from her skin. What the fuck was he thinking? Nereids were one of the more sexually free races. They didn't mark their females.

His dick bobbed against her back as he walked them to the other side of the small pool, and he clenched his teeth. He got the distinct feeling that mating his Mageia would be a true test in control.

"Feels so good. I could fall asleep in here." Her voice slurred a little, and she let out an adorable yawn. Would she really fall asleep in his arms? It was like his beast was purring inside. It wanted to mark her, fuck her, mate her.

A second later, he heard her breathing even out. With her head resting against his chest, she'd actually fallen asleep. She turned a little and rubbed her face against his chest. His heart nearly stopped; in all his centuries he'd never had a female cuddle into him like that. He just stared down at her, speechless, humbled that she trusted him to watch over her sleep. Long eyelashes fanned out on her soft cheek, and he brushed aside a lock of hair that had fallen over the side of her face. She weighed nothing. He stifled a groan as he slid his dick to rest under her and tried to relax. Her small hands came up to ball next to her head, and he stayed like that, listening to her steady heartbeat and sleepy noises.

Sirena, is there anything I can do for, um, sore muscles, for Rain? Well, that was awkward.

She answered back in a second. *Where are you now?*

In my cavern at the island.

I'll drop off a jar of something you can massage into all of her sore spots.

His thumb circled softly over the soft skin of her arm as he lounged.

A few minutes later Sirena added, *I left it at your door, with some stuff Alyssa packed up when you took Rain. The cream works quickly.* After a pause she spoke again. *You might consider bringing her to the manor.*

Why?

Bathroom and kitchen. She's mortal and needs those things.

Son of a bitch. Ever the practical sister, she would think of something to make him even more un-fucking-comfortable.

He blew out a breath, shaking his head.

Drake, is the beach house free? Drake liked his comforts and made sure they had options throughout Earth and Tetartos Realms. He hadn't been thinking clearly, or he would have thought of the beach house much sooner.

Chapter 15

Guardian Manor, Tetartos Realm

Brianne looked up into the bright sapphire eyes of her dream lover and smiled. He was leaning over her, looking broody, and she found it amusing. It felt as if she'd been dreaming forever, and she loved every hot second of it.

His eyes flashed, focusing on her lips. He seemed mesmerized by them.

"Beautiful," he murmured and claimed them with his. The bed was so soft beneath her back that she felt as if she were in the clouds. She loved to fly high and sift the clouds through her fingers. She imagined Vane with wings and grinned wider at the image. She wished he could fly with her, but that was impossible unless she carried him.

No, he could never have wings. That was something Apollo had attempted in his twisted experiments so many long centuries ago. Splicing DNA between Geraki and Ailouros races had created creatures that were vicious, dangerous. Griffins were never able to retake human form after they were mutated. They were too unstable to control, so the God stopped trying to combine the animals within the Immortal races. The bastard destroyed them when his experiments failed.

She shook off the depressing thoughts. It was not the time. She and Vane may never be mated, but she could fantasize, and she had, for nearly a hundred years, as they played their games. So long that she couldn't believe that neither seemed tired of the game yet.

He flipped her onto her stomach and settled against her. "What else do I do in your dreams?" His purred words made goose bumps rise over her skin. He'd asked her that same question over and over, and then given her every hot sexy inch of his beautiful cock every time.

"Whatever you want to," she said with a smile into the bedding. She felt him tense, not expecting her to give him free rein over her. She chuckled, feeling light and carefree.

"Anything?"

"Yes." She moaned as he flipped her hair to one side and started kissing her neck.

Before she knew what he was thinking, she was flipped and straddling his hips. His eyes were full of something. Mischief? He nipped at her lip, and then kissed away the sting.

"Then show me your wings."

"What?" The word choked out. She was shocked that he wasn't making love to her again or doing something hot and dominant like she loved.

"I want to touch your wings. Change for me." His voice sounded rough.

"You don't want to have sex?" She frowned at him. She'd never had a lover stroke her wings. They were strong, big and very sensitive. She wondered how it would feel having his hands on them.

"I'm going to take you again, Brianne. Don't ever doubt that. I want to see your wings first. I want to touch them, maybe even stroke

them while I fuck you from behind." He purred.

Her breath rocked out. She loved his dirty mouth. Loved the images he painted and just how wet they made her.

"I'll show you mine if you show me yours, kitty." She smiled at him.

"Gladly. Now change."

She bristled at his demand, but her beast was itching to be free. Dying to show herself to the male that had always made her flutter.

She felt the transformation in her muscle and bone, and moaned at the change. Her wings broke free. It felt so damn good when she changed. Her talons wrapped over his shoulders, gently; she knew her features and body changed and grew more angular. Small fangs broke from her gums. It wasn't a big change, but his breath rushed out, and his eyes heated. Her beast thrilled at the way he responded.

His hands went from her ass to her jaw, his thumbs stroking her cheeks. She leaned into the touch, and her eyes lowered, it felt so good. He bent in and kissed her, his tongue slid over her fangs, and she jolted. She'd never kissed anyone while transformed; it was different, hot. She nipped his lip and grinned at him. He set her down. "Turn," he demanded and then flipped her around and started petting the soft feathers.

She grinned at his impatience, and then nearly purred at how incredible it felt. Her back arched as jolts of pleasure ran through her wings and over her body.

"Oh, my little lark, the things I'm going to do to you while I stroke these. Mmm, so damn gorgeous. The browns and reds are beautiful with your red hair."

She was thrilled with how much he enjoyed her other form, but she felt the rush she always got from transforming. She needed to fly.

She was excited, aroused, but more, it was so much more.

She whipped around, catching him off guard and making him growl. "I wasn't done."

"Your turn." She wanted to pet her kitty. She felt the need to play, fly while he ran below her.

He raised an eyebrow and then smirked. "I have ways to work off all that adrenaline."

"I know you do. Now change," she demanded.

He winked at her before transforming into his big lion form. She retracted her talons and ran her fingers through his snow white fur. He was so soft. She wanted to rub her body all over him. He was hers. At least here, in her dreams, where she allowed that kind of closeness. It felt like the dream was lasting years. They'd made love over and over, slept within sleep, and now they were sharing their beasts. It was something more than she'd dared imagine, something she would hold close. These dreams were ones she'd conjure over and over again. It was just too perfect.

She felt uneasiness just under the surface, but quickly pushed it aside. This was her time to do whatever she wanted, and now she wanted to fly.

Chapter 16

Kane's Compound, Tetartos Realm

"The Guardians have a price on my head," Cynthia said inside Elizabeth's mind. Kane made sure to share the mental connection when she made contact with the Earth Mageia, just as Cyril had always done. He wanted to know why it had been over a week with no report on her progress in getting him more Mageia.

"I think I've found a female with something unique. The ones in the covens are too protected, but I've found one on the outside. The problem is that she's protected herself, and I haven't been able to get to her. Plus, the other covens are searching for me. The bastards are playing the role of the Guardians' pets."

"How long?" He didn't have the patience to listen to her excuses. She was a bitch that sold out her own to gain her a little youth serum. He didn't give a shit about her problems.

"It'll be a week and a half before we're able to get to her."

"Do it." He was not pleased, but it wasn't as if they had a working serum, yet. It may take that or longer for Ian and Jayr to figure out what Cyril had taken to the grave.

"I'll need another vial. It's much more dangerous now. The price should reflect that." Her cold voice came through the link and made his skin itch. She and Elizabeth were fucking made for each other.

He shook his head in irritation, not that Cynthia could see it, but Elizabeth could. "No. Get the job done, or I'll get someone else." He was bluffing. If finding another contact had been an easy option, he would have had Elizabeth do it before now.

"A week and a half," she responded.

"Do it," he demanded and watched Elizabeth smirk at the other female's task.

"Take her back to her cell," he instructed Angus and walked away, leaving his second to deal with the bitch. He needed to get reports from Ian on the mating serum so Jayr at the hidden facility could look them over.

Chapter 17

Guardian Beach House, Tetartos Realm

Rain was still asleep an hour later. She hadn't even woken up when he'd wrapped her back in the blanket. She turned into his chest as he started carrying her out of the cavern. Shit, what did he do with that? His stomach twisted. She was so small and vulnerable, and he would keep her safe. She was his now, and his beast loved it.

She made noises and moved around, snuggling her small body tighter to him. His dick hurt like a bitch, but as much as claiming her scared the shit out of him, he felt oddly content having her in his arms. He moved them out of the tunnel, back into the bedroom, and was hit with the scent of the two of them in the air. The towel he'd used to clean her up was still on the floor. He took a deep breath as he laid her on the bed. She rolled to her side, and he forced his gaze away from her to throw on his clothes. Within seconds he had her back in his arms and out the door. He wondered if she always slept so soundly. He picked up the bag Sirena left them before walking out onto the warm sand and porting them away.

She let out a throaty moan when they reformed. The same blending sensation hit like a blast, slamming his dick into his zipper. That sexy sound and his own intense reaction told him just how screwed he was. It was going to be torture getting her into the house and not taking her when they got there. She was sore, and as much as he hoped the springs miraculously healed her, that probably wasn't the case. He needed to rub that cream on her sweet abused pussy, but that thought only made him want her more.

Her ass wiggled in his arms, and he looked down into her eyes.

"What's going on?" Her voice came out throaty and scratchy from sleep.

"I ported us to the Guardian beach house."

"Why? How long was I out?" He smelled how wet she'd gotten from teleporting. He stifled a groan and bounded up the steps and through the door.

He picked the first room down the hall just past the kitchen and living room area. They were all big and comfortable, and if she didn't like it, she could pick another one. He just needed to get her out of his arms before he pinned her to the nearest wall or bent her over so he could see her sweet ass in the air. Fuck.

He nearly choked out the words to answer her questions. "There are more conveniences here. You were out for over an hour."

She licked her lips, and he was sure she was doing it to torture him. Porting with her was a fucking problem. They weren't leaving the beach house anytime soon.

"I haven't been sleeping much."

Her words hit him hard. There wasn't any accusation in them. He figured she was still too drowsy for that. All he knew was she sounded sexy as hell, and he was an asshole. She hadn't been sleeping because of him. He set her and the bag on the bed and stepped back. He couldn't believe the strength of the mating frenzy.

He stood near the door, trying to get his shit together before he slid off his jeans and climbed on her like a fucking bastard. "Sirena said she put some cream in the bag to ease the soreness." If things were different, he would spread her wide and apply it himself. He knew his limitations, and touching her pussy when he was that far gone would go from soothing her to pushing his fingers, then his cock deep inside her within seconds.

She sat up on the bed and started rummaging through the bag. She kept the blanket at her breasts. "There are clothes." She sounded relieved.

He'd rather she stayed naked, but they still had to talk. He sure as hell wasn't looking forward to it, but he'd said they would.

"Sirena said Alyssa packed you a bag when I took you."

He saw her lips tilt into a small smile. He knew it wasn't for him, more likely for her friend's thoughtfulness. He stared at the small dimple that appeared on her cheek. He wanted to trace it with his tongue. Shit.

"I'll be on the patio," he said, turning to leave. He needed to get somewhere her scent didn't linger. The pain wasn't nearly as bad as before, but he wanted her. Worse after smelling her juices flow after porting her there. Her small body was readying for his possession, and he was dying to be back inside her tight little pussy. He ran his hands through his hair and walked into the kitchen. He hoped she used the cream.

He went straight to the fridge, which was always stocked with beer. He'd need to get some food for her. Immortals fed off the world's energies, but she wasn't Immortal, yet. *Conn, can you have someone drop food off at the beach house? I'm not sure what Rain likes to eat, so variety would be good.*

No problem. I'll drop it off inside the back door in a few.

Thanks, man.

He pulled out a bottle and twisted off the cap. He stood inside the fridge door, feeling the cool air over his heated skin, and took a few long pulls. He grabbed another and considered what she might want to drink. A smile tilted his lips as he remembered her comparing the taste of his kiss to her favorite sweet wine. He bumped his head into the freezer door, to clear his mind of more heated thoughts. Wine it was. He knew the one his sisters preferred and grabbed a bottle.

Wine, corkscrew and a glass in one hand, his beer in the other, he headed to the big patio. He took another long drink of his beer after opening the wine bottle and pouring her a glass.

He sat with his feet up on another chair and looked out to the surf. It was calling to him. It always did. He wasn't sure what to do now that he'd claimed her. He was off patrol, probably until he completed the mating ceremony, but they were inundated with beasts and fucking possessed. He frowned, not thrilled at leaving his brothers to do all the work.

How long could he hold out for Sirena to come up with something to prevent Rain from seeing his blood memories? No one so innocent should see that.

He heard and felt when she came out onto the patio. He got up from his chair as she sat next to him and stared at the wine. She smelled of shampoo and coconut. Her wet hair looked sexy as it fell around her face. She was in a short tan skirt and purple tank top that hugged her beautiful breasts.

He cleared his throat. "I poured you a glass." Was she remembering comparing him to the wine? He hoped not. "There are plenty of other things to drink. Are you hungry?"

She shook her head as if in a daze. “What’s going on? Now you’re concerned? I really don’t get how you can hate me so much and then flip so fast to being sweet and acting like you give a shit about me.” She didn’t shout, just stared at him, a little wrinkle over her nose.

Chapter 18

Guardian Beach House, Tetartos Realm

Rain watched Dorian, waiting. He was gorgeous sitting in the partial shade, looking out to the beautiful beach. She wondered where exactly they were, but in the end it didn't matter.

He was in the same clothes he'd worn when he'd barged into the treatment room at Paradeisos. His large body lounged back in the chair. A bottle of beer dangled in one hand. He gazed off for a moment, letting her really study him. His hair was wild and looked wet as it stuck out in every direction. She stared, remembering just how soft those strands were. His entire appearance was deceptive. She wanted to believe that things would go smoothly now that he'd claimed her, but that was a child's dream, nowhere near realistic. Things were likely to change at any moment. She sat waiting for an answer to her question. She needed to understand what was going on in his mind. Figure out what he'd do next, and be prepared.

"I never fully realized how much it affected you. I was too focused on not allowing the mating to happen; I never took into consideration that you would suffer. I've always thought the Immortal suffered the brunt of the frenzy."

"Why couldn't it happen?" She knew some, what Sirena had told her, but she needed to know from him.

"There are things you don't know about me."

She debated whether to tell him she knew some of it already, but he floundered for long moments, so she prodded him along. "Sirena explained some."

His head turned to her, eyes flashing darkly. "I should have guessed she would."

"Considering you were hiding, someone had to tell me what was going on. She tried to explain away your desertion. I appreciated her attempt at making the rejection more about what you'd been through and not so much a complete denial of having me as a mate," she mused wryly.

She raised an eyebrow, daring him to deny he'd been an ass.

He let out a self-deprecating laugh and took another drink. "If you know, then you understand that I couldn't keep an Immortal alive. How do I, out of all the others, get a mate? As my mate, your big gift is a target on your back."

"Bullshit. I was already a target because Alyssa and I are close."

"Rational or not, nymph, that was a huge part of my staying away." His eyes pierced her, and they looked ancient in that moment. He dressed like a young male with his bright tee shirts and blue-tipped hair. It was so easy to forget just how old he was.

"Please don't treat me like an idiot. That might have been part of it, but that's not all."

He eyed her and nodded. "There were so many reasons I'd come up with, and that was just one of the big ones. Would you want to take something so rare and precious when you were the reason your friend was never going to have that? Because of your bad judgment? Drake said that fighting in the rings wasn't a good idea, that getting too close to the Immortals wasn't a good plan, but I didn't listen,

Cahal died and never gets a mate. But I do? *I'm* the lucky one? Over my brothers who deserve it so much more?" He frowned and shook his head. He looked back out to the sea and took another long drink of his beer, finishing it and setting it on the table in front of them.

She sat pondering that. She could understand the guilt. He was a Guardian meant to protect, and he would see his friend's death as his fault. Even if it wasn't. It didn't make what he'd done to her any better, but at least she understood where his mind was. It was a lot like Sirena had said. Guilt, fear... Would she have felt the same if she'd gotten Alyssa killed? Maybe. "Would your friend have wanted you to suffer? You didn't kill him, Dorian."

He looked at her again. His eyes hard. "I didn't save him either. He was there because of me. He was killed because of my shitty taste in females. I knew she was a bitch. That she wasn't a good female, but I arrogantly assumed I could handle anything that came. I never imagined she would work with Cyril. I should have, she was that twisted." His voice rose with each word. He honestly felt that he caused his friend's death.

She shook her head, irritated. It was obvious that he wasn't loosening the hold on all that guilt. Did that mean he was going to run again? Not knowing what was coming was frustrating. "Wow, you're right. As a God among men, you should have known what was going to happen. It really is your fault that he died because some sick bitch got greedy. I'm sure your friend would love how you've honored his memory."

His gaze snapped to her, surprised.

She added more matter-of-factly, "I would have thought something simpler would have worked. A memorial. Maybe naming your firstborn after him, but hey, suffering and making me suffer along with you was good too." She shook her head and leaned forward to grab the wine he'd poured; she needed it now.

She was just lifting her hand for the drink when she was hauled into his lap, his mouth landing over hers. Her breath caught in her throat, and her lips parted, letting their tongues tangle. He kissed like nothing she'd ever known. It was enough to make her breasts ache and panties wet.

Enough. You've made your point. It wasn't rational thoughts that ruled me. His words were a slow glide inside her mind.

They rule you still. It was jealousy that finally made you claim me. If you hold onto the horrors of the past, where does that leave me? You'll only run again. She directed the words, hoping that they connected as her mind started to blur with what his mouth was doing to her.

I'd already decided to come for you. Drake said the same damn thing about Cahal. He also pointed out how much I was making you suffer. It was never my plan to hurt you, Rain. I just wasn't thinking about anything but my own guilt and fears.

Having him inside her mind felt so damned intimate. She loved and hated it all at once.

It did hurt me. I know you don't know me, but the rejection felt personal. I deserved some kind of explanation. I didn't enjoy the pitying looks from your brothers as I walked around constantly aroused. I didn't earn the shitty things you said to me, and I really didn't deserve to have you spying on me the entire time I suffered. Alone.

He broke the kiss and looked at her, regret and pain filled his eyes. The back of one knuckle trailed down her cheek as his eyes searched hers. She knew he already housed too much shame for his friend and she was only adding to it, but she needed him to see that there was more happening besides what happened a hundred years ago.

"You're ripping my heart out, Rain. No, you didn't deserve any of it, and I'm sorry. I said those things to drive you away. Everyone told me how great you were, but that made me hate the thought of claiming you even more. I don't deserve a mate, Rain, but I won't leave again. You're mine now. Tell me how to make it right."

Her heart ached at the heated tenderness in his eyes; she knew just what he hoped would make it up to her. Damn male. He was so damaged, and now he was hers, and she didn't know how to fix him.

Their breathing was ragged, and she felt his hard cock throbbing as she straddled his muscled thighs. She blew out a breath. She was already more than happy to screw him again. Feed the damn hunger that was only slightly sated from their first time. "I don't honestly know what will make it right. I don't trust you not to run off and trample my feelings again. I guess only time will tell." She should move off his lap, but she didn't want to. She wanted to feel all of him again. It was stupid. She would only tie herself tighter to him, but her body had suffered long enough. She wasn't going to do it anymore. The cream Sirena put in the bag was amazing. Her bruised pelvis felt completely healed.

"Are you still hurting?" Her whole body tingled at the silky tone to his voice. "I wish I knew what you were thinking right now."

She narrowed her eyes at the reminder that he'd been in her head. "I'm glad you enjoyed hearing all of my personal thoughts. Why don't you open your shield and let me hear what you're thinking?" She raised an eyebrow in challenge.

He sat there for a moment just staring at her before grinning seductively. Shockingly, his thoughts began sifting through her mind.

Pain. Arousal. Guilt. Hope that she'd used the cream. Hope that she didn't hurt anymore, because he wanted inside her more than he wanted to breathe. He wanted to bend her over the patio table and eat her pussy and rim her little ass.

She panted and circled her hips on his lap as images of him pushing inside her body filtered into her mind. So many positions. She thought she might die from the need he stoked. Soon it cut off, and she fought for breath. She wanted him, so much. Her skirt was up to her hips, and his palms were caressing her ass as she moved against him. They would talk again later, for now she needed him to stop the ache.

"My thoughts stay along those lines," he murmured next to her cheek. The fingers of one hand pushed back her hair, and he ran his tongue over her ear and neck. His other hand pulled her hip into his jean-clad cock. "I love your neck."

She moaned as he spoke against her sensitive flesh. Her hands went to his shirt, and he leaned forward, allowing her to slide it over his head to fall on the ground next to them.

His eyes flashed. "You want my cock right here? Where anyone could see us if they port in?"

The image of Conn or Bastian walking up and watching her ride Dorian's cock filtered through her head. She knew he was showing her his wicked side.

He grinned seductively as her tank top joined his shirt on the ground. His fingers quickly flipped the snap to her bra, and it followed her top. He lifted her higher and nipped at her hard nipples. She felt the hard muscles of his torso between her thighs. "These are so damn beautiful. Your tight little ass and these gorgeous breasts haunt me nearly as much as that piercing. I saw it the first time I looked through your eyes. I watched you trail water over your tight nipples and over your pussy and wanted to show you just what the water could do to you."

She moaned at the thought of him watching her get off. "What exactly can you do that I can't?" She could barely speak the words. He made her dizzy. His body was so hot, and her hands were all over his tattooed shoulders. The ink depicted a view of looking through rippling waves.

He tilted her chin up to look at him. His eyes danced with heated playfulness. "I can command it to be so much harder than you can. I can push it deep, just like my cock. Use it to hold you down as I pump inside your hot little pussy. Do you want that, Rain? Do you want me to be dirty with you?"

"Mmm." She was incapable of speech at the moment. She'd never experienced anything so damn hot, and she knew it wasn't just the mating that got her. It was him and his dirty mouth.

She was too far gone to stop. She unbuttoned his jeans, the backs of her hands grazing his hot abs, and she nearly groaned. Before she was able to caress the cock that came out to greet her, she was lifted up and carried inside. Her skirt and panties met his pants on the bathroom floor. She knew the shower was big; she'd just used it. She stepped in and turned around. The water came on as he crowded her against the wall. She was more excited than she ever dreamt possible. He was going to do hot and wicked things to her, and she was dying to experience every bit of it.

"This has possibilities," he said as he looked around the huge stone shower enclosure to the big bench in the middle. "Lie on your back, and spread your thighs for me."

Her breath caught, and her pussy clenched with thoughts of

what he wanted to do to her. She knew it would feel good. His eyes lost some of their playfulness, and in their place was hot, hard male. He looked down at her naked body, and his eyes flashed bright. Steam filled the space, and soon water was everywhere, shackling her wrists next to her head. She never dreamed being restrained would make her so damned hot, but it did. Her hips moved on the hard bench. The water never felt like that when she manipulated it. Soon, more was running over her breasts, caressing her stomach, down to her pussy, where it probed. He watched it and molded it to push into her body as he stroked his cock. "I won't push it deep, just enough that you want my cock to take its place."

She moaned. "So good."

"Do you want more, Rain? More water filling you, pushing into your hot pussy?"

She was so close, but it wasn't enough. The water pushed inside and moved over her ass. He was using it to torture her.

She couldn't breathe; she was so damn hot. Her chest rose and fell with each breath, and she saw he was doing the same as he watched the water push inside. The liquid slid deeper. Gods! "Dorian, no more." She panted. She needed so much more than the tease. It was excruciating, and she made noises, demanding something hotter, harder.

He knelt between her thighs. "Are you still tender?"

She shook her head.

"Good." His mouth replaced the water. More liquid came to pour over her breasts while the other currents were still clasped over her wrists, flowing over her palms and fingers with enough pressure to add to the sensations racking her body. His tongue flicked over her piercing. "Lift your legs back."

She obeyed without thought, knowing instinctually that whatever he commanded would make her come harder.

"That's it, Rain. Show me your sweet pussy."

She needed to come so badly. Her channel pulsed as his tongue worked her. She wouldn't last long. He held her legs back and licked her slit, then spread her cheeks and licked her tiny back entrance until all thought disintegrated. Who knew how fucking hot that was? The entire time he watched her. Her neck hurt from lifting her head to keep eye contact with him as he tormented her body. His mouth moved up to her clit and sucked hard. The climax came strong and fast, rushing over her until her hips bucked.

He lifted his mouth and stood, wet and intense.

"Let me up."

His muscles were twitching along his chest and stomach, and his cock looked angry.

The water fell away, and she sat up, shaky as she watched him try to catch his breath. He was attempting to get control.

"There is nothing like the taste of your come." He groaned as he pumped a hand over his shaft.

She wanted to know what he tasted like. Twice now he'd gone down on her, and she'd yet to return the favor. She couldn't wait to slip him into her mouth. Make him beg. She got on her knees in front of him and pushed wet hair off her face. Steam still filled the space and ran along his skin.

His eyes got brighter as he looked down at her. "Lift up," he said, and the minute she did, a towel slid under her knees. More telekinetic Guardian power. His hands went to her cheeks as her fingers wrapped around him. He pulsed at her touch.

She looked into his eyes as she licked up the underside of his cock. It was so long and thick she knew she'd never take it all, but she'd do her best to make him come. Hard, like the release he'd given her. With only a handful of experiences, she hoped she could make it good, make him wild. "Tell me what you like," she said, and his eyes flashed above her.

"Suck on the tip, Rain. Wrap your lips around it and suck hard," he instructed. His fingers pushed wet hair off her cheek, and his thumb caressed her jaw as she sucked on him. "Just like that. Now rub your tongue along the ridge. Oh, fuck, yeah."

She took a deep breath as she tasted his pre-come and moaned around him.

"Gods, you're beautiful sucking my cock. I love watching it disappear between those pouty lips. Now, take it as far as you can down your throat." He watched, seeming mesmerized by the sight. It made her wet all over again. "I can smell how hot this makes you, Rain." His voice was rough, and his eyes saw all the way to her soul. She pumped her hands as she took him deep. She moaned again when she got more of the sweet fluid that slipped from his cock. "Suck harder, and swallow when I'm at the back of your throat." She did and was rewarded when his hips pumped toward her. He demanded more, and she wanted to give him everything. "Keep swallowing and breathe through your nose, you can get me deeper. Gods, so damn good. Take me to the end, but I want to come all over your tits."

She pushed herself further and swallowed as his hands gently caressed her cheeks. Tension made his stomach muscles twitch, and she knew she had him.

“Fuck!” he shouted as he pulled out and shot all over her chest. It felt hot jetting onto her skin. He bent and moved his hands from her cheeks to rub the fluid all over her swollen mounds. She moaned, so ready to come again she thought she’d combust from want.

“Shit, that was so damn good.” He looked down at her with too much emotion for her to decipher. His cock was still hard, and she hoped that meant he planned to put it to good use. She was dying after making him come. His scent was all over her, making her even needier. She was hot and achy, so ready.

His eyes heated, and before she had time to think, he had her up against the tile wall. Her legs wrapped around his waist, and she felt his cock between them. His lips were on hers, licking and sipping from her mouth. *I like the taste of me on your lips. Sucking me made you so damn wet.* A comment, not a question. His hands were on her ass, sliding her up and down his shaft, his cock running right along her piercing, making her break the kiss to mewl incoherently. She needed him deep, not teasing her. Her eyes closed, and her head rocked back on the tile. “Do you want my cock, Rain?”

“Yes.” She moaned.

“Then guide me in.” He lifted her until the head circled her slit, and it was torture. One hand moved from his shoulder to grasp him. “Tell me how deep you want it, Rain. Do you just want the tip? Are you too tender to take it all?”

She moaned deep. “All,” was all she could say, her lids lowered as she watched him.

His chest was heaving as he watched his shaft sliding inside. “Watch your pussy suck me in." Her upper back rested against the wall as he fed her his cock. She watched, mesmerized that he could go so far inside. So slow, so hot, he filled her up to the root and moaned. His hips circled, and just as slowly he slipped out to the point where he was barely inside. "See how shiny and wet you get me. I fucking love seeing your juices coating my cock. It's so damn hot in there, and I can feel you pulsing around me." His eyes pierced her with hot intensity. "Your pussy was made for me. It clenches and pulls me deep."

"Yes, stop teasing me. Fuck me." She groaned in frustration. His words were killing her, and she was having trouble catching her breath. She needed it all. He searched her eyes before pushing back inside. "Damn it, Dorian. I won't break. I need it harder."

He drove in with force, not like the first time, where she'd been bruised. His shoulders were taut, his eyes on hers, watching.

"Yes. Don't stop. I need to come so bad." Her fingers dug into his shoulders.

"Watch," he demanded, and her eyes moved back to where they were connected. His hips slammed in. He was still tempering his strength, but it felt so good. In and out, she watched as his cock sank deep, and his fingers caressed her ass cheeks. One digit circled her back hole, and that was all it took for her to fly. Her body jerked as she shouted. He held her tight, all the way against him, and she felt his come jetting inside. Strange electric pulses sent her back into another orgasm.

The tendons were straining at his throat as he groaned through his release.

Mind-blowing. She didn't want to face their bigger issues yet. He cuddled her to his chest, and she felt sleep claiming her.

Chapter 19

Guardian Beach House, Tetartos Realm

How is it? Dorian asked Conn through the link. It had been three days since he claimed Rain. Three fucking amazing days of feeding the frenzy and catching up on sleep.

Quiet since yesterday. Alex had a feeling about a location on Earth, and Jax and I are checking it out. Her and Uri's powers seem to be expanding, his brother said. If Alex had a feeling, the chances were good that something big would come from Conn's search. Her ability was unpredictable, but it had helped them in the past.

Anything else? He felt marginally better about being out of commission now that things had settled down. He only hoped it wasn't the eye of the storm, meaning they'd soon be hitting the other side.

The others are out trying to figure out what the distractions were for. So far we have no idea why there were so many attacks, but that could change at any moment. How's Rain?

She's good. Dorian closed his eyes for a second. Rain was asleep in his arms. He hadn't wanted to move her; he was getting used to her falling asleep on him. She'd been doing it from the start, and he liked it.

Conn obviously didn't buy it if his chuckle was to be believed. *I bet. Good luck making up to her. She's worth it, so don't fuck up. We all like her.*

I know. He growled in annoyance that Conn was right. He also wasn't happy that his brother was so close to her. He was feeling possessive, something completely foreign to him. He sure as hell was not turning into Gregoire. That male had serious issues, and Dorian didn't want that to be him. It would make the ceremonies to come so much harder.

He took a deep breath, trying to rein it in. The problem was that he really liked her. She had spirit and so much more. It all started while he was hearing her thoughts, and it had only grown as they'd spoken when he let her up for air and food. He moved his nose closer to her. He loved her scent. He was so damn lucky they had the cream Sirena had given them. He couldn't get enough of her, and she seemed to be right there with him the entire way.

Everything she did affected him. Just watching her eat was torture. He'd taken her on the patio table after a bit of fruit juice dripped onto her delicate little chin. The sight of it had been too much for him to take. The frenzy was still too strong. She might not trust him with anything but her body, but that she gave freely. She had to know he was getting addicted to her.

When are you finishing the mating?

Soon. As soon as Sirena came up with something to prevent Rain from seeing his memories when they blood bonded.

Gotta go. Good luck, man. With that, Conn was gone.

He'd spoken to Drake briefly. The dragon hadn't said much but to get his shit together before he came back on patrol.

Rain stirred in his arms, and he kissed her head. He'd never felt so much tenderness for another being. He wanted to hold her and protect her from everything. It was a compulsion as disconcerting as the possessiveness. He wasn't sure what to do with any of it.

"Who was that? Conn?" she asked on a sleepy yawn.

He'd worn her out, and the thought made him grin. "I thought you were asleep."

"I was. Your chatting woke me up." She sounded disgruntled. "What's soon?"

They hadn't spoken about the actual mating, and he wondered what she knew of it. Theirs would not be the same as Alyssa and Gregoire's. "We need to talk about a few things before doing anything."

She looked up at him, alert and watchful. "Such as?" She moved to sit with her knees to her chest and her hands wrapped around them. He knew she was agitated. He wanted to soothe her, but he knew she was preparing herself for what he'd say. The protected way she held herself said it all.

He was not thrilled to be having this conversation. "What exactly do you know about mortal mating ceremonies?"

She looked uneasy. "I believe Sirena explained it all to me."

"Then you know that I'll have to share you?"

Her cheeks flushed, and she nodded. "Is that something that concerns you?" she whispered. The sweet nervous look on her face made him inhale deeply. Sometimes she was all sass and bluster, and others she was beautiful and vulnerable. Innocent.

"Yes." He watched her expressions closely. She wasn't an experienced female; he knew that. "Have you ever been with two males?" He wasn't pleased with how that question made him want to fucking snarl. He'd never had a problem sharing females, had enjoyed it often with Cahal and even some of his brothers for centuries, but the thought of sharing her ate at him.

"No," she said, color tinting her cheeks.

He nodded, not liking anything about what was coming. It would be another fucking penance. She'd be taken to new levels of pleasure while he endured and hated every damn minute of it. He needed to touch her. He pulled her beneath him, wanting her heat against his body. His beast fucking hated the protected way she held herself as they spoke. She softened instinctually at his touch and it made him want to sink his dick inside her small body and stay there.

"I have to let an Aletheia have you. Can you handle that?" He watched her eyes as she nodded. "I'll want to take you at the same time, and I'll want you focused completely on me." He knew that without thinking. It was the only way he'd get through it.

He scented her sweet pussy heating at the idea. He was both thankful and irritated by her reaction. The thought of another male taking her grated, but knowing she'd get off hard was better than her being scared or upset by it. Any female that he'd shared seemed to love having two cocks fill them. He would make it good for her. All the while he'd be in complete hell. Even now, his skin itched at the thought of another cock anywhere near her pouty lips or sweet pussy and ass.

"Okay." His traitorous dick throbbed. His old kinks were fighting with new emotion, and it all screwed with his mind. How did the more possessive males even get through the experience? It was the only way to turn a mortal into an Immortal. Rain would have to be filled with Aletheia semen, and it wasn't something that worked without contact. Sirena had tested that back in the early centuries of mortal matings.

He paused. "You know after that is our blood bonding?" This part of the discussion he dreaded almost as much as telling her he planned to give her sweet ass to another male.

He rubbed a hand over his face. What the hell was wrong with him?

"Yes," she said, a hint of suspicion in her tone.

"I don't want you to get my memories when we blood bond." He heard her harsh intake of breath.

"So we've had three days of a lie? You have no intention of finishing the mating." She wiggled to get out from under him, but he held her still.

"That's not what I said." He hated seeing the pain and anger in her beautiful eyes. "We will complete the mating. I'm just hoping that Sirena can find a way out of you seeing my memories."

"And if she can't find a way?" she shot back.

"Then we do it." He gritted his teeth, hating that he really wouldn't have another option. He would finish the mating, but that didn't mean he wasn't planning to give Sirena plenty of time to find an answer. "We don't need to finish it soon."

"So you decided for us." She bucked, but he refused to let her up so she could run from him. They weren't finished.

He understood that she was pissed off, but she didn't have a fucking clue what he was trying to save her from. At first it was about not wanting her to see his failure, but now it was so much more. She didn't deserve his nightmares. No one did. "You don't know what you'll see, Rain. The horrors I've experienced were fucked up."

"You're embarrassed."

"Hell yes, I am. You'll likely see the lowest moments of my centuries-long life, but that's not the only reason I don't want to do it. You have no idea what it was like watching your friend's slaughter. Having twisted bitches drug and taunt you with that death, naked because I'd just fucked the worst of the bunch." He glared down at her and saw her eyes flash when he'd said he fucked Calista before she'd killed Cahal. She needed to know the reality of it. "I'm sure you'll get earlier shitty experiences too, back so many centuries ago that they're only sick blips in my life, but I doubt you'll be spared that. You have no idea what it was like in Apollo's breeding labs, being treated like cattle! And you never need to. That sick shit will never touch you."

He hated the whole fucking thing. Yes, it would humiliate him. She might be feisty, but she was fucking pure, and that shit would torment her. The past three days getting to know small things about her only cemented his decision. It was no longer about his humiliation as it had started. It was about protecting her.

"Is that really how you see me? Too weak to share your pain, to be a real mate? I may be young compared to you, but I'm sure as hell strong enough to share your horrors. Don't automatically assume I'm lacking." Her voice was filled with fury as she said the words.

"My trying to protect you from this has nothing to do with whether I think you can handle it. The point is that I don't want you to. The lightness about you should never touch the dark shit that I've lived through. Seeing the things I have will haunt you. I don't fucking want that. Be angry all you want, but I still plan to try to protect you."

Her eyes flashed with anger, and then, a moment later, it switched to resolve. That didn't bode well for him, but he wouldn't budge. "Let me up. I need to go for a swim."

"I'll go with you."

"Whatever. Just stay out of my way while we're out there."

He moved off her, and she shot out of the bed. She was beautiful and so damn perfect for him. Her hot ass swayed as she went to the closet. His beast loved her, and he cared about her. More than cared. He liked to think it was the frenzy, but it was more. Being in her mind for that short time when he'd claimed her changed him in a big way. He pulled at the back of his hair; he could use a swim. It had been days, and he fully intended to watch over her while they were out there. He knew she wouldn't appreciate it, but she was mortal, and he wasn't taking chances with her safety. Sea creatures could be fucking huge in Tetartos. He couldn't imagine her controlling some of the larger breeds. It didn't matter what her power was.

Chapter 20

Guardian Manor, Tetartos Realm

She woke up to an odd sensation. Her head was snuggled into a hot male chest. She smelled his sexy scent and knew right away she was still dreaming. There was a distinct fuzziness at the corners of her sight as she stretched, rolling over onto his naked body. He lifted one lid and pulled her back down next to him. It seemed weeks had passed in constant dreams. She loved it and hated that eventually she'd wake and the sick feeling in the pit of her gut would be there waiting for her, like it always was.

This dream had been so different from the rest. She'd let go completely. No games, no power struggle, just living as she would if she were a different female. They'd done so many wicked things. She still felt his fingers on her wings. She moaned at the images in her head.

"Sleep." His voice held a tinge of gravel. Strong arms pulled her tight, tucking her head into his chest as he rolled onto his side facing her. The way he held her felt distinctively possessive, and she chuckled.

"My dream Vane is such a cuddly kitten."

"Sleep," he growled, which only made her giggle like a young female into his chest. He apparently didn't enjoy mornings, though her dreams seemed to always be in the light. She noticed a dark canopy hanging above the bed, blocking out some of the sun.

Well, why the hell not? Her dreams were her own private place to experience the things she would never allow in reality. She'd asked her dream lover to make love to her, and he had; then she'd fallen asleep in his arms, another first. Why not spend some time cuddling? In her opinion, it seemed pleasant enough. She'd always been drawn to his scent, and she inhaled deeply. Even in dreams he was a treat she couldn't resist. She rubbed her nose and cheek over his skin and freed one of her hands to slide over his back and narrow hip, tracing the indent that vee'd to his cock.

"Woman, let me sleep," he grumbled and tightened his hold before rubbing his cheek in her hair. She couldn't imagine him really being like this, but she kind of liked the dream version. In reality he was probably up at dawn to make sure his beautiful hair was perfect. He was such a fussy kitty. So at odds with his strength and power.

She couldn't see anything. He had her tucked too tightly against him. She relaxed a little. Maybe just a minute longer and she would bend him to her will. For now she wanted to see what else he would do. How the dream would end.

"How long does cuddling usually last?" she asked, curious. It was comfortable, but if it was going to last hours, she wasn't game for that.

She was lifted up so fast it caught her off guard. His face was inches from hers; both eyes were open and annoyed. "How the hell would I know? You won't let it fucking happen."

She raised an eyebrow. Geez, testy much. "So, we're done?"

He let out an irritated snort. "What did you want to do, your royal larkness? We're obviously stuck in whatever dream shit this is. I just wanted to relax since we're the only ones here."

What was he talking about? "What are you talking about? It's just a dream, and you're fucking up my happy time," she said, and she jumped up, glaring at him. Her heart was beating out of her chest. It had to be a dream.

"Well, if it's a dream, songbird, it's one that we're sharing."

He flipped her underneath him, giving her his considerable weight. With one eyebrow cocked, he said, "Since when do you know you're dreaming and don't wake up?"

Chapter 21

Guardian Beach House, Tetartos Realm

Rain wasn't going to argue with the asshole. He wanted to swim, fine. She didn't have to talk to him. She just needed a little time to herself to process. She wasn't stupid enough to think he'd let her go with the sea beasts alone. As if they'd harm her, she snorted. He was about to learn she wasn't completely powerless. At least not in the sea. Just everywhere else, she thought derisively.

They'd had mind-blowing sex for days. She wasn't sure what to make of the time they'd spent together. He'd been tender and hot. They'd talked about her shop and her selling it. She'd thought they were bonding, stupid her. It was just sex and idle chitchat to keep the frenzy fed.

He thought she was breakable, and she kind of was. At least until they finished the damn mating he seemed to never want to complete. So, he planned to hold out in hopes that he could get out of sharing his nightmares with her? Did he really think that would happen? Idiot!

It's not like she wanted to see them, suffer through his horrors, but that's what mates did. She ground her teeth together as she slipped into one of the bikinis Alyssa packed for her. She was thankful her friend thought to get a bag of her things together. Her friend knew all of her favorites, and she'd packed well.

She grabbed a towel from the bathroom and headed out

through the living room and kitchen area and out through the patio door. She drew in a deep breath when she saw him standing there gloriously nude. His firm ass and muscled back were to her as she made her way down the steps. She almost tripped on her own feet as she tracked his body.

He turned around and watched her closely. She hated that his eyes were so damn stunning. Every inch of him was perfection. From his blond, spiky hair, to his sculpted body, all the way down to his beautiful tanned feet.

She walked right past him and dove into the shallow surf. The water caressed her skin and soothed some of her fraying nerves. She broke through the surface and took a deep breath.

She submerged again, going under wave after wave. It felt good getting out into the ocean. Relaxing, she turned to float on her back for a bit, and the water rocked her gently. After catching her breath and getting lulled by the movement, she flipped back over, sliding underneath the liquid before jolting. He was right beneath her. Scared the crap out of her. She'd known he was close, had felt a pull to him, but she hadn't realized he was directly below her. She came up coughing water. He was a damn menace. He surfaced a few inches in front of her.

"What the hell! Why'd you scare me like that?" She needed a minute of peace, not him completely in her space.

He looked different, and she realized he was bigger. His features more angular and his eyes were brighter, almost glowing. She swore even his teeth were bigger. She sputtered a little. "Are you in your other form?"

"Yes." He looked at her, and she saw the ancient glint in his eyes. The confidence that seemed to shadow him, even though she knew his past must have taken it down a notch. She wondered at just how arrogant he must have been before everything that happened with Cahal.

They treaded water together while he watched her. He seemed more alert, a little dangerous.

She looked down through the clear water and saw his dark grey tail. She wanted to see all of it. His form was different than the other Nereids she'd seen, not that she'd ever been that close to a Nereid before. It made sense that he would look different, darker, more deadly. He was pretty much the God of Nereids, and now she thought of their iridescent tails and knew they were nowhere near the male in front of her.

"Are you controlling them?"

What? She looked around, understanding. "Yes. And no. They're curious. They just want to say hello." She looked at the creatures circling them. She had projected waves of soothing thoughts to them from the moment she entered the water. They were getting closer, wanting attention, and liked to be near her. They were always drawn to her. Some were huge, but none would ever attack her or each other in her presence. She'd made it clear that they were to be peaceful around her.

"You can actually talk to them? I felt something when you entered the water, and again now." His eyes were a little wide. She assumed he knew of her abilities.

"In a way." She could send them instructions when she was in the water, but she got back emotion, not words.

"They're curious?" he asked, looking around with narrowed eyes. "They never come near me. I don't like that they're so close to you."

"Stop being an ass, or you'll upset them. They can feel it, and they're not thrilled with you near me any more than you like their presence."

She sent more soothing thoughts out. A smaller young beast sidled up, and Dorian frowned. "Stop it, Dorian. I can feel your worry and aggression. He's just a baby. He's curious and wants me to pet him." She did. They were out just past the wave break, and she was treading water with one hand as she petted the young creature. It always made her heart swell knowing how much they loved her. The little guy was a few feet long with a hard shell-like casing over his head. She rubbed just behind that, over his back, and felt his happiness. She smiled down at him, knowing Dorian watched it all warily.

"Be careful, Rain. I will teleport your ass away if the little bastard's venomous spikes come up," he growled.

"Stop it. I'm serious! He's fine. He would never hurt me." The sea creature fluttered his back fin as she rubbed him. It would have been soothing and peaceful if Dorian wasn't killing the experience for her. She sent the little one back to its mother, who wasn't far off. Rain felt the being's agitation, a reaction to Dorian's blustering, and she nearly growled herself.

"If you're going to stay, then you need to get a grip. I am not powerless here, so stop treating me like I am."

He blew out a frustrated breath, and she could tell he was struggling as he looked at all the creatures around them.

He finally shook his head. "Incredible. Gregoire said that you had power with sea creatures, but even *I* felt it. I've never known a Mageia to have such tremendous power within their element." With a furrowed brow, he continued scanning their surroundings.

Her chest expanded at the compliment. Deep down she'd wanted him to see what she could do. She'd thought he was a little more aware of her ability than he seemed to be, but she was glad he hadn't known. It felt so much better seeing his reaction. She needed him to know that in the water she wasn't weak. She wasn't oblivious to her mortal limitations, but in the water, with her creatures around her, she was strong, powerful... loved. Her body may be weak, but that didn't make her so.

"Thank you," she said softly, and meant it. She was a little surprised that he'd felt her ability; it had to be because of their connection.

"I still want to swim for a bit," she said, needing to move.

"Then swim with me." His voice held a seductive quality that sent tingles all over her skin. She'd come out there to clear her head. Touching him would do the complete opposite, but he tempted her. Always.

"I can take you deep." His voice ran over her and hit every hot nerve. She hadn't missed the double meaning as he inched closer and ran a hand over her waist. "Show you hidden gems further down. You can share my breath."

She nearly groaned. He was getting to her; the picture he painted made her pussy clench. Damn him. What was wrong with her? He knew just how to make her surrender. She looked longingly into the water. She'd always wanted to explore the depths, but she couldn't hold her breath long enough to truly enjoy it.

She thought for just a second before agreeing to a temporary truce. "Okay."

He grinned wickedly, and she saw his slightly sharper teeth. He was beauty and danger all wrapped in one sexy package, and the bastard knew it.

"You might want to tell your entourage to move, my little sea goddess."

She shook her head and tried not to grin back.

His strong arms pulled her into his warmth and stole a kiss that made her dizzy. Her fingers gripped his shoulders tight, and she forced her legs not to wrap around him.

"Take a deep breath, and let me control the movements."

He turned her so that her back was to his warm, hard chest. One hand snaked around her waist, holding her, his thumb rubbing over her skin. The gentle caress knocked her off balance. She shook it off and sent a message to the beasts that they needed to give them space.

She heard his whispered, "Amazing," before he carried them under the water.

He turned and dove, gradually gaining depth as her ears popped. He pushed them through the water, and she knew he was tempering his speed for her comfort, but holy hell, his tail was undulating behind her in such a way that made her want to turn around and straddle his waist. Gods, she wondered what those sexy movements would feel like against her clit. The gentle caress of his finger combined with the seductive flow of his tail was keeping her on edge. She bit her cheek against the desire he stoked with each pulse of his hips against her ass. She'd never see all she wanted to with that kind of distraction. They eventually stopped near a reef, and she stared in wonder. It was stunning, so many colors. Every time she needed to breathe, he turned her around and kissed her. The first time she was so surprised she blew it all out. He grinned and gave her more.

Where are your gills?

He frowned as if offended, and she nearly lost all of her air again trying not to laugh. *Nereids don't have gills.*

She wanted to wrap her legs around him and stay deep in the water forever. He kissed her again and flipped her back around so she could see.

After what felt like hours sharing breath and exploring the depths, he finally took them up. The creatures had followed them for a while. Others had come and gone, finally relaxing in Dorian's presence, mainly, she knew, because he'd stopped sending out aggressive vibes.

The minute they broke the surface, he kissed her long and hard. "Wrap your legs around my waist. I want you so damn much."

She felt his cock under the silky smooth second skin of his tail. He rubbed her up and down over it, and she moaned. Even that felt bigger than before, but he was larger in general. Stronger.

They were back on the beach before she drew her next breath. Her back met a soft towel over the warm sand. The port back gave her that same melding sensation. His mouth was on hers, his tongue probing and tasting as his fingers ran over her face and neck. *The things I want to do to you. Creators! I need to calm the fuck down. I want your mouth, your pussy, and I'm dying to feel your sweet ass all around me. I want everything, Rain. All of you.*

She swallowed hard at the images he fed her. It was so damn hot. She moaned as his lips moved over her jaw and down her throat. He moved the triangles of her bikini top aside and toyed with her nipples, pinching them a little harder than he'd done before. It gave her intense jolts of pleasure that bowed her back.

"That's it. Can you come from me playing with your nipples? From suction or pinching them, maybe some sharp slaps..."

She moaned, trying to find words but failing. She was so wet and needy beneath him. "I don't know."

He was watching her face as his hand plumped and manipulated her. His eyes were penetrating, demanding. Her tender lover gone, in his place was something more. He pinched her nipple a little harder and she whimpered.

"That's it. You like a firm hand, nymph." He slapped her breast, a quick sting he gently massaged away. She keened and pushed her swollen flesh further into his palm. His eyes were intent, scorching as he watched her.

"Have you ever allowed anyone inside your pretty ass?" he asked as he continued to pull and pinch, tracking her every reaction with heated eyes.

She swallowed hard, panting. "No." She'd never been tempted, until him. Dorian could coax her to all kinds of wickedness, he already was. They'd done so much in a short time. What little experience she had was fast trysts, nothing long enough to do anything different.

When they finally mated, the Aletheia would take her there. He would fill every inch of her with come to start the process of Immortality.

"I'll be your first, Rain," he whispered in her ear, and the words heated her blood. Her breasts were swollen tight, and he was driving her insane just playing with her hard nipples. He kept torturing her, plucking and teasing, hard and then soft. He gazed back up at her, and his eyes held so much intensity, more than just heat. "You'll be so tight I'll have to work my way inside. Once I'm there, I'll hold you down and take you slow, giving your ass time to stretch around me. After that you'll be mine in every way possible."

She moaned hard. What was he doing to her? Her pussy flooded, not just from his fingers, more from the hot, possessive words she craved.

His hands left her breast and pushed her bottoms aside, running his knuckles over her pussy. His lips came down and sucked on one hard nipple at a time, nipping as his fingers turned and pushed deep before coming out and spreading the liquid up and around her pussy. *I love that you're so wet. Your pussy smells like heaven. I want to lick up every sweet drop, but you'll need every bit of it for what I'm going to do. Is this pussy mine?*

"Yes." She was too far gone.

Come on my fingers. I feel how close you are.

She shouted and climaxed. It was if her body was waiting for the words.

So damn perfect. I want you on your knees.

Her breath stuttered out. He was destroying her, making sure she always craved him. Soon she wouldn't be able to live without his cock and his hot words. It was scary and exhilarating.

He slipped her bottoms off and untied her top, leaving her nude on the sunny beach. The danger of being caught added to the need. She doubted anyone would disturb them, but what if they did? She gasped when he flipped her over onto her hands and knees.

"I love the sight of your beautiful ass in the air. Put your chest on the towel, Rain."

She moaned and did as he said, arching her back so that her ass was tilted up. She couldn't help the wiggle of her hips as she spread her legs wider.

"Fuck. So damn gorgeous." The fingers of one hand trailed over her spine; gooseflesh rose everywhere he touched. She held her breath as he pushed his cock inside. He loved her on her knees, and she loved it when he took her that way. He smacked her ass and rubbed his hands over it as she whimpered and pushed back into him. Her pussy constricted. So damn good.

She felt his fingers rubbing around where her lips met his cock, felt the juices easing the connection between their bodies. A second later his wet thumb was circling her ass, and then he pushed. She groaned as her hips tilted higher. "You love it every time I touch and lick you here." His other hand massaged her hip and ass. "So beautiful. I love the line of your spine and curve of your ass offered up for me." Images flashed in her mind, and she groaned. He was showing her what he saw. Through his eyes it looked so good.

I'll never sate this craving for you, whispered in her mind. She watched his thumb penetrate deeper into her back entrance as his cock slid in and out of her pussy. She couldn't help the climax that rolled out in wave after wave. She clenched and throbbed as her fingers dug into the towel. Electric jolts pulsed, and she knew that he was coming. Even if he hadn't shouted or she hadn't felt the warm jets that filled her, those currents would have told her. Whatever that was, it always sent her back into another harsh release that sapped her energy and left her limp and relaxed. Her eyes felt heavy, and her knees started giving out as he slipped from her.

She was lifted into his arms and rested her head on his chest. She felt him kiss her forehead, so tenderly. He seemed to do that a lot. Her heart constricted. Every time he took her, she felt even more connected to him, the links more solid. The odd swirling sensations in her body were getting more demanding. She knew from Alyssa that it was her life force pushing to complete the bond. She wondered if it felt the same for him.

Sleep, whispered in her mind as her back met the soft bed.

Chapter 22

Guardian Manor, Tetartos Realm

Alyssa and Gregoire met them in the war room at the manor. It was a large space filled with electronic equipment and a huge solid wood table in the center.

"How are you?" her friend asked with a hopeful grin. Alyssa's eyes were searching, concerned, but mainly eager.

Rain wouldn't kill her friend's joy by telling her that Dorian was amazing in bed, but planned to hold out as long as he could before actually completing the mating. No, not when her friend was hoping for happy news.

"Good," she lied. Not really a lie, because she loved the sex and the time she was spending at the beach house. It was holding back her feelings for him that was becoming more difficult. They talked some, but it usually ended with her braced over a hard surface panting for breath as he claimed her body. He was quite serious about using that healing cream on her after every bout, which only added to the soft feelings rolling through her. He was both tender and demanding with her, and the combination was lethal to her heart.

Havoc came into the room with Uri and Alex, and the pup bee lined right for her. In his excitement, he knocked her into the wall. She was glad it was there; otherwise she'd be on her ass. He wiggled into her side and wagged his butt. She chuckled as she scratched behind his ears. He was such a greedy and sweet pup, but had no idea that he was so strong, too used to all the Immortals he could bound into without budging them an inch.

"Havoc." Uri's tone was of warning, and the hound's pointed ears went back before he licked her hand softly.

"Sorry, Rain, he's getting bigger and doesn't know his strength," Alex said regretfully.

"It's okay, boy. I understand," she murmured down as he looked up with soulful red eyes.

She felt Dorian's eyes on her and caught the concern and tension on his face. She just shook her head; she was having a hard time getting used to his worrying about her.

She looked back down and petted the pitch-black beast. She smiled as he rubbed against her side. She was sure he'd grown in the days she'd been gone. He was already higher than her waist.

Alex's voice brought her attention back to the others. "Pretty soon his strength won't be a problem for you at all." Her beautiful sapphire eyes danced as she smiled.

Rain smiled back, not wanting to kill the mood and tell them that it wasn't likely she'd be Immortal any time soon.

"When do we get to start designing your mating gown?" Alyssa asked with a big excited smile. Her friend loved sewing, it was her business, but Rain didn't want to think about a gown she probably wouldn't be wearing for a long time. The conversation was going south, fast. It's not like she could tell them that it didn't look like she'd ever be mated. It was painfully obvious that Dorian would just keep holding out until Sirena came up with something. She'd seen in his eyes that nothing was going to change his mind.

"Who knows?" Rain finally said as if it were no big deal.

Alyssa frowned at her.

She smiled at her friend. "Don't worry. It'll happen." When she started getting grey hair, she'd probably have to put her foot down and demand it. She wasn't about to withhold sex; she'd only cause herself pain if she denied them some relief. Not to mention, that was the one truly amazing thing she got out of it all.

The whole thing frustrated her. She honestly didn't want to see his horrors any more than he wanted to show them to her. Not for his reasons, she had entirely different concerns. She knew those memories would rip her guts out, and she'd end up more enthralled with the irritating male. Seeing what he'd been through would only show his strength and character. She was better off not experiencing any of that until he cared for her. He acted like he already felt some kind of stronger emotion for her, but she couldn't trust it was real. She mentally shook her head, for now at least, she could hold out her heart, live in the moment, and experience the good without getting addicted to him any more than she already was.

She was saved from further conversation when Conn came in, smiling warmly at her. "You doing okay, Rain?"

"Yeah." She smiled back; she really liked the wolf. He'd been a sweetheart since the moment she moved into the manor. He'd given her a tour and told her about the others and how the place ran. In general he'd gone out of his way to make her comfortable, and when she needed to find another place to stay, he'd arranged the cottage for her. She owed him. He had such a dark bad-boy thing going, with all the tattoos and piercings, but he had a heart of gold. He was even there when she'd faced off with Drake about selling her business and moving for her safety. When she'd balked at Drake's high-handed bossiness, Conn had been there to turn up the exhaust fans and laugh it off. She was pretty sure the Guardian leader wouldn't have barbequed her, but it was a tense few moments as she watched smoke filter out of his mouth.

She felt Dorian's approach even before he slid an arm around her shoulders. She looked up at him, unsure about the display of affection. He'd been talking with Gregoire and Bastian on the other side of the room. As their first outing together, the entire thing was awkward as hell. Now, with his arm around her and a distinctly hardened jaw, she wasn't sure what the hell was going on. Was he feeling possessive? She looked at Alyssa, who only beamed back at her. Traitor. She tried really hard not to like it, but damn, she did. She huffed out a breath.

I'm fine with this, whatever it is, but pee on me or start acting like Gregoire and we have issues.

His gaze shot down to her before he burst out laughing.

Conn smiled and shook his head before walking over to take a seat.

Dorian lifted her up and kissed her, right in front of everyone, before leading her to the seat next to Alyssa and Gregoire. She was still fighting off the effects of his kiss when she sat down. Her cheeks felt flushed, and she was angry that he would get her all heated when she was stuck sitting there with no outlet.

Drake came in after several of the other Guardians, as well as Erik and Sam, Alex's brother and his mate. It felt odd attending an actual Guardian meeting as if they were already mated. She felt it when Dorian pulled her chair closer to his and rested his arm over the back as they faced Drake.

Their leader opened with, "Everything's been quiet for a week. Too quiet. We still have no idea why there were so many hell beast attacks and demon-possessed. We can all guess that it has something to do with someone taking over after Cyril, but we don't know for sure. Conn."

The wolf sat in front of a laptop and reported what information he had. "Uri hasn't found anything useful out of any of the possessed we detained, but he and Alex had a *knowing* that appears to be leading us to Cynthia. The location was the home of a Mageia who has a rare ability with air. She's similar to Rain in that she can communicate with winged creatures." Conn grinned at Rain. "We took her to a safe house a few days ago and made it look like she's off visiting the Denver Coven for the week. She's not fucking happy. She was already warned by one of the covens that Cynthia was preying on their own. She had set up some impressive protections, but was still being watched."

"Good," Alex said, looking relieved. Her powers were kept secret. The abilities were those even the Gods hadn't had. They seemed to be getting stronger after her mating with Uri. It took about a year before mated pairs' powers completely blended. Rain wondered what they'd be able to do then.

Conn spoke again. "We've marked and bugged the cars of the Mageia watching her. I should have a location soon."

Uri added, "We won't have a lot of time once we find Cynthia. A week seemed a realistic time for her to spend at the coven; longer and we're concerned that Cynthia might look for new prey. We'll have to hit before that time's up, and it's coming. The bitch is smart, and she'll get suspicious and likely go back into hiding if the female never goes home."

"Why can't we just put the Mageia back in the home and let Cynthia's idiots grab her?" Jax asked as if that was the smartest option.

Alex answered. "We already cleared it with Drake. We can't use her as bait. She needs to be away from it all," the female said with certainty. "We bought all the time we safely could. It'll work. We just won't have a lot of time for recon." Alex shook her head and frowned at Jax like he was an idiot. He just winked back at her, causing Uri to narrow his eyes at the cat.

Drake moved on. "Sirena."

The healer sat there pensively for a second before nodding and speaking. "Vane and Brianne are, for the most part, fine. I'm hopeful they'll wake within another couple of weeks. Brianne will probably awaken first because less poison got into her system." She took a breath before adding, "I'm going to continue doing tests *often*, since I keep getting anomalies. I'm not really sure what it all means yet. It's subtle, nothing life threatening."

Rain wondered what Sirena was keeping from them and saw the other Guardians eying her.

"What's really going on?" Erik asked Drake pointedly before anyone else had a chance.

Alex seemed to be looking off into space as Vane's twin questioned what was happening. The big dark-haired Demi-God looked angry and concerned.

"I agreed that Sirena would discuss her findings with Brianne and Vane before she imparts any of her thoughts to anyone else. It's not life or death, so you wait," Drake said matter-of-factly. He didn't seem pleased with any of it, but it wasn't like he was a warm and fuzzy dragon anyway.

Rain felt the tension grow thicker. Worry for one of their own was obviously getting to them.

Erik eyed Sirena. "We'll talk when this is over."

"Erik, I know you're Vane's brother, but don't piss me off. It's none of your fucking concern until Sirena has more than guesses." Smoke filtered out of Drake's mouth.

Erik narrowed his eyes, and Rain wondered if the male had a death wish.

Alex grabbed her brother's hand and shook her head with an odd look on her face. "He'll be okay."

Chapter 23

Guardian Beach House, Tetartos Realm

Dorian's mouth was on hers the minute they reformed at the beach house, their home for the week since he'd claimed her. Their tongues dueled until she was moaning deep. What had started out tender with him was getting increasingly more dominant. She wrapped her legs around him as he pinned her to the wall. *I'm going to do such dirty things to you tonight.*

Gooseflesh ran along her skin.

Do you want that, Rain?

Hell, yeah, she wanted every hot inch of him in any way she could get it. Pathetic, but so damn true. *Yes.*

Good. He carried her to the bedroom and slipped her clothes off first and then his. "I'm going to stretch your snug little ass, Rain. I'll have to give it to the Aletheia, but I won't let him be the first for anything."

She swallowed. The possessive gleam in his eyes was just making her hotter.

He leaned down and kissed her quickly. "Get on the bed, nymph. During the mating, your pussy and ass will both be full of cock. I'm going to stretch your ass with a toy and fuck your sweet pussy tonight so you know just how good it is with no one else."

The image he projected was hot. A part of her loved that he didn't want to share her. She refused to feel guilty about doing what had to be done, but would she feel bad about enjoying it? She worried she might. Every time he talked about it, she got so wet at the idea of two males focused all on her, and it made her stomach clench.

She should feel guilty for loving his struggle, but it made her feel wanted.

He moved some pillows. "Lay with them under your hips. I'm going to take my time."

Her breathing grew even more erratic. Creators, what was he going to do to her. Her thighs were already wet, and he hadn't even touched her pussy or breasts. She crawled onto the bed and lay over the pillows with her head on the comforter and her ass in the air.

"Spread wide for me, Rain."

She groaned and complied.

"So hot and wet."

Outside the door, Bastian said through their link.

Her head turned to Dorian. "What's outside?"

"He just picked a few things up for me. I'll be right back. He won't come in." He nearly growled.

A second later she heard packaging tear and looked back. "It's a plug to stretch you tight muscles. I'm going to slide it in and fuck your pussy while it's lodged in your ass. Once you come all over me I'm going to take out the plug and take your ass nice a slow. The lube I'm going to use is special and will make it good."

She closed her eyes at the image of him pushing the tapered toy inside her.

"Arch back for me. I'm hungry." His voice came out gravelly.

A hand ran over her back as the plug and a small jar were tossed onto the bed, right next to her head.

Soon both his hands were caressing her spine and hip. "I love the line of your back like this, all arched with your ass high, ready for whatever I want to do. You smell so fucking edible." He groaned, and so did she. Gooseflesh rose all over her skin as she waited. The anticipation was killing her.

"Your pussy is so damn wet, Rain."

She felt his lips between her shoulder blades and hissed out a breath. His cock nestled between her cheeks as he leaned over her. She couldn't help moving back into him. His shaft was warm and hard against her. His tongue trailed up her spine to her neck. The sensation made her squirm and sent tingles all through her body. She fisted the blankets as he slid his cock back and forth, massaging her crack.

He lifted from her, and she missed the heat of him. Warm breath filtered over her pussy a second later as his big hands massaged her thighs before moving up. A heated smack landed on her bottom, and she groaned at his wet tongue soothing away the light sting. She circled her hips for more, loving when he was rougher with her. She knew he always tempered his strength with her, but the sting was good.

"My little sea goddess loves to be spanked." She heard the grin in his voice. "We really need to explore that further one day, but now I have so much more in mind."

She sighed into the soft material of the comforter. The wet sensation of his tongue over her pussy made her back bow further, giving him all the access he needed to make her feel good. His tongue was ruthless, and his hands came up and spread her wide, licking and sucking until he met her ass and rimmed it with his tongue. "I can't wait to get in here," he said and then moved away, making her groan in irritation. She wanted to come.

He chuckled and smacked her ass again before picking up the things he'd left next to her on the bed. She heard the lid of the jar open and waited, anxious and ready. "Offer me your ass, Rain." Shit, he was killing her, but she tilted her hips higher. "When I push it in, you need to push against it. The lube will make this easier." He palmed her ass and spread her wide, waiting... tormenting her.

"I'm going to show you how fucking beautiful it is with your ass all stretched around the plug, but it'll be even more gorgeous stretched around my cock." He groaned, and images started filtering into her mind. His fingers as they applied the clear lube over her back entrance. Soon she was watching his finger enter her ass. "Fuck, just like that. Take it."

She pushed and arched; it tingled and felt so damn good. The fingers of his other hand slid over her lower lips, and she saw liquid rush from her body to coat the digits.

"Gods, you're soaking my hand. Who's pussy and ass is this, nymph?"

She gasped and pushed back for more, and he added another finger to her ass. They glistened from the lube as he slid them in and out.

"Tell me," he growled.

"Yours." She barely formed the word she knew would get her

what she needed.

He groaned. "You grip my fingers so hard. I can't wait for your ass to swallow my dick." The black rubber toy replaced his fingers, and she felt deliciously stretched. He pushed all the way in until the base met her cheeks. She whimpered mindlessly, caught up in the sensation. She needed to come. It was all too good. Too wicked.

"Damn, I can see just how much you love having your ass filled." He circled the toy around and around, and she keened uncontrollably.

"Oh, Gods, Dorian, make me come. I can't take anymore."

"Do you want my cock filling up your pussy?"

She couldn't breathe. His words thrust her over some unseen edge into agony. *Yes.* She was beyond getting her voice to work. She needed more.

He groaned and fed her the image of his cock sliding under the toy, and she just about came off the bed. She felt him push inside her pussy and thought she'd die if he didn't finish it. *Please. I need.*

She heard his heavy breathing as he pushed inside. "So fucking tight."

It was intense. With the toy in her ass and his cock slowly tunneling into her pussy, she'd never felt so stuffed and so hot.

"Can you take more?"

She nodded into the bed. Her shoulders were tense, and she was probably ripping the bedding as she clawed it. Never had she felt so raw.

He pushed until he was all the way in.

Damn it, Dorian. Fuck me hard. She was beyond begging. She knew he was holding back. Since bruising her pelvis the first time, he always held back.

He growled behind her. Hard fingers gripped her hips as he started thrusting until he hit just the right spot. She came hard around him. He shouted, and she felt the electric current that sent her over again, violently.

Her breathing was ragged, and she thought she might pass out when his cock slid from her body. He leaned in and kissed her cheek. “So amazing. Can you take more, Rain, or have I worn you out?”

She felt hot tingles all over her body. He wanted more, and she was only too happy to give it to him. She was tired, but the thought of having his cock in her ass was heating her all over again.

“More.”

“Ah, Gods, you’re fucking perfect.”

She heard the drawer open and knew he was getting the cream. She smiled. He made sure to gently caress it over and inside her pussy after every time they’d had sex. His finger gently pushed the soothing cream inside her channel and over her lips. His fingers slid to her piercing, and she moaned. She was still sensitive, but he was gentle. She felt his fingers glide back to the toy.

“Push, Rain.”

She did as he pulled the toy from her body. She groaned when it came free.

“I’ll go slow. Tell me if it’s too much.”

She moaned. *Show me.*

He groaned and showed her what he saw as his cock slid just inside her body. Her piercing moved, and she knew he was using his telekinesis on it as he claimed her ass. He was so much bigger and longer than the toy, but she pushed back, begging for more of the biting stretch, the manipulation of her piercing making her wild.

"So fucking hot and tight. Your ass is sucking me so good. It won't be long before I'm filling your ass with my come."

She was close again after only moments. His heated shaft in her ass was so much better than the toy; she felt so damn full and out of control. Claimed.

She pushed back one more time and came hard as he filled her ass. Her body spasmed when the pulsing current hit deep inside her body.

She lay there panting for long moments. "Is that electric thing normal?"

"I think it's my beast. It's only happened with you." His words made her heart ache.

"You can electrocute?"

"No."

She didn't know what to say to that. He pulled slowly from her body, and she groaned. A wet cloth smoothed over her pussy and ass a second later. The inside of her thighs were next.

More cream from the nightstand was caressed over her ass, and she was thankful. It already felt a little achy. She'd never taken a male there, and it needed a little soothing. She felt like her heart could use a little of that special cream too. That had been intense. It was the last piece of her body she had to give, and she felt… possessed, claimed, even more than she had before. She didn't know what to do with the emotion.

"Would you like a bath or sleep, nymph?" he asked softly.

"A bath sounds nice."

She heard the water turn on in the bathroom and looked forward to relaxing her raw nerves.

"I'll bring you some wine." His lips were at her ear, and she loved the feel of his warm breath on her skin.

She got up slowly, and he watched her closely. "Wine sounds good. I just need a second." She needed to rinse off before getting into the tub. His getting her a glass of wine would be perfect.

She was just stepping into the water when he came in with two glasses. The temperature was perfect. She moaned and watched as he stepped into the tub with her. He just assumed that tub time was for him too. She mentally shook her head and tried not to be too happy for his comfort. He seemed to enjoy touching her all the time, and the affection was addicting.

She settled back between his thighs and rested against his chest, taking what she needed whether it was wise or not.

She sipped the wine he handed her and relaxed a fraction. They sat quietly for long minutes, and she was glad the tub fit them both comfortably.

"How are you feeling?"

Physically. "Fine." Mentally, she was starting to get the sad feeling inside. Would he ever share himself with her completely?

Chapter 24

Guardian Manor, Tetartos Realm

"Alyssa, I think your damn nerves are screwing with mine. I need air. Are you two up for going out to the patio?" Rain paced from the media room toward the balcony and opened the door to the cool evening breeze. Dorian was with his brothers, going to take down Cynthia, and the stress was getting to her. She was worried for him, which was ridiculous. He would be fine. She was turning into Alyssa. The problem with that was that Alyssa and Gregoire were bonded, committed completely to each other. She just felt silly for worrying over Dorian. Rain listened to the chatter on the Guardian link and filled in Sam, since she wasn't mated to a Guardian and couldn't hear what was happening.

She craved the same connection that Sam and Alyssa had with their mates. Every time she had sex with the stupid guppy or they swam with the sea creatures, she ended up feeling closer to him, yet he still planned to hold out on committing to her.

"I'm all for some air," Sam said with a bite to her tone. She, like Alyssa, was having a hard time not being out there in the fight. Rain had no such problems. She was still mortal and didn't doubt for a second that she'd be a huge liability.

"Come on, Havoc." Sam called Uri's hellhound. He bounded off the couch and looked just as happy to get out as she was. The hound had only gotten to take Erik and Alex to Earth before Uri brought him back to sit with them. It was a huge Guardian secret that the animal was not only capable of breaching Tetartos' confinement spell, but could take a passenger. Sirena was still trying to figure out how that was possible, but Rain just hoped that meant she'd get to visit the other Realm someday.

Rain closed the balcony door and walked downstairs and out to the courtyard. It felt so much better, easier to breathe out there.

The three of them sat in patio chairs. She didn't know Sam well, but what she did know, she liked. The female was from Earth, and Rain remembered her saying that her parents were relocating to Tetartos.

"When do you think your parents are going to get here?" she asked Sam.

"Actually, I think I've convinced them to stay on Earth and move into one of the coven communities there. I don't think they'd be happy being so isolated out here." Sam looked pensive.

A lot had changed in the last week.

Sam continued, "They have so many more conveniences there, and Drake would have wanted them to live here in one of the cottages. It just sounded too much like roughing it for my mom, who likes her malls. When they thought there would be no chance for me to see them again, it made sense." She said the last on a whisper. No one was allowed to know that Havoc could take passengers to the other Realm. It was strictly guarded information, but for Sam it would be the only way to see her family.

Rain nodded. Her parents lived in one of the cottages now, but they were introverts. The other day she and Alyssa had gone and dropped off some of her mom and dad's paperwork to their old boss who believes they moved to another city. It wasn't smart to be seen with Dorian, though she worried whether the scene at Paradeisos was being spread into the Realm. Supposedly Tynan squashed it, and Cesaro was being kept silent along with a handful of others that had seen her being hauled out of there over Dorian's shoulder.

She nearly groaned at the thought of what he'd done next. The frenzy was still riding them. That wouldn't stop until they completed the ceremony.

A small smile tilted her lips, thinking about her parents' reaction when she'd finally spoken to them about her and Dorian. Drake had wanted her mom and dad out of Lofodes because of their association with Alyssa, but now they needed to stay close because of her mating. They seemed more than fine with the cottage and the manor was only a short distance away. In reality, as long as they had their books they were happy.

Rain scratched Havoc's butt, which he'd pointed in her direction when she sat down. She thought about what Sam said about Earth and sighed wistfully. "I can't imagine what it's like to go to a mall and try on shoes and clothes. Oh, and go to clubs, or amusement parks, or even a movie theater."

Sam chuckled. "I kind of took that stuff for granted. I do miss some things, just not the traffic or the smog," the blonde said. "Fighting hours of traffic every day to sit in a tiny cubicle isn't pleasant, but sadly it sounds wonderful now that I've got nothing useful to do. I'm really starting to hate that Erik won't teach me to fight. He just growls and postures. Alex finally took me to the gym and showed me some sparring moves. I was a jogger not a gym-goer. I've never fought anyone in my life or even hit a punching bag, so needless to say, I suck." She looked frustrated.

"At least I have my business. You're both welcome to slave away for me. I have plenty you can do," Alyssa said.

Both she and Sam looked at each other and chuckled.

Her friend frowned at them. "What? You two have better ideas?" She actually snorted at their lack of enthusiasm, which only caused more laughter to erupt from them.

"It's really sweet of you to offer, but I wouldn't know what to do with a needle and thread."

Alyssa's mouth dropped open, appalled, which brought tears of mirth to Rain's eyes. "Really? I'm not so backwards that I don't have sewing machines." She huffed. "Gregoire set me up with the most advanced equipment." She puffed up talking about her sewing room and what her mate had done.

In between fits of hysterics, Rain defended her friend. "I've seen it. He went crazy buying stuff. Half of it she doesn't even know how to use." She didn't realize how much she needed to laugh. It felt good.

"Of course I do. I read the damn instructions. That one machine is simply defective."

The three of them had a hard time stopping the laughter once it started. It relieved a lot of the anxiety she was feeling with Dorian on Earth. She knew she could still communicate with him, but she didn't want to distract him in the middle of a fight. She didn't like what they'd said about Cynthia using advanced weapons with the potential to do serious damage to an Immortal. They might even be able to sever his head, which meant death. Immortality wasn't infallible.

Chapter 25

Guardian Manor, Tetartos Realm

Brianne woke in a small bed that was definitely not hers. She scanned her surroundings before deciding it was fine to move. She was groggy as hell. What happened? Her muscles were stiff, and her ass was planted in the infirmary. That meant she'd been injured. Mentally taking stock, she knew that all her limbs were where they were supposed to be, and she didn't feel anything wrong. She whipped the thin blanket off and scowled at the horrendous gown they'd put her in. Why not leave her naked? She wasn't shy. Her brothers never helped Sirena with her healing, and those were the only ones she might be slightly skeevy about seeing her nude. Once her brain started working, she'd call her sister and bitch-slap her for putting her in the stupid getup.

She shook her head, trying to clear the fog in her mind. She stretched and inhaled deeply, surprised at catching the one scent she'd grown to crave. It was dangerous to her, but so intoxicating. More now than ever before. Her heart stuttered, and she jumped from the bed, her muscles feeling the pull, but she didn't give a shit. She whipped aside the curtain that obscured the top of the bed next to her. She knew what she'd find. Who. Her brain was so damned fuzzy. Had Sirena given her drugs?

She tried to shake off the cobwebs as she searched Vane's face and sheet-covered body for whatever injury had landed him in the bed next to hers. She didn't find anything. Her stomach clenched as she listened to his steady breathing and tried to relax.

He was sleeping and didn't appear injured. He had to have already healed. What the hell were they doing there? She didn't dare touch him, keeping her distance was a necessary precaution. The last thing she needed was him waking up to her pawing at him as if she cared. She scoffed at that thought, but the draw to touch him was stronger than it had ever been. Something was making his scent so much more intoxicating than before, and it was affecting her hormones.

She frowned. His beautiful golden hair was splayed out on the pillow. His eyes were closed, and his jaw had a day's worth of stubble. She balled her fists to stop from feeling what it was like. He was too fussy to allow whiskers. She really wanted to do more than touch that rough hair; she'd much rather hop in the bed right beside him and do wicked things to him as he slept. She grinned at such deviant thoughts. She stretched her arms over her head again and tried to think while working to shake off her weird reactions. Why were they there? The stubble meant Vane might not have been there long, right? Unless someone shaved him. Damn, that could have happened. Her aching muscles indicated that she'd been there well over a few days.

Blips of memory started coming back to her. *The fight, hell beasts, and then Vane there fighting alongside her. The rush, then irritation at being tossed out of danger. Him getting distracted, and the ofioeidis biting down, so close to his head. She'd panicked; the beasts hadn't been the same as the ones she fought before, a new breed, so much stronger than the others. Blinding terror racked her as she and her brothers cut the beast's head off and dislodged the venomous teeth from Vane's flesh. She'd shouted at him, furious that he'd gotten hurt. The bastard wasn't supposed to get injured, ever. She'd wanted to mutilate the beast for harming her male. No, not hers, never hers, but her mind hadn't been rational. Obviously, or she would never have ripped his leather aside and sucked at the poison as quickly as she could. With venom, every fucking second counted. She'd split blood and venom over and over as her brothers watched. Now they knew. She'd been avoiding that. Never wanting them to know the extent of the relationship, her weakness. It had all started out as something forbidden. She should have exiled him from Earth; instead she'd met and screwed him like a bitch in heat every damn chance she'd gotten in the last century. Damn! Damn. Drake and her brothers would know what she felt. They'd pity her. She'd been too demented to guard her emotions when trying to help him.*

She rubbed her face. Maybe it was better to face her brothers now while she looked pathetic and sick. There would be lectures, questions. She knew it was coming. She looked down at Vane again. When would he snap out of it? She still needed to kick his ass. The whole thing was his fault. First in thinking to fight beside her, as if she'd needed help, and then because he'd gotten hurt and scared her.

Why didn't that matter as much? She couldn't take her eyes off of him, wanting to pull off the sheet covering him and see if his cock would respond to her lips. Shit. She just needed to get her heated response to the damn male under control. She didn't want to have it out with her brethren while horny, but she was dying for confirmation from Sirena that Vane would be okay. They were both hit with the same venom; he would be fine. She obviously was, so he would be too. She believed that.

He'd better be having sweet dreams, because when he woke up, his ass was hers.

More memories struck. She sat back down to catch her breath, and closed her eyes. Had they been sharing dreams?

Gods, she hoped that wasn't real. If it was, so much more was on the line when he woke up. She heard her brothers on the Guardian link. She had to dress in case they needed her, but she really had to stretch out her muscles before she did anything.

Chapter 26

Cynthia's Hideout, Earth Realm

Conn and the others had done as much surveillance as they could after figuring out where Cynthia had been hiding. It was a fortress, under a new alias they hadn't known about. It was in a corporation her maternal grandfather set up decades ago, and Cynthia had managed to hide it well. The property was miles of fenced and tree-lined acreage. They'd checked the place with all the electronics they could, and now they waited. They had as much footage as they could get in the few days since the meeting at the manor.

Dorian wore a spelled vest; they all did.

He wished he was back at the beach house with Rain. He knew she was holding back, not wanting to give anything more than her body, but his reasons for not wanting to blood bond had only grown stronger. He ran his hands through his hair. He fucking... cared for her. Shit, he wanted to protect her from his ugliness indefinitely.

"Nothing's changed in the last few days, still five guard stations with rocket launchers," P said through the link. The last time they'd gone after Cynthia, they'd found out too late that she not only dealt in human drugs, but she was well fortified with military-grade weapons. The first round of raids went smoothly, but by their second round, her Mageia were waiting.

"Guards in goggles, likely heat-seeking to know what they're aiming at. Stay back until I signal," Drake said, flying in the opposite direction of P. He'd partially transformed and had to fly higher because the green scales of his wings glinted in the moonlight, whereas P's were pitch black. P and Drake wouldn't normally change form on Earth, but Cynthia was just too good, and the best option was to strike from above. She'd managed to down eight Guardians last time. No easy feat. That was not happening again.

"She's spelled the building. It'll take a minute to break through and then secure the guards with the long-range weapons. Don't stay in one place long in case we don't get them all. I have no doubt she'll have even more safety precautions in place," Drake growled through the link.

They'd considered gassing them, but without having a good idea of the layout, it wasn't a good idea. They didn't want it obscuring their vision and senses if the crazy bitch ran again. Drake and P would have to subdue the Mageia with long-range weapons as quickly as possible and disable the missiles too. It was in no way the ideal situation, so they were prepared for anything.

Blaring alarms sounded a second later. Dorian waited next to Bastian and Conn. Others were in groups around the entire perimeter, including Uri, Alex and her brother, Erik.

You good, man? Conn asked.

Yeah, I've got this. He wasn't going to be left behind, and since feeding the frenzy, he wasn't in the dangerous shape he was before. Yeah, he'd still fight with a semi, but not a full-on hard-on. It was doable.

None of them wanted to take the chance that Cynthia would get away again. She was the only link they had to Elizabeth and whoever was in charge of Cyril's people. They didn't think anyone would follow Elizabeth. She was just too damn sadistic; she'd always been twisted. They could see someone using her for her ability, yes, but her as a leader, doubtful. That meant someone else was pulling the strings and having Cynthia find them test subjects. That had to stop.

He, Conn and Bastian stood waiting for their cue to teleport in.

Dorian wanted to check on Rain but stopped himself. He'd left her with Sam and Alyssa at the manor; she was fine. He really needed to get his shit together. He was fast becoming addicted to her sweet body and so much more. She was so damn perfect. Caring, strong and beautiful. Her power was beyond anything he'd ever seen from a Mageia. Even he couldn't do what she was able to. Once they mated and their powers fully melded, she truly would be his sea goddess. Rain was everything he never imagined having in his life.

He really needed to get a hold on it. The longer Sirena searched for a way around her seeing his memories, the bleaker the option seemed. The blood bonding had to be done. It was the final step that would lock in her Immortality. Sirena thought she might be able to come up with a drug to dull the memories she'd see, but who knew if and when that would happen. The longer he waited, the more he imagined ripping apart any Aletheia that touched her. He would have to share her, she wouldn't gain Immortality without it, but fuck, she was his. He understood a little better why Hippeus were forced into chains when they mated a mortal. Gregoire's race was fifty times more possessive than any of the others. Nereids weren't known for even a little possessiveness, yet his was getting stronger every day.

Conn seemed off. He kept looking into the trees away from the house and inhaling. *Are you good?* He frowned at the wolf.

We're in, Drake said.

He and the others ported into the property. He chose to land in the trees, alert for any movement that would indicate Cynthia leaving. The alarms were blaring. Others were teleporting to the roof and into the second-floor windows. He felt, then heard an explosion to the left.

Fuck, landmines under the fruit trees on the east side of the house. Sander is down. Getting him back, Jax said.

Son of a bitch. He was glad the side he was on had mature trees to land in.

On my way, Sirena sent, no doubt Jax had broadcast an image of where to meet. It would take too long to take Sander to the manor and through the spells to the infirmary. Sirena would teleport him there if she needed to.

He ported to the side of the house. He, Conn and Bastian stealthily moved in, but no Mageia were coming out to meet them. Gunfire erupted from the other side of the home.

Can someone cut that fucking alarm? He felt Jax's annoyance. It was loud as shit and hard to discern anything else, which was the point.

Working on it, Conn said as he slipped through a side entrance to the massive home.

He watched and stole through the same door, rounding a corner as Bastian came in behind him.

A Mageia appeared around the corner and shot just as Dorian teleported behind him, the asshole had skills, and the butt of the weapon nearly cracked back into his jaw. He dodged, and the bastard pulled the air from his lungs as Dorian grabbed his hands to cuff him. It was a decent attempt to fight, but the spelled cuffs would drain that power. The room's furniture crashed from the air currents the

Mageia was trying to manipulate until the metal shut it down.

Half the upstairs is cleared and no sign of the bitch, P said.

I have her scent. Cynthia's in here, Jax said, recognizing it from tracking her after the last battle.

Dorian secured the Mageia's feet in a long zip-tie in mere seconds and stuck him in the corner to retrieve later, then followed after Conn. Another bound guy was left in a corner. The blaring alarm was making it impossible to hear anything the male was saying, and he didn't care. He and Bastian looked at each other, watchful of their surroundings. He slid into a hall and handled another asshole who charged through a door ahead of him. There were too many damn rooms and hallways in the place. The downstairs was easily twenty thousand square feet, which would have been much easier to search if there weren't sitting rooms and hallways all over the place.

Why aren't hordes of Mageia on our asses? There were a few, but not like the last time. He caught up as Conn had one down and cuffed. An assault rifle was on the ground next to them.

We took care of most of them before you got here, P said through the link.

Asshole.

P chuckled at the comment. His brother generally kept to himself, and Dorian understood why. The son of Hades had his own issues. He nearly snorted. Fuck, they all had their own issues.

He spotted a Mageia slip out of a hidden door in the wall as Conn walked passed. Dorian was on him before the bastard could pull the trigger on the Glock he'd raised. Conn turned with a raised eyebrow as Dorian secured the bastard.

There are hidden doors in the walls, he informed the others.

No one's found the alarm? Jax growled through the link.

Obviously not, asshole. Keep bitching, though, cuz that's making it so much better, Dorian responded. He was just as irritated.

Fuck off.

Shut up! Drake snapped.

It reeked of perfume the further they went. Someone had to have broken a bottle of the sickening stuff.

Another wall slid open, and three Mageia came out firing in both directions. The area was too damn small, and a bullet grazed his neck while another hit his vest. It burned like a bitch, but he gritted his teeth and knocked one weapon away and flipped the bastard to his stomach. He was hit with another fucking bullet to the thigh. He felt Rain's panic through the link and was getting ready to reassure her when he felt her. Next to him. Everything happened so fast. Their eyes connected, and he saw his own horror reflected in hers. His heart stopped as everything moved in slow motion. He grabbed for her as two more Mageia filled the room. The bullet hit, and he instantly felt her pain, her fear. Her warm blood on his hands as he covered her small body with his. Her body went limp in his arms.

Gregoire, Rain just teleported. What the hell's going on? Alyssa's voice was panicked through the link. He ignored all other chatter. He didn't fucking care what the hell was going on other than getting Rain help.

Fuck! Sirena, get the hell over here. Rain's been shot! He gave Sirena the visual of his island on Earth and teleported them out. He needed her on his bed. Safe in his home. He needed her to be okay.

He'd never felt so scared in his entire life. He smelled her blood as he lay her down on the bed. She cringed in pain, but didn't say a word. His own injuries long forgotten, he fought through the buzzing in his ears. The blending of their bodies still affected his damn dick, but his panic quickly killed it. "It's going to be okay. I've got you. Sirena will fix this," he said while using the blanket to put pressure on the wound. They were both bleeding all over the bed, but it didn't matter. He kissed her head and shook as he waited for his sister.

Just stay with me, he said in Rain's mind.

Damn it, Sirena! Where the fuck are you!

Her breath was hissing out. It was a lung; he knew it. Better than her heart. Fuck. He kissed her lips, still putting pressure to the wound.

Everyone out now, Jax's voice came booming through the link. Fuck, that didn't sound good, but all he could think of was her jerking attempts to breathe, and Sirena still wasn't fucking there.

Sirena came rushing through the door. "Let me see."

He moved but refused to leave her side, he just kept kissing her forehead. Shaking, he was fucking shaking so hard.

"It punctured her lung." He watched his sister work and saw the bullet fall away. Finally, Rain took in a deep breath, and he slowly relaxed.

Sirena pulled the bullet from his leg. The neck wound was only a graze. It probably looked ugly, but it was already closed.

"Go take care of Sander. I'll heal," he told Sirena when she moved to look at his neck.

His sister's gaze was hard. "No more. That was close to being deadly for her."

He nodded. He wouldn't wait any longer. No fucking way was he taking another chance that she'd die on him.

Sirena left, and he looked down at his little mate. So much terror had filled him when he'd seen her. "Does it still hurt?"

She cleared her throat. "No."

His head touched hers, and his hand went to her heart. He was still trying to breathe through it all, and feeling her heart beat was the only thing loosening the vise around his lungs.

What's happening? he asked through the link. Fuck! He'd abandoned his brothers in that hallway.

We're good, man. Take care of Rain. We all got out before the place blew. Jax scented the explosives at the last second. Her people were not so lucky. We only got one out, and Uri is interrogating him now.

Conn's words relaxed his muscles. He couldn't have left her even if they'd needed him. He didn't want to take his hands off of her. He closed his eyes. He'd never forget the surprised agony on her face as she'd been shot. Son of a bitch.

Her hand went to his neck, and she spoke softly. "Why didn't you let her look at this?"

He couldn't move or open his eyes. "It'll heal in a few minutes. Just give me a second and we'll shower." He took in a deep breath. "What happened?"

He heard her swallow. "I felt when you were hurt, and I panicked. I don't know how it happened. I wanted so badly to see that you were okay. The next second I was moving through thick air and then I was there. I didn't know I could even do something like that. We're on Earth?"

"Yes." He breathed out. He stayed touching her. This was his fault. He never imagined her teleporting to him through the Realms. Alex had done it when Uri was hurt, but Rain was mortal. He clenched his jaw. Not for long.

"We're completing the mating tomorrow. Only because I don't think I can make it fucking happen sooner. Not with my brothers still having to clear out Cynthia's. I can't see something like that ever again. Right now I need to clean all the blood off of you, because the scent of it is still scaring the shit out of me." The words came out with so much raw emotion he almost choked on it.

Her hands were in his hair, and he needed her so bad. Fuck, he was still shaking. She was too damn fragile until he made her Immortal.

"I hate what you'll see."

"I know," she replied softly as she massaged his scalp.

He lifted her into his arms and carried her into the shower area. He peeled off her pink top and little shorts. Everything was covered in blood, and he clenched his jaw tight. He would burn them.

Once they were both stripped, he lifted her and set her down under the water. He quickly washed the blood from his own body and proceeded to clean every inch of her as gently as he could. Squatting down, he lifted each foot and soaped them. His eyes wouldn't leave the spot where she'd been injured. It was pink, but closed. He kissed it over and over before resting his head on her stomach. She hadn't said a word, just let him care for her. He was too raw. A few inches could have meant her life.

"I'm okay," she whispered as she stroked his wet head. He felt the water caressing his skin and knew she was manipulating it to soothe him. He wanted to make love to her, but the bed was ruined, covered in blood, and he'd rather the whole thing be burned with her clothes. He took a deep breath.

"Tomorrow won't come soon enough. I need to take you back to Tetartos and keep you safe for one more fucking night." He blew out a breath. He needed to go for a swim to calm the fuck down.

"Dorian, please. Don't. I'd rather stay on Earth for the night," she whispered, and he heard the longing there. "This is the one place I've always wanted to see."

"I can bring you back with Havoc once you're Immortal. I'd already planned for that." He saw her understanding, but disappointment shone in her eyes, and it nearly broke him. Fuck, he'd give her anything. "I need to keep you safe. I almost lost you."

"You got me out of there, Dorian. Just let me see a little of Earth. I know you'll keep me safe." It went against his instincts, but the look on her face slayed him.

"We'll have the night here, but you have to listen to everything I say." He couldn't believe he was doing this.

Her eyes brightened a little. They were finally losing some of the glassiness from the shock and pain. "Really?"

Shit, he would wrap her in Kevlar if he had to. They would stay in his other home. The island was small, and he knew instinctually she'd want more than the sight of a secluded island.

"Yes." He stood up and lifted her into his arms. "I'm taking you swimming first. It will do us both good right now. The sun's just going down here."

Chapter 27

Dorian's Island, Earth Realm

Rain was still reeling from the raw emotion she'd seen on Dorian's face. He'd looked more than panicked, he'd been horrified. The sight of it nearly split her heart. She knew just how much he cared for her in those harsh moments when his emotions were completely exposed and then after, when he'd cared for her.

Her brush with death pushed him into completing the ceremony, and she was glad. She was still quaking inside, and she never wanted to feel that weak or scared again, ever. Her stomach still felt shaky. When she couldn't breathe, she'd thought for a second that it might all be over. No more. A swim was exactly what she needed. Then she'd be ready to explore.

She'd been surprised and happy to hear he planned to bring her back. She hoped that would be soon, there was so much she wanted to experience there, but she needed to shake off the nerves. If they'd gone directly to the beach house, she wouldn't have rested, and she would have hated that she'd had to come back so soon. She wanted to see everything she'd seen in movies or read about in books and magazines. She'd sold all of that in her shop, and she loved anything Earth related. She was infatuated with it.

He lifted and carried her out to the beach. The sun was getting ready to set, and the sky was a magical mix of orange and pink swirling through the blue. It was beautiful. She took a deep breath of the salt air and hoped that would settle her nerves. She had a feeling that it would take a while before anything truly relaxed her.

When her body started porting to him, she'd been caught completely by surprise. It felt like she moved through rubber before reforming next to him. She'd been disoriented as she saw his horrified expression. He'd been covered in blood as he grabbed for her, and then she'd felt the blinding pain of the bullet; everything had been so loud. It left her unable to breathe and scared. His shaking and putting pressure on the wound had hurt, but when Sirena finally got there and healed the damage, she was able to breathe again. She still felt a ghost of the pain and knew her mind was making it up. The wound was no more than a pink circle. Her hand went to the marred flesh. Now, even still shaky, she was so damn happy to be alive.

"The sea life is different here. Much more mild and tame than in Tetartos, and the waters are a hair cooler."

His thumb massaged her side as he held her. He kept moving until they were in the warm surf. She felt his body change while she was in his arms, and then they were off. It was much the same as before. The creatures were much smaller, sleeker, beautiful. He kissed her over and over, giving her his breath.

Between Dorian's touch and the water, her raw nerves finally settled into something manageable.

The next time he flipped her around to give her air, she quickly wrapped her legs around him and rubbed up against the bulge there. She was ready for so much more. Confirmation that she was still alive. That they both were. Seeing the blood on his neck freaked her out. He could have been taken from her with those weapons.

He teleported them to the shore. "I promise to take my time

later, but now I need to be inside you. Are you wet for me, Rain?"

She moaned. "Yes." She was always ready to take him. Always wanted him. Always would, he was intoxicating.

"Good." Still standing, he held her ass with one hand and guided his cock inside with the other. "Fuck."

She held onto his shoulders as he controlled her all the way down his shaft. She circled her hips, loving when he was deep.

"I need to feel your come all over my dick."

"Yes." She swallowed as he thrust inside her. He stood in the sand with the sea behind him, the sun an orange dot against the horizon, and it was beautiful.

"Look at me."

She gazed up, finding his eyes nearly glowing with feeling. He controlled everything, sliding her up and down while her piercing rubbed over him, making her burn. She gasped while his hands massaged the mounds of her ass. He let her body weight take her down, but she needed more.

"Harder." Soon she was sputtering incoherently.

He gave her more, slamming her down to the root. She was consumed by him, but she hated that she knew he was tempering his strength. It was obvious in the taut lines of his neck. This would be the last night he would need to be gentle with her body. She could only imagine the rough sex they'd have when she was finally able to experience all of him. Could take every bit of wildness that she knew he kept leashed from her.

Her release boiled over, making her cry out as he followed her. All the while staring into her eyes. Watching every play of emotion on her face. He lifted her up and claimed her lips, and she honestly thought she could kiss him forever. Something about his full bottom lip always got to her. Coupled with the wicked things his tongue was capable of, she was moaning into his mouth. Her hands were at his jaw, tracing the hard line with her fingers.

When they finally broke the kiss, she was dizzy and ready to do it all over again.

"I love the dazed look you get every time we kiss."

She sighed as she looked into his curious eyes. He wasn't teasing her. "I've never felt kisses like yours."

He smiled down at her. His eyes were soft, loving. "I feel the same, little nymph. Now let me get you to bed, and I'll kiss you until you fall asleep."

She liked the sound of that. "Isn't your bed ruined?"

"Yes, but not the one at the other house."

She heard him ask Conn to bring some of her stuff to his other house. After he dressed and covered her in one of his bright shirts, he teleported them away.

"Where is this?"

"It's our Florida home," he said offhandedly as he moved to open the glass doors. They seemed to be at the back of the house, and she stood there for a second, processing the odd ping in her heart at his calling the home theirs.

She cleared her throat. "How many homes do you have?"

"This and the two island homes, plus there are suites in both Guardian compounds. The one on Earth and the manor on Tetartos."

She looked around some more. It wasn't as big as the beach house on Tetartos, but it was beautiful, and she saw a pool and hot tub on the next level down. The property was surrounded by trees and shrubs. Excitement ran through her at the thought of being on Earth. It was different when they were on the island and obviously so far from humanity. She stifled the urge to peek out the front door. Behind the house was water, with a long dock lit with tall lampposts all the way to the end, where a boat bigger than Tynan's sat. She grinned. Out in the night she saw the lights of other vessels in the water, and even though it was dark out, it seemed the sky was so much lighter than it should be.

He picked up the bag that was leaning against the glass. She was thankful he'd asked Conn to drop off some of her clothes. She eyed the bag, concerned that a male had packed it. Odds were good that nothing matched, and there would be no underwear. She shook it off, at least she wouldn't be wearing his tee shirt when they explored the next day.

They walked through a big open kitchen and living room, down a hall into a spacious bedroom with a giant bed and a small seating area arranged on tile and decorative rugs. It was cozy. He dropped her bag and lifted her into the big comfortable bed. "Rest now. I promise to take you sightseeing in the morning before we have to head back to Tetartos to get ready for the mating."

She lay there and started getting nervous as he took off his clothes and got in next to her. His skin was warm, and she sank into it like she always seemed compelled to do.

"Is there a certain Aletheia that does matings? Sirena never explained that part," she asked against his chest.

The lights turned off, and he tucked the blanket at her back. She loved listening to his heartbeat; it relaxed her. It made her feel safe and comfortable. She'd spent every night curled into him just like they were doing. In the beginning she'd been too exhausted to move, but later it had become a habit. One he perpetuated by pulling her against him after sex and using the soothing cream on her pussy. She smiled.

She was nervous about the mating now that it was really going to happen.

"There are Aletheia that do the ceremonies."

She could almost feel him thinking next to her.

"Have you slept with Tynan?"

She looked up at him, thankful there was some light coming through the curtains. His brows were furrowed like he wasn't looking forward to her answer. "No."

His muscles seemed to relax.

Before, she loved his jealous tendencies, now she worried that it was taking a toll on him and would be a nightmare during the ceremony to come. At least he wasn't as bad as Gregoire. Thank the Creators for that, but it was more than she'd imagined when she learned he was her mate. Nereids were known for sexual excess, not jealousy or monogamy. That's probably why she was thrilled every time he displayed it. She felt special.

"Would you be comfortable with him?"

She looked up and into his eyes, what she could see of them in the shadows. He looked pensive. She considered his question. If she had to have sex with another, Tynan was attractive, but pretty much all Immortals were. She wasn't sure about doing the ceremony with a male they both knew. Would it be easier or more difficult because they'd likely see him again? "Yes. I would be more comfortable knowing he's trustworthy. The question is will you be okay if it's with him? I don't want things to be uncomfortable if I go to the island with Alyssa."

He lay there for a moment, one hand behind his head, his thumb running circles around her back as she rested mostly atop him. "Do you have any special feelings for him?"

"I like him as a person." She watched him, concerned he needed other assurances. She whispered, "I have feelings for you. I barely know him."

I'm happy to hear that, nymph. It won't be easy, but I promise to make it good.

She moved her leg so that she was straddling him. "I want you."

His hands moved to her hips as he ground his hard cock against her. "Do you?" he said, grinning at her.

Chapter 28

Kane's Compound, Tetartos Realm

"Not my problem." Cynthia was panicking over the Guardians finding her again, and she actually wanted Kane's help in hiding from them. They needed to find another Mageia contact on Earth if he was going to find females there. Kane ran a hand through his short dark hair. He couldn't believe she was so careless that the Guardians found her again. She was a liability.

"We're done here," he said, only half listening to the sputtering pleas from Cynthia through the connection. He looked at Elizabeth. "Cut the connection. I want you to work at finding another contact. If you don't have something in the next week, you die." He was sick of waiting for other test subjects. Ian thought he was close to trialing a formula, and he wanted to make sure the Mageia scientist had all he needed. He felt the moment that Elizabeth severed the connection with Cynthia.

He looked at Angus, his second. "Take her back to her cell. I have things to do." He didn't miss the narrowing of Angus's eyes. No one wanted to be in control of the bitch, but he didn't trust anyone else to do it. Angus and he had been partners for the entire time they'd been with Cyril. He raised an eyebrow at the blond male.

Angus blew out a frustrated breath and prodded Elizabeth to move out the door. She gave Kane a deadly glare as she walked out into the tunnel going the opposite direction of where he was headed.

He was agitated and needed to get out of there. He wished, not for the first time, that he could teleport, but he was full Aletheia, not the son of a God like Cyril. He rubbed the back of his hair. He hated everything about the situation. For more than a century he'd waited for Cyril's experiments to produce results. Ian seemed to think they were close to some kind of breakthrough. He needed to be patient, but he worried that answers wouldn't come soon enough for Isaura.

Chapter 29

Drake's Mountain Home, Tetartos Realm

Brianne hadn't wanted to distract her brothers during the fight, so she'd dressed and listened. Now that it was over and Sirena had healed Sander and Rain, she needed to know what was going on. Drake had come to the infirmary while she'd been helping Sirena with Sander. Poor thing had been big-time messed up by that damn bomb, but he was finally patched up and back to his crabby self. Drake had waited until Sander left before telling her and Sirena to meet at his mountain home.

She quickly cleaned up and teleported. Walking in to the huge living room, she saw him standing by the fireplace; he never sat. The fireplace took up almost an entire wall in the nearly two-story room. Ancient tapestries hung on the walls alongside swords. It felt kind of homey and very old world. Drake's longish blond hair was mussed. Not like Vane's perfect hair.

She wondered if he built the space so large so that he could take his dragon form and lie in front of the fireplace, twitching his tail. She grinned to herself. She sure as hell wasn't going to ask him that.

She was agitated, knowing she'd have to come clean. That and she was all too aware that Sirena wasn't telling her something important. She knew that Vane should be waking up in another week, but having to meet at Drake's didn't bode well.

"How are you feeling?" Drake asked. He wasn't warm and fuzzy, but he cared for all of them in his own way. She knew that without any doubt. He had kept them all marginally sane during the early centuries after they'd become Guardians.

"Fine. My muscles were just tight as shit when I woke." She tried for something to avoid the topic she knew was coming. "Do you think we'll find any clues in the rubble at Cynthia's?"

"No. I'm sure she had tunnels, and she'll be long gone. The explosion was smart; the scent made it impossible to track her." He tapped a hand on the mantle of the stone fireplace. "I don't think she will have left any clues. The human authorities are all over the place now. Once they're gone, I'll have someone double-check."

She sat on the couch and tried to relax. "I guess I missed a lot while I was out."

A fire was lit, giving the room a warm glow. She crossed one leg over the other and jiggled a foot in the air as they waited for Sirena to arrive. What was taking so long? Her sister was fastidious, but this was ridiculous.

"How long?" Drake asked with a raised eyebrow. She didn't have to wonder at what he meant. She guessed that meant chitchat time was over. She hoped Sirena got there soon, though she was sure the healer would take Drake's side.

"Too long," was her best evasive answer.

Sirena finally walked in. The tap of her heels on the stone sounded deafening in the silence after her answer.

"Brianne," he growled.

Damn. "A century, give or take."

That caught him off guard. His eyes went a little wide. That was a huge reaction from him, which wasn't necessarily good news for her. She looked over at the flames behind the grate.

"Are you fucking kidding me, Brianne!" he roared, and smoke billowed from his lips. "Do orders mean nothing now?"

Shit, he was really pissed. "Vane, Erik and Alex were helping out with the possessed on Earth, and you said yourself that we were supposed to avoid them so we didn't have to exile them to Tetartos. We needed the help too much to worry about separating them from humanity."

"How is fucking him avoiding him?" Drake snarled. The room was filling with smoke.

She just stared at the dragon, her mouth open. "I never tell any of you guys who to fuck. I can't believe you're going to tell me."

"Brianne, I'm not your fucking father, but I gave an order, and you blew it off. I'm not happy everyone keeps hiding shit. First hellhounds, then a mate and now this. I took Uri's ass to the mats. I don't ask for shit other than you all do your fucking jobs and don't make things harder for us." Smoke filtered from his lips. His green dragon eyes were old, a lot older than they should be. He carried the weight of the Guardians. He watched over the sleeping Gods so that none of the Guardians would be tempted to off the bastards, and she knew he rarely slept. Sometimes he may seem a little cold, but he took his duty seriously.

"It wasn't hurting anything," she said, knowing that it didn't matter. She had gone against his orders.

"*Wrong*. Sirena, explain her fucking blood work," he growled, emerald eyes flashing dangerously.

Sirena finally spoke, and she looked exhausted and worried,

which scared the shit out of Brianne. "It looks like both your and Vane's cells have mutated. It's like there is a connection melding between the two of you. I'm not sure what that means. It's different than anything I've seen. Similar to a mating, but we know that's impossible. The races never blended in Apollo's labs. He tried to create mixed species on his own, but that failed. One body has never been able to house two animals."

Brianne sat in shock as her sister took a deep breath before continuing.

"I'm not sure if it's something to do with the ofioeidis venom or if it's been there longer. I need to keep doing tests on the both of you."

Brianne sat there, her muscles so tense she thought they'd snap. Connected? Mutated? What the hell did that mean?

"Your fucking actions had consequences. A damn century with a male that could never be yours was a bad fucking idea. What happens if this mates you in some weird way and we lose you to the animals? Will I have to fucking put you down?" Drake was furious and, more, worried, though she only caught a glimpse of it in his hard gaze. Her stomach lurched.

"We haven't said anything because we still don't know what's happening. It's your choice to tell the others. I'm not sure what any of it means for certain, but I'll be taking blood samples often so I can figure it out."

Chapter 30

Guardian Manor, Tetartos Realm

Rain was almost ready. Alyssa was doing the last checks on her dress.

"I can't believe he took you shopping," Sirena said with a smile.

"Yep. In the stores by the beach. He also took me to breakfast in a car. Then we walked around before coming back. He was twitchy and growly the entire time, and holy hell, if anyone got too close to me, he scared the shit out of them." She grinned and continued. "It's different than in the movies. You experience the smells and sounds that are so different from here," she explained to Alyssa.

Sam smiled as Rain recounted her morning adventures.

Rain felt lighter, almost giddy. She hoped they went back soon. She wanted to experience it all. Now, she just needed to get through the mating ceremonies to come.

Sam, Alex and Alyssa were there with the three female Guardians, Sacha, Sirena and Brianne, most drinking wine as they listened to her. Brianne had been tight lipped, claiming that she was still feeling some effects from the poison.

"Did you talk about the mating?" Sirena asked.

"Yes." Rain felt nervous as hell. Excited about what would

happen but worried at what his reaction to sharing her would be.

Dorian had contacted Tynan and Conn that morning. Conn would be there as a witness and to watch over the blood bonding. Of the brothers, she felt most comfortable with the wolf, but the whole thing would be emotionally trying, and she knew it.

"Done." Alyssa tied the dress at the back of her neck so Rain could stop holding it over her breasts. It fell beautifully with a long gather that vee'd almost to her belly button. Her entire back was exposed in the pale pink silk gown. It was so low it nearly showed her ass.

"You look beautiful," Alyssa said, smiling, and then she flushed, and her hand went to her stomach.

"Are you okay?"

"Yeah, just the weird blending thing again." Her friend gave the same answer she'd been giving for a while.

"What are you talking about?" Sirena asked, concerned.

"It's no big deal. I just keep getting a weird sensation in my stomach, and my power surges. I'm sure it's just normal power-melding stuff."

Rain watched as Alyssa looked to the others. Alex and Sam frowned right along with Sirena.

The healer looked at her closely, and then her mouth fell a little, and her eyes grew wide. "Let me see," Sirena said, and her hands went to Alyssa's stomach. A second later, Sirena's mouth fell completely open before saying, "Son of a bitch!" Her hands roved over Alyssa's stomach again as a hush filled the room.

"What?" Alyssa said, and her pale eyes went instantly to panic.

Gregoire was there within seconds.

"What the hell is going on?" he demanded as he came up beside Alyssa and pulled her into his chest.

"You're pregnant," Sirena whispered reverently before breaking out in a big watery smile.

Both Alyssa and Gregoire stared at the healer for a split second, and then Gregoire turned to his mate and dropped to his knees in front of her. His big hands caressed Alyssa's stomach, so gently. He gripped her hips and pulled her stomach to his face. "Gods! Sirena, will she be okay carrying my child? She's so damn small," she heard him say softly, a hint of panic in his voice.

Alyssa's fingers slid into his hair as she smiled down at her mate. He was holding her so gently, and Rain saw a tear slide down her friend's cheek as she massaged her fingers through Gregoire's hair, soothing him. There was a light smile tipping Alyssa's lips, and she looked happier than Rain had ever seen her.

The moment was heart-wrenchingly beautiful, but private. She and the others left the room as quietly as they could, leaving Sirena to answer their questions. Alyssa whispered down to her mate, still smiling at him. So much love. Her friend was going to be a mother. She'd be an aunt to a little warhorse. Her hands went to her chest.

"I didn't think it was possible for at least a decade?" Alex said, obviously still shocked. Sam and Alex were equally affected by the new development. Anxious and pale. They both set their drinks down on the nearest table as if the alcohol burned their fingers.

"It's not surprising that Gregoire and that huge-assed horse dick of his knocked her up so fast," Brianne mused.

Four sets of wide eyes turned to Brianne.

"What?" She looked at them, wide eyed and innocent. "You can't tell me no one else was thinking it." She turned to Sacha with her hands palms up. "You've seen his warhorse. I'm surprised he hasn't broken Alyssa in half. My respect for that female went up fifty notches when she didn't run screaming from him when she caught sight of that thing. Shit, we all know she was a virgin."

Sacha, of all people, burst out laughing, and they all stared at the usually quiet Kairos. Her beautiful bronzed skin was flushed with amusement, and she looked even more beautiful.

Brianne had been quiet up until that point, saying that the venom was making her drowsy. Apparently not anymore. Rain just shook her head, grinning while trying not to picture Gregoire's dick.

Sirena came out, a big smile on her pixy face.

"How are they?" Rain asked. She needed confirmation that her friend would be okay. Alyssa *was* small, and Gregoire was one of the largest Guardians.

"She'll be fine. It's Gregoire I'm concerned about. He's working himself into a panic, and I fear that a new level of possessive craziness is moving in. Alyssa might beat him senseless before it's all over." Sirena smiled at that.

Sam and Alex shared a look and moved in front of Sirena, each settling one of the healer's hands on their stomachs. Sirena chuckled. Rain, Sacha and Brianne just grinned. Sirena shook her head. Neither were pregnant, but now the question was whether or not there would be more pregnancies in the near future.

Alex and Sam quickly picked their drinks up off the table, and Alex downed hers and was looking to the patio bar as if she were planning to head there for a refill. Rain tried not to laugh too hard at the look on Alex's face.

Rain wasn't sure how she felt about children. She'd never considered anything that far out of reach. A decade seemed a long time, but now... What if she got pregnant with Dorian's child? She pictured a small blond boy with spiky blond hair playing in the water, and she smiled. She'd be fine with whatever happened.

As it came time to leave for the ceremony, she turned to the others. She was sure Alyssa needed time to wrangle her mate. She wouldn't hold it against her friend if she didn't make it. She might be a little sad, but not upset. Alyssa's life just changed in a huge way.

"We should get to the Temple," she said. She was anxious to reach Dorian, and Sirena smiled knowingly before grabbing her hand and porting.

Rain took a deep breath as she stared down the long tunnel.

Alyssa came up next to her and squeezed her hand, and Rain was relieved her friend would be there. "Congratulations."

"Thank you. Now, let's get you mated." Alyssa beamed, but Gregoire scowled at his mate touching Rain.

She shook her head and grinned at her friend's crazy mate. His frown settled into something that resembled chagrin. He truly was having a difficult time. Alyssa's hand left hers, and Gregoire tucked her into his side. She was flushed and beautiful, and Rain was immensely happy for her.

At the end of the tunnel the others walked into the cavern ahead of her. When she entered the glittering gold room, Dorian was there waiting. His eyes glittered with heat as Rain moved toward him. His beautiful bright eyes roved over her dress and down to the bare feet that peeked out from under the fabric. The material was light, a soft tease against her skin. She still couldn't believe this was happening.

She felt rested, happy, and anxious all at once.

Dorian took her hands in his as Drake began. It was weird, but she couldn't hear anything. It was if they were the only two people in the world. The Guardians were all there, along with Erik and Sam, but she didn't see them. Didn't hear anything but her own heartbeat.

The Temple they stood in was coated in gold, and she remembered standing there less than a month ago and seeing Dorian for the first time. Looking at him now, she realized how far they'd come in such a short time. She took a sharp breath at the beauty of his exposed chest. Soon, he would be marked as her mate. She saw the sexy vee that disappeared into his low-hanging black pants and her mouth watered a little. She was a very lucky female.

He said his vows in the old language, and she somehow understood every word. It was a binding pledge to honor and care for her, with his body, soul and in blood for eternity. She felt the words flow over her like a soft blanket for her soul.

Sirena, who stood at their side, lifted Rain's hand to make the sacred permanent mating symbol on Dorian's chest. Two serpents intertwined for eternity would always cover his flesh, proclaiming that he was hers. She felt the heat of power and saw his eyes flash. His lips parted as the serpents began forming on his flesh.

The minute it was done, he lifted her up and kissed her deeply. She melted into his arms. His hand went under the back of her dress to the dips above her bottom, and she moaned before breaking the kiss.

"Set me down. I want one too." His eyes flashed with hunger, and then she turned her back. She heard his intake of breath when he saw her bare back exposed to her ass. It still seemed as if they were the only ones in the beautiful golden Temple. As if they were in a Realm of their own.

Soon power flowed from Sirena's hand through his, this time marking her skin with a thinner, more feminine version of the serpents running the length of her spine. From between her shoulder blades to just above her ass. She had faced away from him and tried not to moan at the biting sensation when the hot mark rose on her skin. She knew hers would be a soft plum color instead of the obsidian of his. She clenched her thighs as liquid flooded her. It was so damn intense. The minute it ended, she was in his arms and halfway out the tunnel.

His eyes were penetrating, and his jaw locked tight. "I've never seen anything more fucking beautiful. I'll see that mark every time I bend you over." He groaned. "I'm going to trace every line with my tongue the minute you belong completely to me."

Her eyes went to his chest, and her lids lowered. "I want to do the same to yours." She heard his teeth grinding as she traced the mark with her fingertip.

Chapter 31

Temple of Consummation, Tetartos Realm

When they reformed on the soft sand, she felt his hesitation. Arousal and heat ran wild just beneath the surface of her skin, and she breathed through it.

A few seconds later Tynan and Conn ported right next to them. Dorian's eyes were locked on the male that would touch her.

Tynan looked ill at ease with the situation as he said, "I get it, D."

The two males walked up the steps into the Temple, giving them a moment alone.

She smoothed a hand over his jaw, and he shook his head, still staring at the doorway into the Temple. "I'll get through it. Hopefully, without killing him. Your eyes need to be on me the entire time. I want it to be good for you, *it will be*, but I'm walking a fine line." He looked down at her and put his forehead against hers.

"Okay," she agreed, understanding. She'd die if she had to watch him having sex with another female. It didn't change the fact that it had to be done.

He carried her up the steps and into the massive stone room with mosaic tiles depicting all forms of sexual excess. There was a huge ornamental bed in the center. Each doorway surrounding the big room was open to the night air. Silk curtains billowed with the soft sea breeze coming in. A soft glow shone from the hundreds of candles arranged throughout the space.

He set her on the bed, watching as she tucked her feet under her body. She knew that he'd met with Tynan before the ceremony and had made the Aletheia well aware of his boundaries.

Conn walked out of the room, leaving the three of them. He was to watch over the blood bonding and be there in case Dorian lost his mind with Tynan. She knew the wolf was standing sentry outside for this part of her Immortal ceremony.

Dorian took a deep breath and leaned in, kissing her until she was clinging to him, her arms twining around his neck, holding him as he made her dizzy. His hands went to the tie at the back of her neck and released it, letting the fabric fall to her waist. She grew more heated knowing that she was on display.

He doesn't taste your sweet pussy, and he won't touch these. His hands came up and plucked at her nipples to show her just what was off-limits to Tynan. Her back arched, pushing the swollen mounds further into his hands. *I can smell how wet this makes you. I think we need to explore the fact that you get so wet being displayed. You want me to fuck you while others watch, don't you, nymph? You want them to see you impaled on my cock.*

She moaned, knowing he was right. It really did turn her on. His mouth tilted against hers, breaking the kiss.

He stared down at her for a moment as his thumb came up and caressed her bottom lip. "Tynan's going to use your pretty mouth now, and you need to drink every drop."

She swallowed, trying to get through the fog he created in her mind.

It was beginning.

He moved, discarding the silk pants, and she caught sight of his chest again. That mark said he was hers, and she loved it, wanted to lick it. She wanted him never to wear a shirt again so that every other female could see it.

He looked up at her, grinning, and she realized she'd been directing her thoughts to him.

"Close your eyes, and let him slide between your lips while I make you come," Dorian said, and she looked over as Tynan got onto the bed. He was naked and stroking his hard cock. He didn't say a word, just looked torn as though he hated his life when he moved in front of her. She felt for him. This couldn't be anything like the sexy interludes he was used to.

Dorian climbed up behind her, his chest at her back, and she closed her eyes and let herself fall into whatever happened. She felt the warm tip of Tynan's cock rub against her lips. She opened, sampling his pre-come. He tasted sweet, good, but nowhere as incredible as Dorian's addicting flavor.

She felt the heat of her mate against her back; big hands moved over her stomach and up to caress her breasts. Her piercing moved back and forth, putting pressure on her clit, driving her wild. He was using his ability to make her crazy.

"Suck him deep, and make him come, Rain."

She could hear the strain in his voice. She sucked hard and heard Tynan's deep groan. His hands were at her cheeks, and he was being gentle as he slid in and out of her mouth.

I need you to use your hands, pump him and play with his balls. Make him come hard and fast. I'm starting to lose control, Rain.

Watching him, knowing that mouth is mine and it's wrapped around his fucking dick.

She lifted her hands and pumped the base as she swirled her tongue. The intense manipulation of her nipples and clit was driving her insane.

You have to stop. I can't concentrate, she begged.

Good, he growled in her mind, making her pussy clench. He was losing it, and it was making her hotter.

One of his palms drifted down her stomach, slipping inside the dress at her waist. It slid lower over her mound and jewelry, and two fingers dipped inside her.

Do it, Rain. Make him come knowing that I'm in your pussy and you're hot, wet and ready to fucking come all over my fingers. Tell me who your pleasure belongs to.

You. Damn him, he was killing her. Her hips were circling for more as she sucked Tynan off.

She pumped her hand faster, used harder suction until finally Tynan came down her throat with a strangled groan. She was still strung tight as she swallowed. She was panting and so close. She leaned back against Dorian's chest and ground her pussy into his hand until she exploded all over his fingers.

He caressed her through it, and when she finally opened her eyes, she saw Tynan watching them, tension bracketing his mouth. His cock was already hard, and she knew they'd only just started. She took a couple of deep breaths.

Dorian laid her down, resting her head on a pillow, and slipped the dress from her waist. She was nude and so ready for more. She watched him, knowing that he needed her eyes on him. Which worked well since she couldn't tear her gaze away.

"Show us your pussy, nymph."

She whimpered and opened her legs. His fingers played with her clit and dipped into her juices to coat first one nipple followed by the other. His fingers slid back in, and he painted it over her lips.

Tynan moved in and plunged his cock inside, and she bit her lip. She didn't know what to do. It felt good to be filled, but wrong because it wasn't her mate. Dorian shook his head and leaned down to lick her lips. How could he want to kiss her when she'd had another male's come down her throat?

I'll always want to kiss you. He blew out a breath and looked down at her with regret. *There is nothing wrong in what we're doing. Most others do this purely for excitement and to get off. I don't want you to remember this night with guilt. This night is sacred to us. Tonight we make you Immortal, and you and I will bond for eternity. It's not supposed to be about me being a jealous dick. I'm fine. I don't like sharing you, but I love watching you come, and believe me, nymph, tonight you will come over and over.*

She searched his eyes and realized that Tynan had stopped moving. Dorian looked back and nodded, so the Aletheia pushed in again, and she bit her lip. "We're going to make you come hard, Rain." He kissed her, his tongue slipping inside her lips to taste and tempt her. He seemed to have found some peace with what they were doing, and she felt a million times better with his lips on hers.

I want your lips around me. I want to replace his taste with mine. Will you do that, Rain? Will you make me come down your throat as he fucks your sweet pussy?

She moaned and nodded. Gods, what was he doing to her. He

licked off the juices he'd painted on her nipples, and her fingers went into his hair as he nipped and pulled at them. His eyes flashed wickedly at her when he moved to straddle her chest. She could feel Tynan's strokes, and it was hot and exciting.

Dorian traced her lips with his cock. Her hands came up to stroke the base, but he grabbed them and restrained them against the pillow on either side of her head. *Now suck me.* His hips tilted and rocked his shaft into her mouth as she sucked hard. He growled, and his head went back. He looked so animalistic. More than he'd ever had, and more liquid slipped from her body to coat Tynan's cock. She moaned around his shaft, loving that he pinned her down to take what he wanted. The near feral gleam in his eyes was setting her off, and she bucked her hips, wanting to come so damn bad. *That's it. Take what you want, buck and fight me as I pin you down and fuck your mouth. Know that Tynan's inside your sweet little pussy, but soon it'll be my cock in there as I give him your perfect ass. You'll be stuffed full of cock, Rain. More full than you can imagine.*

She moaned, and his cock pushed deeper into her throat. *Swallow,* he demanded as he pushed in a little more. *Your soft lips will never take another cock besides mine.* She kept swallowing, taking what she could; then he pulled back until just the tip was inside. He pushed in again, and she could tell by the quickening of Tynan's thrusts that he was close. His strokes were getting harder, and she felt her walls clenching around him. There was a tug against her clit as Dorian manipulated the piercing again to drive her over the edge.

Come, Rain.

She did, doing her best not to clamp her jaw down as she screamed through it. She heard Tynan's shout a second later, and her pussy heated with hard jets of come. Dorian's strokes got faster as she sucked and licked the underside of his cock. She saw his muscles tense, and then he pulled back just so the head was out of her mouth, his hand pumping his thick cock in front of her lips. "Keep your mouth open and swallow it all. I don't want my dick to shock you." He'd done the same before. Making sure to never stay in her mouth in case the electrical currents could hurt her. She doubted they would, and she had every intention of testing her theory when she was Immortal and could heal if she was wrong. Her mouth opened wide, and his come pumped past her lips and onto her tongue. She swallowed every last drop and then lifted her head and licked the tip. He groaned and looked a little wild.

She was flipped around so fast she couldn't process what was happening. His legs were over the edge of the bed, and she straddled his hips. His cock firmed beneath her, and she rubbed against it. "Lift up." He positioned his shaft at her entrance and slid his cock home. He pulled her chest down over him, thrusting up so that he was buried all the way to the root. He captured her arms behind her back so her breasts were pushed tight to his torso and her ass was exposed and vulnerable. She moaned, knowing just how she must look with her pussy stretching tight around his cock and her ass offered up. Her breathing was erratic. This was what she was anxious for. Ever since he'd put the toy in her small back hole, she wanted to know what it was like with two real cocks inside her. She refused to feel guilty that it turned her on.

She could barely move, but her hips bucked uncontrollably.

"Use plenty of lube. I want it to feel really good for her."

She couldn't see what was happening behind her, and it added to her arousal. After a moment she felt Tynan's fingers slicking lube over her ass and gasped. She was having trouble staying still with Dorian's cock impaling her. He was bigger around than Tynan, and he stretched out her walls.

I need to move, she begged through their link.

Soon. His voice vibrated back to her, almost a growl.

Her ass was invaded with slick fingers, pushing and caressing, and she tried tilting her hips for more, rubbing her clit hard against Dorian.

He grunted, but held her so tight she couldn't move her face from his chest. She gasped when she felt the other cock. "Push against me, Rain," Tynan instructed, and she did.

They all groaned when he lodged the head inside. "So tight. Damn. Is it hurting you?" Tynan asked.

"No," she keened. It was the total opposite. She wanted more. Wanted to feel them both deep. Needed to be full.

"Do it," Dorian ordered Tynan.

The Aletheia's cock inched further inside her ass as she panted and shimmied for more. The lube made her skin tingle in the best way. It added to the sensation of her hard nipples pinned against Dorian as she was filled with two hard cocks. She mewled as her ass stretched. Tynan's fingers gripped her hips gently as he sank inside. "I'm in," she heard him pant out. She was so damn full she didn't know what could feel hotter until they started working in tandem and she lost all breath. One out, the other in, massaging her walls and making her cry out for more. The thrusts gained speed as she mewled into her mate's chest, and release claimed her, hard. They kept fucking her, and she thought she would lose her mind until she felt Dorian tensing. He came, and the jolts rocked her over the edge all over again.

"What the fuck?" Tynan groaned and came in her ass. She wondered if he was feeling the electricity too.

She was dizzy and achy, but so damn sated she couldn't move if she had to. She felt Tynan slip from her body. Dorian's voice came out gravelly, a little remorseful. "Thank you."

"Happy mating, my friend, a vial of my blood is by the chalice."

She felt Dorian's nod. She knew he was talking about the fact that to digest Dorian's blood she needed a drop of an Aletheia's mixed in. The entire thing sounded disgusting, but it was the only way.

Dorian released her arms and started massaging them. He pushed her hair off of her face and kissed her gently.

"Rest."

Chapter 32

Guardian Manor, Tetartos Realm

Brianne lay awake in her suite, her mind rolling around all that Sirena had said. Mutated cells. What did that really mean?

She was debating avoiding sleep again like she had the night before. If he truly had been sharing her dream, he knew she felt more for him than just loving his cock. Damn, she hoped that wasn't the case. She chewed on her lower lip. If she slept, would she find herself back there with him?

She closed her eyes tight. She'd done things there she never would have done had she known. She'd let herself be vulnerable.

So much was happening in their world. All the matings after so many centuries, and now a pregnancy so soon after Gregoire claimed Alyssa. It would have been exciting if she didn't have the sick feeling something more was happening. The Creators wouldn't be back, but they'd warned the Guardians before leaving that the Gods would one day be needed. Was that time closing in? She hoped to hell it wasn't. The last thing the Realms needed was Ares and Artemis awakening, sick bastards that they were. What possible use would they be to anything good? They were one of the main reasons the Guardians had so much trouble. They'd spawned the damn Tria, for fuck's sake. She pinched the bridge of her nose and considered sleep for the millionth time.

In the end she decided it was better if she went to him again. Maybe do some damage control.

Her eyes closed, and she lay there waiting. After several deep breaths, she finally relaxed and felt it take her under.

"Where were you?" dream Vane demanded. His hands were on his hips, and his eyes flashed accusingly.

Shit. She really was sharing her dreams with him, wasn't she?

He stalked toward her, and she tried for flippant. "I found another hot locale and was snoozing there."

He grabbed her, and she released her talons, free to attack. She didn't like the look in his eyes. She'd always made him prove his strength, that he was worthy before she let him fuck her. Her beast loved the game and the fact that he was the only one that could best her, aside from her brothers. Only now it felt forced, not what it used to be.

"So we're back to this, then?" he growled.

"We're not back to anything. We were only having fun, Vane. So I got a little kinky in my dreams."

His hands held her arms behind her back as he glared at her. "Kinky? I don't think so."

Her heart raced, and her eyes shot open. Damn him. Now she didn't even get to sleep. She was screwed. Worse, she had no idea what the whole connection thing was until Sirena did more tests. She jumped out of bed. She needed to fly.

Chapter 33

Temple of Consummation, Tetartos Realm

Dorian owed Tynan. He'd treated the male no better than a prized stud, and he hadn't deserved that shit.

He ran a hand over his face. "Are you okay?" She'd come hard all over his dick, wrung the come from his body when she'd clamped around him like a vise.

"I'm okay. A little sore, though." She waggled her eyebrows.

His lips tilted as he stared down at her beautiful face. He knew she wanted him to apply cream to all the sore spots. "I'll make sure to fix that. That's the only trouble?"

She nodded. "I feel good."

He saw Conn standing outside, looking at the sea. They needed to get the blood bonding over with, but it made his gut clench just thinking about it.

She looked up at him, knowing. "I'll be fine. I have to see it."

All his horrors and failures would be lined up for her, he knew it. The only memories she'd see were his strongest, and the vast majority were not good.

He kissed her and got up to get the cream, glad he'd asked Tynan to bring it with him. He wouldn't need the male's blood. He'd arranged for some of Uri's to complete the bond. He really owed Tynan, big time. Maybe he would buy him another boat and have Bastian teleport it over. Yes, he'd get him a bigger boat. The male loved to sail.

He uncapped the jar and moved to the bed. She was snuggled up on her side, watching him. She painted a gorgeous picture. He moved her over onto her stomach and slid his fingers in to apply the healing cream to her abused pussy and ass. He would be taking her again after the blood bonding.

He looked forward to her becoming Immortal, taking Nereid form. She really would be his sea goddess, and he didn't doubt for a second that he would be chasing her through the waters. He was eagerly anticipating not having to temper his strength when he was taking her. Until he could stop holding back and give her everything and not worry about harming her.

"Let me clean you up, and then we'll have Conn come in and watch over the blood bonding."

She nodded, and he lifted her into his arms and carried her over to the cleansing alcove in the corner. The water started flowing from the ceiling mount, and he took his time cleaning her before drying her skin.

Conn.

His brother came in and smiled at them. He grabbed the chalice and ceremonial blade, and then pulled out a vial from his pocket. Uri's blood.

He took her lips as Conn sliced into his forearm. He didn't want her to see that.

I'm going to bite your shoulder as you drink from the cup, nymph.

It happened very fast. She drank, and he sank his teeth into her smooth skin, partially transforming to use his sharp fangs. She flinched, and he quickly licked at the sting as his beast hummed inside at being able to mark her.

Her memories started flashing in his mind.

Loneliness as she played by herself as a small child. Her mother and father sitting to the side with books. They'd share smiles, but wouldn't take the time to play with her.

Hunger as she walked through a market. A small hand darting out to swipe a piece of fruit, panic when the shop owner turned. A female child about the same size, with brown hair and pale green eyes, making fruit fall in the other direction, a distraction. Adrenaline, running as fast as her small legs would carry her. Relief, then excitement as the other child followed her. Laughter as they played and talked.

Another flash.

She was older, so was the green-eyed girl. So much happiness filled her when she pulled a pan of something from an oven. A hug from the other girl's mother. Complete joy from the affectionate touch.

Swimming in the sea. Her creatures surrounding her, loving her. Exhilaration, excitement, freedom. Hugging their backs and letting them take her far out into the cold water.

Elation, pride. Showing a grown Alyssa her empty shop with boxes and shelves. They smilingly started rummaging through the inventory.

Disappointment and sadness as she stood at an Emfanisi and faked a smile for Alyssa. Knowing that she would age and die. Berating herself for believing she might find a mate. Resolve to live her life to the fullest.

Lying in a bed. Regret and disappointment filling her heart as she looked at the spots of blood on the bedding, wondering why it hadn't been as amazing as she imagined.

Sirena telling her she was mated and being hit with the biting pain of rejection.

Blinding intensity and pleasure as he made love to her the first time. So much heat and lust... connection.

Him seeing her with her creatures. Pride, longing for him to see her as powerful, special, worthy.

Pain, panic, need to get to him. Moving through rubber and reforming. Blood, pain, unable to breathe. Seeing his fear and knowing he really cared for her. Worry she might die and lose him.

Him saying the words to bind himself to her, the flow of Sirena's power as the mark rose over his skin. Love. Heart-wrenching love.

He came back to himself and just stared at her. She was his. He nearly choked from the emotion slicing him deep. She loved him so damn much it nearly broke him. He never imagined seeing so much pain, hope, strength in such a young female. He lifted her into his lap and waited, swallowing. He would give her the fucking world on a damn platter.

Conn's back was to them, and he thanked fuck for that. He was raw.

"You can go, Conn," he whispered.

His brother nodded and left. Never looking back.

Her eyes opened, and he'd never seen anything more beautiful. She took deep breaths, and he saw the tears pooling in her eyes. Fuck. She hadn't even cried when she'd been shot. He kissed her lips.

It's over. I'll make it go away. Let me love you.

Yes. Even in his mind, her voice was raw.

She clung to him as he devoured her, trailing his tongue over her jaw and down her neck. He could never take the memories away. She knew him at his worst, and he was sure the only good things she'd seen in his mind were her. She was the only pure, beautiful thing in his world, and he'd almost lost her when he'd rejected her. Denied her. Them. Never again. She was his, and he would fucking cherish her every day as the gift she was.

Chapter 34

Kane's Compound, Tetartos Realm

The alarms were shrieking when Kane returned from the hidden lab. Why the fuck hadn't Angus telepathed him? He searched for the link to his second and couldn't find it. Anger and concern hit him hard. Was his second dead? He stalked the halls, snapping two hellhound necks on the path to his room. What the fuck were the Tria doing sending their beasts to attack him. He snarled as realization hit... Elizabeth.

He sliced into the neck of another beast with his dagger. Dead Mageia littered the halls, and he raged as he continued to the tunnel leading to his suite.

"Hello, lover," Elizabeth purred as he entered. She had another bastard with her. Reve. The Kairos was so mild tempered, and Kane had never imagined the male would turn on him to help the bitch.

Three hounds attacked at once, and he moved quickly to dislodge one, but another got his teeth into Kane's neck. Fuck. He wouldn't make it to his weapons. He wished he was able to teleport. He broke one more neck before hitting his knees from the paralyzing bite. The damn hound wasn't letting up.

He glared daggers at Reve, who just shook his head. The male had no loyalty. Fucking coward.

"What happened to Angus?"

Elizabeth's silver eyes glittered with pure excitement, then tilted to the side. He saw Angus's bloodied and abused body on the floor. "Dead, but not before I had some fun. He had some interesting memories of you going off somewhere with the reports you get from Ian." Son of a bitch. Kane was glad he hadn't shared the location with the male.

He was done. Guilt and pain ate at him. He'd failed his sister. Her madness at losing her mate, because of him, would only continue. He wouldn't make it out of this. Soon, she would take his blood memories, and it would be another bloodbath at the hidden facility, or worse. The sick bitch was capable of so much worse.

"Why?"

"I never could have come up with all the lovely serums Cyril had. I never would have thought to give souls as payment for the hell beasts if it hadn't been for him. He's gone, though. Now, I have everything available to me, and you were no replacement for Cyril. I could never have taken him down so easily. I owe some gratitude to whoever killed the bastard." She smirked evilly.

Licking her lips, she slinked closer to him. He didn't give a shit what she had planned. She'd done it all before. His gut clenched remembering the early years when he'd been at her mercy like so many of the others. He glared at Reve again. He should have disposed of her when he had the chance.

None of it mattered now. All he cared about was Isaura. Elizabeth would do unspeakable things to his sister, if only because she meant something to him. The bitch was sadistic. Even the children in the lab wouldn't be safe. He closed his eyes and contacted the only male that could help them now. He could only link with another Aletheia, and there was only one that could make sure his sister was protected.

Urian.

Kane's life was already forfeit. He knew it by the look on Elizabeth's face. Her evil smile indicated that he'd soon be wishing for death. Like Angus had. He looked at his friend's defiled body, covered in blood, the head off to one side. He felt a pang of sickness and regret that he hadn't killed her. He would soon pay dearly for that mistake, but Isaura didn't have to. Pain was radiating down his arm from the hellhound biting into his shoulder. He was bleeding out, and the venom was slowing his movements. He only wished it would all end him, but it wouldn't.

He would give the Guardians the location of the secret lab before Elizabeth had those memories. He wouldn't take the chance of the sick bitch getting to his sister before she could be rescued.

It was the last thing he'd ever do for her. Regret washed over him, knowing he'd failed to make amends. To give her back the life that he'd taken from her.

Chapter 35

Guardian Beach House, Tetartos Realm

Rain stretched her arms high over her head. Relaxed. She was content and happy. They'd spent the last few days in bed. She'd woken after the blood bonding, and he'd loved her over and over until she actually felt the connection of their mating and Immortality flowing through her. It had been blindingly intense, powerful.

She actually felt stronger.

"Are you ready? I imagine your loyal subjects await their goddess's first transformation," he whispered in her ear. She heard the smile in his voice as his strong arms circled her ribs.

"I'm ready." She was anxious and excited to attempt it. Would she be able to change so soon after gaining Immortality? He seemed to think so. She chewed her lip nervously as they walked through the house and out to the beach below.

"Let me in your mind, nymph."

She got wet remembering just how much they'd shared minds in the last three days. It added an entirely new level of intimacy, having him so completely inside her, every emotion and thought, ranging from loving to hot and kinky. She felt every bit of his pleasure, knew everything he wanted before he demanded it in that sexy growl he'd started using. Everything was stronger, deeper, wilder than before.

He no longer leashed his strength, and her body was more than capable, and oh, so eager for every heated thrust. She licked her lips remembering him taking her hard, slamming her body against the furniture, the walls. It took a day of pushing him, taunting him before he finally accepted that she wasn't fragile anymore. After that, it was like an entirely new world opened up, and they'd done some serious damage to the beach house. She smiled to herself.

Her new abilities were itching to be let loose. The only instruction she'd had so far was on using the world's energies to fuel her body. That had been peaceful nourishment unlike food, undiluted energy.

The lesson to come was the one she'd craved the most, yet gave her the most anxiety. Would she change? Would she get back to human form? She'd never heard of anyone getting stuck. Pain wasn't an issue. Dorian already explained that it would feel good, almost freeing to let her other form take hold. She trusted that; it made sense.

A buzzing had set up residence in the pit of her stomach, and it was past time to see what he meant. It became more insistent as her toes sank in the warm sand.

"I'll be with you. Open your mind, and I'll guide you all the way through it."

She let down the mental shield and felt the itchiness inside growing hotter, heavier. It had a distinct wildness to it as she stepped into the surf. Soon liquid was running over her calves and thighs to her stomach. She closed her eyes and moaned. She felt like she would come out of her skin.

Fuck, that's strong. He was in her head showing her the way, but it was as if instinct was already taking over. She pushed through and felt the change in her muscles. It slid over her skin, and she dove, unable to stop herself. She needed to be covered in her element, needed to swim. She felt her creatures, her companions, moving in. Excited. More kept coming as she tunneled through the water. So many came, following her, wanting to be near, yet giving her space. She sent out the soothing emotion she knew they loved. She mindlessly moved, lost in the beauty of it.

Fucking incredible. So damn beautiful and shit you're fast.

She looked over and grinned at him, knowing he was keeping pace with every inch, every mile she swam. She finally slowed and surfaced. She spun to see how far they'd gone. No land was in sight, and she was shocked they'd gone so far. It seemed as if only minutes had passed.

"I wasn't kidding, you're fucking fast. You easily matched my speed as if you were born to that form." He pulled her into his arms. "You were made for this, for me. I've never seen a more gorgeous female in all my centuries." His hands went to her face, and he looked a little awed.

She basked in it, loved the power of it, the freedom, being able to share it with him. She looked down at her tail. It matched his, steel grey and smooth. She turned her head and saw the sharp spines lining the back, a feminine version of what his sported. He usually made sure to keep them retracted while he was with her; she'd need to learn how to do that. She was just too damn ecstatic to think of anything past what they were doing. She was happy, loved... so deeply. She felt it in his mind.

Creatures filled the water around them. So many they spanned the depths and kept coming. She projected more of what they craved from her.

He looked around and shook his head before kissing her, hot and hard. Her tail rested against his, letting him keep her above the water as his mouth possessed hers.

Chapter 36

The Seas Outside of the Guardian Beach House, Tetartos Realm

We have a situation. One of Cyril's males contacted me with the location of a secret lab. He gave me other information, but said that Elizabeth would soon know. I don't know if it's a trap, but it feels urgent. We need to get there immediately. He asked me to take care of his sister. Protect her. I have a feeling he's dying, Uri sent through the link along with a visual of where they were supposed to go.

Rain was shocked and nervous. What the hell was going on?

Feeling? Drake asked, likely wondering if it was part of Alex's *knowings*.

Yes, we have to go, now, Alex added anxiously.

P and Sander, go with them.

On it, came from P.

Sacha and Jax, wait five minutes, then follow.

Dorian teleported them to the house. "We need to get dressed and get you to the manor in case I'm sent out." His jaw was tight as he donned his leather fighting gear and sheaths that held two swords at his back. He'd brought more and more of his things there. They'd pretty much settled in even though he'd said they needed to decide where she would like to build a home on Tetartos. She still wasn't sure what to do with that.

Son of a fucking bitch! Uri's shocked growl reverberated through the link.

What is it?

Get Sirena in here. We have Mageia children, hundreds of all ages up to fucking ten years old. It's a fucking breeding lab, Uri snarled through the link.

The line went silent.

Sirena, now! Drake ordered.

Dorian teleported the two of them to the manor, still waiting to see if Drake would have more of them go.

Gregoire and Alyssa appeared soon after them. Brianne came in right before Conn, who looked odd, anxious, maybe even a little wild under the surface. He was usually so mellow it caught her off guard. He smiled at her when she frowned in his direction, getting ready to ask what was wrong.

Bastian, get over there. Sirena, where the hell do we put these kids? We don't have room at the manor, and we don't know what's been done to them yet, Drake growled through the link.

Rain sat with Alyssa on the nearest couch, both aware that they wouldn't be called out there. She wanted to ask how her friend was doing, but they were all silent, waiting.

Erik and Sam walked in a minute later as they listened to Sirena coming up with locations to send the children to. Babies were coming to the manor, and Drake gave the okay on that. Uri sent messages out to Immortal warriors that they needed foster homes for the children. Healers in the cities were notified that they would be needed to assist. Sirena ordered everyone around to different facilities, but Drake still hadn't called anyone else in.

I have the lead scientist. He didn't put up a fight or attempt to flee. Getting his memories now so that we don't miss anything here. More instructions came from Uri as he told them where all the information was kept. *I can't get through to the Aletheia. My guess is that he's dead. The sister's mind is gone, and she's dangerous to herself. She's apparently been this way since losing her mate in a battle a century ago.*

Rain's heart lurched for the poor female.

Chapter 37

Brianne's Home, Tetartos Realm

Brianne couldn't sleep. She'd been avoiding it for days, and the lack of rest was taking its toll. Each time she dozed, she was back with Vane, and every time he seemed more angry and frustrated than the last. She planned to avoid the hell out of him.

Sirena had taken more of her blood in between monitoring the children they'd rescued from the lab. That whole thing was fucked up. They now had reports on the research being done to circumvent the mating curse. It was dangerous, and they had no idea where the other lab and Elizabeth were. All the bastards working in the breeding facility had been isolated there for over a decade. Sirena was backlogged, and there wasn't a damn thing any of them could really do. Healing and studying charts was not among any of the other Guardians' skill sets.

She squirmed in her soft sheets; she was hot and horny. She always slept nude, and the supple sheets were only making it worse. Her body was so damn achy. She needed to be fucked. She was going to have to buy more batteries soon.

What Sirena and Drake had said kept rolling in her mind. She hadn't taken another male in the time she'd been with Vane. Too long. She'd always rationalized it because he knew just how to make her beast sing, and that kitty sated her body like no one else ever had. Why take a subpar fuck when she had him more than willing to make her purr? Of course, she'd never tell him that.

She opened the drawer to her nightstand and rummaged in there until she pulled out a long remote-activated vibrator. She slid the sheet off her body and spread her thighs wide. She was so on edge and needed to relieve the tension. She rubbed the length of the rubber toy over her slit, and then swirled it around to get it nice and slick. She only wished that Vane was there with his big pierced dick. He was sheer perfection. She frowned before correcting that errant thought: his cock was sheer perfection.

She rolled her hips and moaned. She pictured him over her, in her bed. A place she'd never taken him. Thank the Creators he didn't know where she lived. If he did, she had no doubt that the Demi-God would be at her door, trying to get through her protection spells. He was not pleased that she'd left him in the dreams and was reverting back to her usual self. He'd called her bluff when she'd tried to make light of the things they'd done there.

Why was his scent so much stronger than before? She forced herself to stay away from the infirmary because of it. Was it the connection Sirena spoke of? Like a mating, but not? She still didn't understand what that meant, and she hoped to hell her sister had answers soon. Preferably before he woke up. Which didn't give much time. Sirena thought he would wake soon. Days, maybe.

She shook her head. All that mattered right then was getting off. Her muscles were too damn tight, and they'd stay that way until she found release. She slipped the toy inside her pussy, lodging it deep before hitting the vibrate button. She slid the fake cock in and out as she groaned and rolled her hips. It was good, not the same, but it would still get the job done.

Snick. Her hearing focused, and she turned off the vibrator and took it out. Son of a bitch. She could smell him. Not possible. Her door slammed open, and a furious Vane stood in the doorway.

Her breath caught, and she jumped from the bed and stood there paralyzed by the wild look in his eyes. Her pussy clenched, so damn primed and wet, and he looked good enough to fucking eat.

He growled when he saw the toy on the bed. He slammed her up against the wall. Her breath left with the force, and she knew he'd caved in the hard plaster. She hummed with need at the sight of his wild eyes. "I'm the one that fucks this pussy." He sounded dangerous as two fingers invaded her pussy. He was hot, wild and fucking possessive. It was not a good idea to fuck him, but she needed to come. She was too primed, and his scent was all over her, inside her.

He pulled his fingers out and slid the flimsy infirmary pants down to his ass. He grabbed her wrists in one hand and held them over her head as he lifted her with the other. "Spread your thighs."

She gasped and did as he commanded. He slammed her hard onto his cock. The scent of them fucking filled the room. She closed her eyes at how good it felt. That bit of jewelry decorating his dick was her undoing. It rubbed just right inside her as she met every punishing thrust.

"Open your eyes!" he demanded, and she did, a little. He was glaring at her. "I told you there was no going back. You're fucking mine, and you know it. I can feel you inside me. Something's happening, and you're not running again, or I promise you won't like what I do, lark."

His thrusts grew even more demanding as they both rasped for breath, losing their minds to the need. She loved every damn minute of it. She shouted as her pussy constricted around him, but he didn't stop. "Again," he demanded, rolling his hips. He was so damn deep she felt his balls at her ass. She groaned hard, coming all over him a second time.

He looked feverish, wild. Beyond feral, nothing like she'd ever seen him before. She worried for only a second before feeling him pulse inside her. She moaned, and he struck. His teeth sank in where her neck and shoulder met. First shock hit, and then another blinding orgasm sent her over. That time even harder. Her beast slammed to get free, to mark him as he was fucking marking her, and she fought it. What the fuck was he thinking? Why the hell had the feel of his teeth in her skin sent her back over? Her mouth dropped open as his tongue lapped at her blood. Oh, fuck what was happening to them? What had they done?

Chapter 38

Cynthia's Demolished Compound, Earth Realm

It had been weeks, yet Conn kept coming back, night after night. Her scent trailed to the next town, but he hadn't found her there. She'd driven away. As soon as he found any clues, he'd be on the hunt. He'd scented her the night of the explosion. He hadn't been entirely sure, and then the battle had started. He'd wanted to go to her, but he'd had to complete his mission. It had been too dangerous. He'd been anxious to get it done. Finish it so he could track her.

Alex and her brothers had avoided exile. Obviously his little wolf had as well. He'd told Drake and the others after Dorian's mating.

So much had happened, but his beast was more focused on finding his little Lykos.

He would find her. She could run, but she wouldn't be able to hide from him forever. Once he tracked her, found her, she'd never want to leave. His wolf was itching to pin her ass down and claim her. She was *his*. A gift he was only too happy to claim. He craved a mate of his own. He only had to hunt her down. Thoughts of the chase alone made his dick pulse. He smirked, his poor little female had no idea what was coming for her.

Glossary of Terms and Characters for Reference:

Adras – Hippeus (half warhorse), Immortal warrior in charge of the city of Lofodes, mated to Ava, father of Alyssa

Ailouros – Immortal race of half felines, known as the warrior class, strong and fast

Akanthodis – Hell creature with spines all over its body and four eyes

Aletheia – Immortal race with enhanced mental abilities and power within their fluids, can take blood memories, strong telepathy

Alex – aka Alexandra, Demi-Goddess daughter of Athena, sister to Vane and Erik, mate to Uri

Alyssa – Hippeus (half warhorse), Daughter of Adras and Ava, mate to Gregoire

Angus – Aletheia, second in command to Kane

Aphrodite – Sleeping Goddess, one of the three good Deities, mother to Drake

Apollo – Sleeping God that experimented with the Immortal races, adding animal DNA to most in order to create the perfect army against his siblings

Ares – Sleeping God and father of the Tria

Artemis – Sleeping Goddess and mother of the Tria

Astrid – Kairos, business associate to Alyssa and Rain

Athena – Sleeping Goddess – One of only three Gods that were good and didn't feed off dark energies and become mad, mother of Alex, Vane and Erik, mate to Niall

Ava – Mageia/Hippeus, mated to Adras, mother to Alyssa

Bastian – Kairos (teleporter), Guardian of the Realms, diplomat for the Guardians within Tetartos Realm

Brianne – Geraki (half ancient bird of prey), Guardian of the Realms

Charybdis – Immortal abused by Poseidon and then sold and experimented on in Apollo's labs, she gave a portion of her life force to create the mating spell, aka mating curse, so that no Immortal could breed with any other than their destined mate.

Conn – Lykos (half wolf), Guardian of the Realms

Creators – The two almighty beings that birthed the Gods, created the Immortals and planted the seeds of humanity

Cynthia – Mageia on Earth Realm working with Elizabeth and Kane

Cyril – Demi-God son of Apollo, Siren/healer, bad guy

Delia – Mageia, power over fire, worked for Rain, abducted by Cyril

Demeter – Sleeping Goddess

Dorian – Nereid, Guardian of the Realms

Drake – aka Draken, Demi-God Dragon, leader of the Guardians of the Realms, son of Aphrodite and her Immortal Dragon mate Ladon

Efcharististi – City in Tetartos Realm

Elizabeth – Aletheia - evil

Emfanisi – Yearly, week-long event where Immortals and Mageia of age go to find mates

Erik – Demi-God son of Athena, Ailouros (half-lion), Vane's twin, Alex's younger brother, mated to Sam

Geraki – Immortal race of half bird of prey, power with air

Gregoire – Hippeus (half warhorse), Guardian of the Realms, mate to Alyssa

Hades – Sleeping God – One of the three good Gods, father to P (Pothos)

Healers – aka Sirens Immortal race, power over the body, ability with their voices

Hellhounds – Black hounds blood bonded to the Tria in Hell Realm

Hephaistos – Sleeping God

Hera – Sleeping Goddess

Hermes – Sleeping God and Apollo's partner in the experimentation and breeding of Immortals for their army

Hippeus – Immortal race of half warhorses, power over earth

Jax – aka Ajax, Ailouros (half tiger), Guardian of the Realms

Kairos – Immortal race whose primary power is teleportation

Kane – Aletheia, bad guy

Ladon – Immortal Dragon, mate to Aphrodite, father of Drake

Limni – City in Tetartos Realm

Lofodes – City in Tetartos Realm

Lykos – Immortal half wolf with power of telekinesis

Mageia – Evolved humans, mortals compatible to be an Immortal's mate, have abilities with one of the four elements; air, fire, water, or earth.

Mates – Each Immortal has a rare and destined mate, their powers meld and they become stronger pairs that are able to procreate, usually after a decade.

Mating Curse – A spell cast in Apollo's Immortal breeding labs that ensured the God wouldn't be able to use them to continue creating his army. Charybdis cast the spell using a portion of her life force and now Immortals can only procreate with their destined mates.

Mating Frenzy – Starts when an Immortal comes into contact with their destined mate, sexual frenzy that continues through to the bonding/mating ceremonies.

Nereid – Immortal race of mercreatures, power over water

Niall – Immortal mate to Athena, father of Alexandra, Vane and Erik, experimented on in Apollo's lab and turned into an Ailouros

Ofioeidis – Huge serpent hell beasts, hardest to kill out of all the hell creatures

Ophiotaurus – Hell beast with the head of a bull and tail of a snake

Ouranos – City in Tetartos Realm

P – aka Pothos, Guardian of the Realms, Son of Hades, second to Drake in power

Paradeisos – Island pleasure resort in Tetartos Realm, owned by Tynan

Phoenix – Immortal race with ability over fire

Poseidon - Sleeping God

Rain – Mageia, best friend of Alyssa

Realms – Four Realms of Earth; Earth - where humanity exists, Heaven - where good and neutral souls go to be reincarnated, Hell - where the Tria were banished and evil souls are sent, Tetartos – Realm of beasts – where the Immortals were exiled by the Creators

Sacha – Kairos (teleporter), Guardian of the Realms, diplomat for the Guardians within Tetartos Realm

Sam – aka Samantha Palmer, mated to Erik, power over metal, Mageia/Ailouros

Sander – Phoenix, Guardian of the Realms

Sirena – Siren (healer), Guardian of the Realms, primarily works to find mates for Immortals in Tetartos

Tetartos Realm – The Immortal exile Realm

Thalassa – City in Tetartos Realm

Tria – Evil Triplets spawned from incestuous coupling of Ares and Artemis; Deimos, Phobos and Than

Tsouximo – Hell beast resembling a giant scorpion

Tynan – Aletheia, owner of Paradeisos Island

Uri – aka Urian, Aletheia, interrogator, Guardian of the Realms, mate to Alex

Vane – Demi-God son of Athena, Ailouros (half-lion), Erik's twin, Alex's younger brother

Zeus – Sleeping God

Up Next!

Tempting Ecstasy

Subscribe to Setta Jay's newsletter for:

book release dates

exclusive excerpts

giveaways

http://www.settajay.com/

About The Author

Setta Jay is the author of the popular Guardians of the Realms Series. She's garnered attention and rave reviews in the paranormal romance world for writing smart, slightly innocent heroines and intense alpha males. She loves creating stories that incorporate a strong plot accompanied by a heavy dose of heat.

An avid reader her entire life, her love of romance started at a far too early age with the bodice rippers she stole from her older sister. Along with reading, she loves animals, brunch dates, coffee that is really more French vanilla creamer, questionable reality television, English murder mysteries, and has dreams of traveling the world.

Born a California girl, she currently resides in Idaho with her incredibly supportive husband.

She loves to hear from readers so feel free to ask her questions on social media or send her an email, she will happily reply.

Subscribe to her newsletter for giveaways, exclusive excerpts and release information: http://www.settajay.com/

https://www.facebook.com/settajayauthor

https://twitter.com/SETTAJAY

https://www.goodreads.com/author/show/7778856.Setta_Jay

Email: settajayauthor@gmail.com

CPSIA information can be obtained
at www.ICGtesting.com
Printed in the USA
FSHW02n1305300818
51897FS